THE KILLER SERMON

THE KILLER SERMON

Kevin Kluesner

First published by Level Best Books 2021

Author Photo Credit: Cole Kluesner

First edition

ISBN: 978-1-68512-041-2

Cover art by Level Best Designs

This book was professionally typeset on Reedsy.
Find out more at reedsy.com

To Jack Kluesner

Thank you for teaching me that anything is possible...

Praise for THE KILLER SERMON

"Kevin Kluesner has written an edge-of-your-seat tale with engaging characters and done the story justice. Highly recommended."—Al Saibini, Retired Special Agent, U.S. Department of Justice

Chapter One

The Shooter

"And he that killeth any man shall surely be put to death." — Leviticus 24:17

Blue Monday. The most depressing day of the year. According to the early morning radio report the shooter heard on his drive into the city, it falls every year on the Monday of the last full week in January. It derived from a formula that considered such things as the weather, personal debt levels, time elapsed since Christmas, the realization that New Year's resolutions would be scrapped again, a lack of motivation, and yet a need for action. He knew it was pseudoscience, but to the shooter, it felt right. The other thing that made this day worth noting was that it was January 22nd, the anniversary of Roe v. Wade.

The shooter shivered despite the four thermal layers he wore beneath his tan overalls and jacket. He'd been in place on the rooftop since six a.m., and it was now nearing seven-thirty a.m. The day dawned a dreary gray, with sunrise a barely perceptible change from night. Even more of a constant was the bitter cold with the thermometer stuck at minus ten. The shooter's nose hairs froze soon after he took his first couple of breaths after jimmying the lock and stepping out onto the roof.

It was quiet when he started his watch, with only the occasional car trudging down a nearby street, causing a muffled break in the silence. Now, however, cars were nose to tail. Honking. Beeping. Doors clunking open and shut added to the din. The wail of a police siren pierced the gloom, as the city threw off its covers and awoke on the bitterly cold morning.

The shooter perked up each time a car turned into the employee lot of the clinic he surveilled. Five cars already, but so far only women he assumed were nurses or office staff had scurried inside. He knew for sure they were women, because he watched each of them through his scope as they emerged from their vehicles. He could make out part of the patient and visitor lot that ran along the side of the building, and he held his crosshairs on a woman with long, dark hair as she got out of her car and walked out of view toward the main entrance. In the employee lot, a small white sign with "Physician Parking Only" in red lettering stood sentry over the vacant space nearest the back door.

The warm, wholesome smell of fresh-baked bread and *shnecks* wafted up from the industrial bakery that took up the two floors below and supplied loaves and pastry under different brands to the grocery chains that served the Milwaukee area.

The shooter shook violently from the cold again and looked at the naked barrel of the 30/30 Marlin lever-action rifle he was half holding, half resting on the roof's edge. Perched in the same spot for an hour and a half, waiting for his target, he was miserable and started second guessing his preparation. He'd thought of lashing an empty plastic bottle to the business end of his rifle with electrical tape. He read somewhere it would serve as a poor man's silencer, dampening the rifle's crack without knocking the bullet off line.

But he didn't know for sure if the bottle trick would muffle the sound of the blast. And he didn't want to take the chance that it would nudge the bullet even a fraction of an inch astray. At one hundred and fifty yards a small error would result in a miss and eliminate any chance he'd have for a clean kill. Besides, he figured, when and if he took the shot, the report could be confused with any number of other city sounds.

The shooter also knew the origin of the sound would be difficult or even impossible to place. With concrete all around, a maze of man-made canyons, the gunshot would echo wildly before it died.

He steeled himself as a black Lexus pulled into the rear parking lot across the street. He didn't want to get caught, but he would accept it if it happened. This wasn't about him.

Chapter Two

Dr. Charles Smith rode in the back of his Lexus LX series sedan, a stack of patient files on the leather seat next to him. He frowned as he studied the open file on his lap, reaching behind his head with a hair tie to corral his long gray hair. He peered over his cheaters and caught his driver's eyes in the rearview. "How much longer, Joe?"

Joe Diener, the large driver who also served as Smith's bodyguard, nudged his sunglasses onto the top of his head and glanced at his phone. "G-Maps says another seven minutes, boss."

Milwaukee's traffic was nothing compared to some larger cities, but two rollovers this morning on different interstates had turned their normal thirty-minute commute into forty five.

Smith was antsy. He looked again at the open file and tapped his right index finger repeatedly on the page by the patient's name. He cared about all of his patients, knowing every one of them came to him at a troubled point in their lives. The reasons why they came to his clinic were as varied as the women's ages, beliefs, or the hue of their skin. But for each woman, the choice she faced was as intense as it was personal. He never judged, and he did his best to ease the pain of their decisions. The woman in the file tried to bury it, but Smith felt she was especially troubled. Was she alone? Was she being intimidated or manipulated? Had she been raped? He kept tapping but, though he tried, he couldn't put his finger on it.

Smith's no-show rate, the percentage of patients who failed to return for their follow-up visit, was less than five percent. But he worried about each one who didn't return to see him. He was anxious to sit down with the woman in the file this morning so he could better understand her situation and comfort her.

When the sedan pulled into the clinic's back lot a minute later, Smith had the files under his arm and was out of the car as soon as it crunched to a stop.

Chapter Three

The rifle's crosshairs intersected squarely in the middle of Dr. Charles Smith's head as he exited the passenger side of the sedan. Diener parked the car and walked around the rear of the vehicle to open the door for the doctor, but Smith was out of the car before his bodyguard could carry out his duty.

Tall and slender, in his mid-fifties, Smith wore no overcoat over his wool Brooks Brothers blazer, even though the temperature was expected to stay submerged below zero all day. He strode up the ice-patched sidewalk to the rear of the Milwaukee Women's Health Clinic. The squat white one-story building looked unimpressive, but Smith was proud of the services he and his team offered here, and the compassionate way they provided them. More than two thousand women from across the state came to his clinic each year, facing an intensely personal and sometimes painful decision regarding terminating their pregnancies. Smith and his staff offered counseling, lab, and ultrasound testing, and abortions that ranged from pill form to surgery for more advanced pregnancies. Smith didn't agree with Wisconsin's current law that prohibited abortions after twenty-one weeks of pregnancy, but he abided by it.

The shooter tried to hold on Smith as he moved up the walkway across the street, trailed by his bodyguard. Wisps of snow swirled in the wind, dancing in front of his crosshairs like cigarette smoke. Smith's long silver hair was swept back and tied neatly, and the shooter's aim swayed from the doctor's nose to his ponytail as Smith hurried to get inside.

When the doctor stopped to insert his key in the door's deadbolt lock, the shooter pulled the trigger 1/32nd of an inch and the 30 caliber, 170-grain soft pointed slug was on its way. It struck Dr. Smith above his right temple, flattened out on impact, and kept boring ahead through bone and soft brain tissue. It exited his left temple and smacked into the clinic's cinder block wall, lodging in a dime-sized crater.

Smith stumbled sideways with the blast and fell backward over a hip-high snowbank. All but one of the files flew out of his hand, and they lay scattered in the snow and on the walk. His keys dangled in the door and the bodyguard froze, his eyes transfixed on the doctor's eyes. Smith blinked once, twice, trying to comprehend what had happened with a brain that no longer functioned. Or maybe it was the last flicker of a connection before the light in his eyes was extinguished forever. Drops of blood sprayed the snow all around Smith, peppering some of the files. As he lay on the fresh white blanket of powder, the snow around his shattered head melted and turned crimson, like syrup being poured to make a black cherry snow cone.

The shooter ejected the spent shell and levered another round into the chamber. The report of the first shot had been deafening, amplified by the concrete all around him. He brought the rifle back into a solid firing position and viewed the scene through the scope. The doctor was down and the bodyguard still. The shooter didn't bother looking for his spent shell casing. Instead, he fished around inside his right jacket pocket. He pulled out a small metal crucifix and dropped it on the icy rooftop. Next, he reached inside his left jacket pocket and brought out a generic red catsup bottle, the kind you'd find at most diners or burger joints, sitting next to a bright yellow bottle of mustard. He flipped the cap off with his thumb and sprayed the crucifix and the rooftop near it with a thick red liquid. The bottle made a slurping sound when it was empty and the shooter pocketed it. Then he set the gun down and moved to the door that led from the roof. At the bottom of the stairwell, he cracked open the heavy steel door that exited onto an alley and waited while a bakery truck rumbled past. He walked two blocks with his head down and slid behind the wheel of his hunter-green Chevy Blazer. He was a mile away from the scene within ten minutes of pulling the trigger. His hands shook as he turned on the stereo and the eclectic compilation CD he'd burned off Napster years ago began playing. Robert Goulet finished "The Impossible Dream," a song from the musical *Man of La Mancha*.

The shooter nodded as Goulet crooned about the world being better off for one man striving with his last ounce of courage. "Amen," the shooter softly said to himself. "Amen to that."

The next song was REM's "The End of The World."

Chapter Four

A bank of high dirty white clouds crept toward the city of Milwaukee from the northwest. Within a half-hour the clouds would slide between the sun and the land, a mottled gray shade that Mother Nature drew across the sky and kept in place for weeks on end during the cruelest of her Wisconsin winters.

Snow spit from the heavens as FBI Special Agent Cole Huebsch pumped the brakes of his nine-year-old Dodge. He'd lost any hope the sun would break through later in the day. His Charger looked more like it was painted battleship gray than the creamy white color that lay beneath a cold, hard veneer of grit and grime. The closest parking he'd found was more than a block down from the Women's Health Clinic. He eased into the spot, bumping up onto the hard-packed, uneven ledge of snow and ice that hugged the two feet closest to the curb. He got out and began an easy jog toward the clinic, the lug soles of his Merrills making a scrunching sound each time one bit into the snow-glazed sidewalk. He slowed as he neared the entrance of the building and threaded his way through the gawkers outside. His breath hung in front of him, dissipating in the frigid air. The uniformed Milwaukee Police Department officer standing sentry at the front door glowered as he scanned Cole's FBI credentials. A woman banged through the door before the officer could wave Cole in, nearly knocking him over as she hurried to exit the building. Long, dark hair flared over her charcoal dress coat, and she had the collar pulled up to her cheeks. Oversized designer sunglasses covered her eyes and most of her face despite the clouds. Cole watched as she almost ran to her car, stowing a reporter's notebook into her purse as she went.

Crap, he said to himself as the officer moved aside to let him in, a little less than thirty minutes after Dr. Smith went down hard on the opposite side of the building.

MPD Lieutenant Ty Igou met Cole as he walked through the doors. Ty wore a natty, dark blue suit and crisp white shirt draped over a muscular six-foot-two frame. He fingered his deep red silk tie and looked down at Cole, who stood a little over five-ten. Cole wore faded blue jeans and a distressed brown leather bomber jacket that was open to reveal a gold Marquette University sweatshirt. It was supposed to have been a rare day off for him. He had a matching but frayed Golden Eagles ball cap on his head.

"You're the FBI guy?" Ty asked, frowning at the way Cole was dressed.

"Good guess," Cole said, grabbing Ty's unoffered hand and giving it a brisk shake. "Now let me try a quick guess: You're the mayor?"

"What?"

"You look like a politician, kid, all dressed up in red, white, and blue. I figured mayor or alderman…nothing higher than that. Of course, you could be a cop, but then I doubt you'd be wasting my time here with stupid questions."

Cole didn't like a pissing match. He liked to do his job and catch criminals. But he knew from experience that sometimes the big dog had to mark his territory early to get the necessary cooperation from local law enforcement.

"I'm a detective and a lieutenant in the Milwaukee Police Department and we're investigating a murder here," Ty stammered. "And I'm nearly forty, so I don't think the 'kid' label fits."

"I'm nearly forty-five," Cole said, stepping forward and invading Ty's private space. His stubble-filled jaw was now inches away from Ty's and his blue eyes looked up and locked onto Ty's walnut brown ones. "That makes you my junior," he continued. "I'm a special agent with the Federal Bureau of Investigation, Criminal Investigation Division. I'm based right here in the Brew City field office. *Any* shooting, much less murder of *any* employee of an abortion clinic, much less a *physician,* falls under FBI jurisdiction. The courts frown on such actions and see them as violations of individual civil rights…which are *federal* crimes."

He paused both for effect and to take a breath and drive home his point. "And you *were* investigating a murder here. Now you're *helping me* investigate a murder. And if I don't find you particularly useful, you won't even be assisting in a murder investigation; you'll be back to chalking tires and writing ten-dollar parking tickets for a living." He fought to keep his voice soft but the tenor hard and sharp. He threw up his hands and added, "Now show me the vic so we can get started."

Ty knew when to shut up and he simply turned and headed inside and down one of the narrow, sterile white corridors. Cole followed and saw the surge of crimson that rushed up the back of his neck.

"Twenty-five dollars," he muttered under his breath.

"What?" Cole challenged from behind.

"Those parking tickets are twenty-five now, not ten."

Ty led Cole back out a side door to avoid contaminating the murder scene, and they made their way around to the back parking lot. "The doctor had two medical assistants, a nurse, an office manager, two receptionists, and a billing clerk," he threw over his shoulder. "We've got each of them sequestered in a separate exam room or office awaiting interrogation," he said. "The doctor also had a bodyguard, but he gives details about as well as he protects."

As they ducked under the yellow police tape and neared the body, Cole reached ahead of him and tapped Ty on the shoulder. When Ty stopped and turned Cole made sure he was looking squarely at him. He nodded and said, "Thanks." Cole knew already he could work with Ty, because the guy was willing to cooperate even though he was pissed off at him.

"My name's Cole Huebsch. 'Hip,'" he said, pointing to his hip. Then he put his right index finger over his lips and said, "Shhhh." He repeated with a grin, "Hip. Shhh. Huebsch." He nodded his head for emphasis.

Shaking his head and smiling in spite of himself, Ty said, "Ty Igou. As in 'I,'" pointing to his right eye, "and 'go,'" pointing his thumb and nodding in the direction of the slain victim.

Smith was lying on his back with his arms up over his head, as if he might push down and make a snow angel. His blazer was open and his feet were elevated, resting on the snowbank. Smith's black eyes were unfocused and glazed over. Cole knew from the way Smith lay that he was probably dead before he hit the ground. All the blood that had soaked the snow red and pink around his head was for show.

"What do you guys have so far?" Ty asked the two crime lab operatives who were looking over the scene and snapping photographs.

"We only set up five minutes ago," the lead tech said. "But it looks like it was one shot and maybe from a car, most likely by a rifle. With a head shot like this, the shooter had to have optics, a scope of some kind. Either that or the perp got incredibly lucky. It'd be a one-in-a-million shot at longer distance with a handgun as the guy's on the move. Anyway, the snow is fresh and we can't find any footprints to signal the perp got close. We've already retrieved a slug from the cinder block right there," he said, pointing to the building about four feet or so up from the frozen ground. "The larger mass supports our thinking that it came from a rifle and not a handgun."

Cole regarded the information and the scene itself. He nodded toward the door. "Are those the doctor's keys in the lock?"

"The office manager thinks so, but she's pretty shook up and couldn't say for sure."

Cole stooped and looked at the keys more carefully. "I'll bet the Lexus fob on the key ring starts that LS 460 parked there. "You'll have to confirm it, but I'd say it's a good bet it's his."

He looked at the pockmark in the building's wall. "If that's where the bullet ended up, and if it didn't have much deflection, then the doctor was either crouched down a bit when he put his keys in the door or the shooter was elevated. Most people I know don't stoop much when they unlock a door, so I gotta believe the shooter was higher than street level."

He paused, imagining the doctor pushing his key into the lock and getting shot as he's turning the knob. He looked around to get a fix on where the bullet might have come from. He looked directly at Ty and said evenly, "Have your people check out that white two-story building across the alley.

I think it's Grebe's Bakery. Have them scour the upper floor and the rooftop. Maybe our shooter left something behind."

He started to leave, but turned back to Ty. "While you're interviewing the staff at Grebe's, see if they have a couple of maple-covered long johns they can spare. Bring your report and the sweet rolls to 3600 South Lake Drive. That's where our Milwaukee headquarters are. Be thorough, but be quick. I'm starved...both for explanations and some breakfast."

Chapter Five

Late that afternoon, Cole sat at his desk at the Milwaukee FBI field office waiting for additional reports to come in. Two years earlier, the Bureau moved from downtown Milwaukee to its current location on Lake Drive in the nearby suburb, St. Francis. The Feds had taken out a twenty-year lease on the four-story, modern, eighty-two thousand square foot building, which previously had been home to an investment group.

He looked out his windows, facing east onto Lake Michigan. The office building was perched within one hundred yards of the shoreline. A former Special Agent in Charge of the FBI's Milwaukee Division dedicated the headquarters in memory of Special Agent W. Carter Baum, who was slain in 1934 by "Baby Face" Nelson at a lodge up in Northern Wisconsin. The Director of the FBI had been on hand for the opening and called it "an awesome location, with amazing views." He predicted the surrounding water, as well as running and biking trails, would provide great opportunities for agents and staff to "heal." Cole hoped so.

Earlier the MPD had found a Marlin 30/30 lever action rifle on the roof of the building he had pointed out from the murder site. That model of gun was one of the most popular deer rifles in Wisconsin. It was relatively light and considered a good brush-busting gun, serviceable for shots up to two hundred yards or better with a scope. It had the stopping power to put down a two hundred and fifty-pound deer or a man with relative ease.

The 30/30 used to kill the doctor had a scope that magnified objects up to four times their natural size. The shooter hadn't bothered to file off the rifle's serial number, and that struck Cole as odd. They'd traced the rifle to a local dealer who'd sold it a week ago at the Waukesha Coliseum gun show, not more than thirty minutes west of Cole's office. Now they were running the lead, tracking down the current owner of the gun.

The MPD officers who found the gun also found a lot of blood up on the roof. The CSI team collected it and estimated they got a good half pint or more. It usually didn't take long to get blood types back from the lab, especially on a case as big as this one. But Cole hadn't heard anything yet. That was concerning. He ran his hands through his hair and wondered what the blood would tell them. Had the shooter turned the gun on himself but lived? They'd interviewed people near the scene after the shooting and some claimed to have heard the shot. Nobody reported hearing a second shot. Crime scene photos showed what looked like a thick stream of blood, a serious wound maybe. But then there was no other blood leading away from where the kill shot was made…no blood spray or drips across the rooftop or down the stairs.

"What the hell?" he said aloud.

Cole picked up another photo from the scene. It had been enlarged and showed a small metal cross. A smudge of frozen blood clung to the side of the cross where Jesus' right hand was nailed.

He took a deep breath and leaned forward, slumping his shoulders and resting his forearms on his desk. He laid his head down on his forearms and closed his eyes.

Cole was a down-to-earth guy, blessed with common sense. He appeared average at first glance, but wasn't really in any way but looks. Even there his eyes, the soft hue of faded blue denim, had a light to them that women were drawn to. How else had he managed to attract his wife, scratch that, his ex-wife? Janet Stone was the drop-dead, perfect blonde who used to grace the top-rated, ten o'clock television news show on Milwaukee's ABC affiliate. Now she read the news for Fox at the national network level. Cole hadn't heard from her in four years. Not that he'd seen her much when they were married. She was always chasing the big news story and he was chasing the bad guys. Some of his cases were big, but most were routine.

Milwaukee wasn't the thrill a minute ride that New York, LA, or DC seemed to be. A few years back, after he solved a number of tough cases, including one that helped put the Midwest's biggest drug dealers in federal prison, he could have had his pick of plum jobs anywhere in the country. But he turned down those opportunities to stay close to where he grew up and what he knew best. He'd been born and raised on the other side of the state in the small town of Prairie du Chien. An only child, he'd lost both parents when he was twenty-two. He hadn't been back to Prairie since the day he helped bury them, even though the city was little more than a three-hour drive away.

Cole knew he had a good life, but it wasn't the one he pictured for himself as a younger man. When he graduated from Marquette with first a bachelor's in English and Philosophy and then a master's degree in Business, he figured he'd have a wife and four kids by the time he was thirty-five. He was almost forty-five now and while he'd had a wife and lost her, he had no children. And it wasn't for lack of trying. Janet's obstetrician thought her slender frame contributed to that. But when the young couple became serious about having kids, they learned that Janet had a genetic anomaly that prevented pregnancy. Cole wanted to be a dad and brought up adoption on several occasions. In the end, the inability to conceive drove a silent wedge between them. Added to the stress and hours of their demanding jobs, they drifted apart and lost each other. After they split up, Cole tried to make up for that emptiness by marrying himself to his job.

Looking back, it was a fluke he ended up working for the Bureau. He'd gone to Marquette because the Division 1 school offered him a wrestling scholarship. A three-time state champ in high school, the scholarship paid for his tuition, fees, and books, and additional grant monies covered his room and board.

He made it to the NCAA final at one hundred and seventy-four pounds his junior year with a record of twenty-nine and one, his only loss coming to a senior from Iowa. He avenged that loss in the final, scoring a takedown with three seconds left in the final period to win the match and the championship. It was the first-ever for a Marquette wrestler. The school dumped its wrestling program two weeks later to make room for women's lacrosse.

Cole and his teammates went from shocked and devastated to outraged, but the administration didn't listen to their protests. Successful alums who'd wrestled at Marquette years earlier came forward, offering to fund the sport, but the administration's decision was final.

Head coaches from Penn State, Iowa, and other wrestling powers offered him a full ride for his senior year. But when Marquette told him he could keep his scholarship, he became a student instead of a student-athlete for the first time in his college career.

Not many young men would walk away from the chance to win a second national title, and the chance to maybe wrestle for their country in the Olympics down the road, but Cole was at peace with his decision. He'd been wrestling hard for ten years and had nothing left to prove, at least to himself. He began dating Janet his senior year.

After graduating, he took out student loans and began a part-time job at a Milwaukee bank, in order to pursue his Master's in Business full time. Two years later he'd worked his way up from being a teller, to a senior teller, to a professional banker. They made him a branch manager when he received his MBA, and they had bigger plans for his future.

One day a year later, Cole was coming back to the branch, carrying lunch for his team. He pushed through the front doors and stopped. He could tell something was out of place. His two tellers were stiff and wide-eyed. A person in a hoodie was addressing them. Cole looked around and saw there were no other customers in the branch.

When he turned back to the tellers, one of them handed the man in the hoodie a bag. Cole assumed it was stuffed with cash. The man in the hoodie said something else to the tellers and then came toward Cole, who was still standing in the doorway with his large, brown bag of Cantonese takeout.

The guy approached Cole, glaring, and said, "The fuck you lookin' at?"

Cole said nothing, just stood still. He hoped the surge of adrenaline flooding his body would be mistaken for fear. He and his staff had been trained to give up the money to the bad guys and let them walk out before hitting the panic button below the counter where they worked. He knew the drill. If a bank employee intervened and got hurt, the bank paid. If the employee intervened and a customer got hurt, the bank paid. Hell, if the employee intervened and the robber got hurt, the bank often paid.

But when the robber got to within two feet, Cole couldn't help himself. He flipped the bag of food in the guy's face and tackled him at the same time. He had the guy face down on the floor with his arms pinned behind his back and calmly told his team to call 911. He was suspended later that day and fired by the end of the week.

The FBI has played a key role in investigating bank robberies since the early 1930s when John Dillinger was making a name for himself. But they evolved to where they only play a lead role in cases where the criminals pose a large danger or threat to the public.

Cole didn't know it when he took the robber down, but before he'd entered his bank that day the guy had already knocked off twelve banks from Indianapolis, up through Chicago, and into Wisconsin. In two of the holdups, he shot a teller in the face for being too slow; one was dead and the other fighting for her life. Cole found out when the police arrived at his branch, that the guy he'd subdued had two 9 mm handguns on him when he'd tackled him.

Two weeks after he was fired, Cole received a commendation for heroism from the FBI and the Milwaukee Police Department. The FBI agent who presented the commendation did a background check on Cole and encouraged him to consider a job with the Bureau. He was twenty-five when he applied. The Bureau accepts applicants between the ages of twenty-three and thirty-seven and only takes US citizens. They want their candidates to have at least a four-year degree and prefer three years of professional experience.

Cole had already passed a rigorous physical test, background check, and medical exam in Milwaukee before heading to Quantico, Virginia.

The physical test consisted of five elements, all of them timed; pushups, sit-ups, 300-meter and 1.5-mile runs, and pull-ups. Each category offered a maximum of 10 points, and candidates had to score at least one point in each and 20 total to pass. The average score was 35. In his class of 40 candidates, Cole was the lone candidate to score a perfect 50.

When he arrived at Quantico, he took a written test that covered logical reasoning and situational judgment and Cole was the first to finish. The day following that test he was called back in and told to retake the test, alone this time.

He wondered what was up, but they offered no explanation. He finished the test faster this time. He was never told why they wanted him to retake the test, or that his scores on the two exams were the two highest ever recorded at the Academy. The person who'd scored the next highest on the test was the agency's current Director. Cole's personnel file grew.

They put him through their 21-week training program and he continued to excel. He learned case exercises, firearms training, and operational skills. He'd grown up hunting whitetail deer, grouse, ducks, rabbits, and squirrels. He was comfortable with shotgun and rifle alike. He worked hard to become proficient with handguns.

When they drilled on operational skills like grappling, control holds and disarming techniques, Cole was at the head of the class. Even his instructors could learn from a world-class wrestler.

Lastly, he learned about interviewing, report writing, advanced interrogation techniques, law, and forensic science. He absorbed it all and soon found himself an agent of the FBI.

The Bureau tried to steer him to jobs in DC or New York, but there was an opening in the Milwaukee field office and he jumped at it. He'd been dating Janet Stone for almost four years and planned to go "home" and propose. He did just that and she said, "Yes."

Chapter Six

Ty came into Cole's office and Cole lifted his head, yawning. He leaned back and stretched. He'd been named the Special Agent in Charge of the Milwaukee Field Office five years earlier, and it was unusual that a SAC would directly investigate a crime, even one as high profile as the murder of a reproductive rights physician. But Cole did a great job developing the agents and analysts under him, and the Milwaukee office had become a kind of farm system for FBI offices in LA, New York, Chicago, and DC. His assistant SAC had just been lured to Phoenix, and he'd also recently lost two senior special agents to San Francisco and New York. Besides, he took the job with assurances from his bosses that he could continue to work cases from time to time. This seemed like the time.

"We've got the name and address of the guy who bought the rifle," Ty announced. He'd been assigned by Milwaukee PD to assist on the case until the Feds could redeploy more resources. "He's from Southern Illinois, Centralia, a little town about sixty miles east of St. Louis. I called the St. Louis field office and they sent two guys out to pick him up. Nobody answered his home phone, so he's probably at work. St. Louis did a background check and there's nothing exotic there. The guy is employed at a local grain elevator. If he's not home they'll pick him up at work. They know the town a bit and said it takes about two minutes to drive from one end to the other, so the whole operation won't take that long."

"Good stuff," Cole said, "but I doubt it'll lead anywhere."

"Why? Maybe the killer's a nut job who wants to be caught, someone who wants his fifteen minutes of fame."

"If that was the case, why didn't he stay on that roof and wave to us after he killed Smith?"

"Maybe he was scared or sloppy. I don't know. I'm not psycho enough to figure it out."

Cole smiled and let out a sad laugh. "But you think maybe I am psycho enough? All I'm saying is that it would be nice if this guy was the murderer, so we could wrap a nice bow around this crappy package and get it behind us." He looked up at Ty and leaned back even further in his chair, almost falling before catching himself. "I have a feeling it's not going to be that easy…not by a long shot. Pun intended." He sighed. "Anything on the crucifix yet?"

"No DNA. The shooter wore gloves and if he ever touched the cross with bare hands he wiped it well enough afterward."

"Not a dead end yet, but also not a road that's going to lead us anywhere any time soon. And what the hell is up with the lab? We should've had the blood type back at least within a half-hour of CSI arriving on the scene. And we haven't heard from them yet."

"They actually called in a report on the blood," Ty said. "Right before I knocked on your door."

"And?"

"They said it isn't human."

Chapter Seven

Cole studied his computer screen and ran his hand through his hair a couple of times. He tended to do that a lot. His lips were pursed and his forehead knotted in concentration. His computer was open to Orvis.com, and he scrolled through the tent sale page of the noted outfitter's website. Each week Orvis dropped the price of select merchandise until it sold out. He didn't like paying their retail prices, but he loved the quality of their clothes. The tent sale was a bit of a poker game for him. He had his eye on three items. The signature twill shirt he wanted was supposed to drop today from thirty-four to twenty-seven dollars, which would be a steal. Would have been a steal, that is, because it was sold out. The H.S. Trask loafers had started at one-eighty and were selling for sixty-three today. When he checked on available sizes he saw only sevens and fourteens. No size ten and no new loafers for him. The last item he was following was a salmon-colored sweatshirt that the site trademarked "world's softest." If Orvis said it was, it probably was. He learned the hard way that timing the tent sale was like timing the stock market. Nobody could do it with any regularity. He wasn't sure if he wanted to pay the forty-nine bucks it would cost if he took it to checkout now, or if he should wait a week and see if it was still available in a Large at thirty-nine bucks. He was mulling this over when someone rapped on his closed door.

Cole looked at the clock on the bottom right corner of his screen and saw that it was a little after six-thirty p.m. He hit the power button on his monitor and it went dark, at the same time he raised his voice to say, "Come on in."

Ty pushed through the door and stepped to Cole's desk, handing the agent a folder. He looked him straight in the eye and said, "It looks like you were right. The guy in Centralia has a rock-solid alibi. The St. Louis agents tracked him down at his job. They know this case is big and they sat on him hard, but his story checks out. This morning he was punched in and on the job at the Centralia mill by eight. The agents talked to the guy's supervisor and he saw him punch in. The supervisor also talked to our guy around nine-thirty or ten; discussing a new project they're going to start work on next week. That means for him to be our shooter, given Dr. Smith was taken down about seven-thirty this morning, he had a total of thirty minutes, give or take, to shoot the doctor outside his Milwaukee clinic, drop his rifle, scramble down from the roof, make his way to his car, and drive to the Centralia plant and clock in. According to MapQuest, it's a six-and-a-half-hour drive from the Milwaukee clinic to the Centralia mill. Dale Jr. might be able to make it in a little less than half that. Unless he borrowed the Starship Enterprise from Captain Kirk and beamed himself back to Centralia after the shooting, we can't make him for the murder."

"Agreed. Even if he had a plane waiting it would take at least a half-hour to get to an airport and get airborne...another two hours of flight time... and another half hour or close to taxi down the runway in Centralia, get to his car, and make it to the mill. No chance. None whatsoever."

"Any reason we shouldn't let him go?" Ty asked.

"No. But make sure we know how to get ahold of him. I don't want to lose any loose threads until we know what this is all about."

Ty turned to leave, but Cole stopped him short with another question. "Did we learn any more about this guy other than his alibi?"

"It's all in the file I gave you. The first key point is that he's a hunter. But there are over one million deer hunters between Wisconsin and Illinois, so that could easily be a coincidence. We also learned the guy owns both a 30-06 deer rifle and a 12 gauge shotgun. No 30/30. He said he was in Wisconsin after Christmas, but he never got to Waukesha or the gun show there. The agents swung by the guy's house after grabbing him and the guy's wife backed up all of this separately.

"Where did he go in Wisconsin after Christmas?"

"Prairie du Chien, little town on..."

Cole put up a hand to cut Ty off, with a look that was part smile and part grimace. "I grew up in Prairie, so I'm familiar with the location."

"Okay. The guy said to get to Prairie he drove through the Quad Cities and up the Iowa side until he got to Dubuque. That route wouldn't take him within a hundred miles of Waukesha. He said he took the same route home, because it's the quickest."

"Did he tell the agents why he went to Prairie?"

"A fishing tournament. That's the only part of his story they noted didn't seem plausible. Who would drive six and a half hours each way for a two-day ice fishing tournament?"

Cole laughed out loud. "It doesn't make sense to you or the St. Louis agents, but they've been holding that Ice Fisheree in Prairie for seventy years now. It's a blast."

"Okay, we don't know what to make of it all yet."

"I can tell you it's not as easy as it used to be to forge a passable driver's," Cole said. "High school and college kids have fooled bartenders with fakes for years, but a few years ago Wisconsin made some changes to cut down on fraud and identity theft. They added ultraviolet ink, raised some of the key letters and numbers on the card, and added a second ghost photo." He grabbed his wallet and slid out his driver's license and studied it. "It wouldn't be that easy to copy for the general public."

"True. But to save money the state is phasing in the new licenses. You only get a new one when your old one expires, unless you want to pay extra. Most people aren't doing that." Ty reached into his jacket and retrieved his wallet. He handed his license over to Cole to examine.

He looked at Ty's ID and then up at the detective, smiling. "Not the most flattering likeness of you." He handed the license back.

Ty laughed and said, "I was actually hoping you'd pick up on the fact that it doesn't have the new identity safeguards, and it's good for another four years."

"So, it could have been easy enough to copy a license like yours. Verify it, but our guy from Centralia probably has a similar license."

"Wait a sec," Ty said, pulling out his phone to do a quick Google search. He scrolled through a couple articles quickly. "Centralia is in Illinois, and Illinois isn't making everyone change to new driver's license technology. They're only making it available as an option. I'll confirm, but our Centralia guy almost certainly has an older technology license like mine."

Cole picked up the file and began reading. "The gun dealer scanned the license he was given. Supposedly the guy he sold the gun to was in a wheelchair. He also remembers him having a scruffy beard and being in a bulky khaki coat. I'd say the whole thing was a disguise," he said, looking up at Ty. "The beard covered the real shooter's face. The wheelchair kept the dealer from getting a good idea of his height. The big coat kept the dealer in the dark about the guy's build. I'm sure the guy made himself look like a handicapped vet to also soften the dealer up. Pretty much anyone would feel a little uneasy about looking too hard at a vet carrying permanent scars from serving his country. So, we learned two things from this. The first is that the license is no doubt a phony. The second is that our shooter is a cunning and devious bastard."

Chapter Eight

A little more than an hour later, Cole was at his desk. He kept foil packets of tuna in his middle desk drawer and he'd gone to the break room and made himself a tuna and Colby cheese sandwich on seven-grain bread. He finished the last bite of his sandwich about the same time he finished sifting through the file in front of him for the second time. Little bits and pieces of ideas orbited around inside his brain, but nothing jumped out at him. Though it made little sense to others, sometimes he needed to drift a bit before having things come into sharper focus.

The right side of a person's brain controls the left side of their body and performs tasks related to creativity and the arts, while the brain's left hemisphere controls the right side of the body and performs logical functions like science and math.

Cole had what some people might call a sixth sense. At times, especially in tense situations, he would get a feeling in the middle of his head. It was neither pain nor pressure, but more like a warmth or pulsing sensation. He first noticed it in high school while wrestling in his first state final. He was a sophomore and was up against a beast of a senior from River Valley who had won the weight class the year before. Cole was down by one point with ten seconds left in the match. His opponent was stronger, more mature, and more experienced. None of the fans packing the University of Wisconsin Kohl Center anticipated what happened next.

Both wrestlers were on their feet, clinging to one another. Cole was trying frantically to find a small edge he could use to his advantage when he felt the warmth in his head. Imperceptible at first, then a small kernel of soothing heat that spread in the center of his head until it was the size of a baseball. Things slowed down fractionally, and he knew with certainty what his opponent was going to do in the next half-second. As his opponent stepped back to try to stall out the last couple of seconds, Cole dropped down and grabbed the guy's ankle. He also pushed into the kid. The combined momentum of the kid trying to step back and Cole's shove made him fall over backward and Cole covered him up for two points and the win as time expired.

The warmth in his head dulled to a kind of numbness and lasted while Cole shook his opponent's hand and his other hand was raised in victory by the ref. It ebbed as he was mobbed by his coach, teammates, and the cheers from the crowd. He tried to hold onto the feeling, but he felt it dissipating, almost like a sedative wearing off. By the time he was bear-hugged by his dad and mom, he almost forgot about it. But the sensation came back to him over the following years when he needed it most. He thought of it as his own secret mini-power.

Cole brought the Orvis page back up and looked at the salmon-colored sweatshirt again. He was leaning toward the purchase and was in the process of pulling his wallet from his back pocket to fish out his VISA card when his desk phone rang. He punched the speakerphone button, "Huebsch here."

"Cole. It's Gene Olson." Olson's deep voice filled the room. Cole leaned forward and tapped the volume bar on the phone to take it down a few decibels.

Olson was ten years older than Cole and had been one of his instructors at Quantico when Cole first joined the FBI. Olson was well decorated and had risen steadily through the Bureau's ranks. He was calling from FBI Headquarters, the J. Edgar Hoover Building in Washington DC, as a Deputy Director, two spots below the agency's top position. Even in the hinterlands of Milwaukee, Cole heard the persistent rumors that Olson was expected to head up the Bureau sometime within the next few years.

"Hi, Gene. Haven't heard from you in some time," Cole said in a warm tone. He got along well with Olson and had come through for the man on numerous occasions.

"Yeah, I know. I wish I was calling to ask if you could get us good seats to the Marquette–Georgetown game next week but, as you can imagine, that's not why I'm on the phone."

"Right. I wondered when you or one of your minions would get around to it. I knew the trouble we had this morning would catch your attention."

"You're a smart boy. It also caught the attention of the Director, the President of the United States, and pretty much every member of Congress. Oh, and did I mention the media has more than a passing interest in your little incident as well? You and your team have been doing a nice job of getting us regular updates, and I appreciate that, but the Director wants to make some changes in how we work this."

Cole thought this might be coming, but he was surprised it was happening this fast. "Let me guess, we're going to transfer the flag, right?"

"Afraid so," Olson acknowledged in a voice that said he had little choice in the matter. "The investigation will be led from our Chicago office. We've got a lot more resources and assets there."

"So, I'll be taking my orders from Jeffers?" Cole's voice didn't hide his annoyance. Collin Jeffers was the Chicago SAC, the head of the FBI's Midwest hub. He'd joined the Bureau the same year Cole had and Cole felt Jeffers was more flash than substance.

"You really think Jeffers will handle this better than me, Gene?"

"No. As a matter of fact, I don't think Jeffers will do a better job." His voice didn't rise but it hardened slightly. "You know that. You've turned down five different promotions over the past seven years, Cole, and three of those were offered to you directly by me. And the funny thing about job openings in the FBI, like most of the real world, is that people typically take the initiative to *apply* for those openings. We came to you, multiple times, because we think you're that good. But the Director wants Chicago leading this and the Director gets what he wants."

Olson softened then, but continued, "Listen, Cole, if this thing isn't put to bed soon, I'll no doubt be sent in to take over. Then I'll be down there and Jeffers will get pushed aside. I hope it doesn't come to that. For now, though, Jeffers is definitely going to need your assistance. You know Milwaukee and

Wisconsin far better than he does, or anyone on his staff for that matter. He only moved to Chicago from Virginia a little over a year ago."

Cole admired Olson and lightened up. "Don't sell Jeffers short, Gene. I'll bet he could tell us where to get the best foie gras or five hundred dollar haircut in Chi-Town. Other than that, you're correct that I could fill in some details for him...if he'll let me that is."

"I've already told him to use you to full benefit. He might be a pretty boy, but he's not stupid. If you help him quell this in a timely fashion, he could grab a higher rung on the FBI career ladder that much sooner. You and I both know Jeffers feels any address in the Midwest is beneath him."

"As long as Jeffers lets me get him and his crew donuts and coffee, I'll be happy."

Olson chuckled. "It'll probably be croissants and brie, but I get you." He paused a bit before continuing. "Listen, Cole, this isn't how either of us wants this to go down. That said, I need you in the game all the way. Figure out who did this and bring the bad guy or guys in. DC won't rest easy until you do, and that means none of us will feel the heat turned down until then. Are you with me?"

"Gene, you had me at hello." They both laughed then before Cole turned serious again. "You know you can count on me. I've always been a team player...maybe to a fault. I'll do everything I can on my end. And I appreciate the fact you made this call. If I'd gotten it from Jeffers first, I probably wouldn't have taken it as well."

"Understood. And though I've given more than my share on this call, I have one more bit of advice..."

Cole was locked in now. "And that is..."

"Get the sweatshirt. That salmon color is perfect for your skin tone!" Olson's loud laugh overwhelmed the volume control before he clicked off.

Cole chuckled and mumbled to himself, "You're right about that," as he typed in his VISA number, expiration date, and security code. That salmon-colored Orvis sweatshirt was as good as his.

Chapter Nine

Michele Fields sat at her open cubicle and focused her deep brown eyes on the front page of the *Milwaukee Journal Sentinel* that lay on her battered metal desk. Her byline ran under the banner headline that screamed *Sniper Kills Doctor* in three-inch type. A smaller sub-head added, *Local gynecologist slain at Milwaukee clinic.*

Michele couldn't claim the headlines, but every bit of copy below and following the jump to page three was hers. She interviewed a nurse, a receptionist, and the clinic manager before the first cop arrived on the scene. She didn't get anything from the bodyguard, but she doubted the police did either. He seemed to be in a state of shock when she saw him.

The police asked her to leave when they realized she was a reporter. She thought she had a lot for the story anyway, so it didn't take much prodding.

When she got back to the *Journal* headquarters she contacted the head of the Milwaukee County Medical Society, Planned Parenthood, and even the mayor for a reaction. Nobody held back. They all professed to be shocked, saddened, and appalled. Michele called Wisconsin Right to Life and got pretty much the same response. She tried to reach some of the fringe elements of the right to life groups but couldn't track any down. She almost hoped someone would condone the use of lethal force or, better yet, take credit for the murder. It would sell more newspapers, and also stoke the community's outrage at the brazen, cold-blooded murder. She would likely get another chance, though. Probably a lot more chances. This story would have legs to rival her own, which were long and toned.

She stood and stretched her five-foot-eight frame, arching her spine and tossing back her long, dark hair. It was seven in the morning and few of her colleagues were in yet. The second floor she was on was a large open room that was half as big as a city block. The interior was filled with cubicles with rows plowed between them. The exterior of the floor was ringed with offices that had doors that closed out the interior noise and windows that opened up on the outside world. Stray rays of natural light crept through a handful of windows and invaded the reporters' cubicled world.

The big room was dimly lit, but pockets of yellow light spilled out of the few cubicles occupied this early. It was library-quiet. Most reporters would come in closer to nine and be there until six p.m. or later, sometimes a lot later. If a story was big enough, you could wrap it up at midnight and still get it in the following morning's first edition.

Michele usually came in earlier than most and stayed later. For as long as she could remember, she knew that men found her attractive. But she wanted to catch the attention of her editors and publisher with her work ethic and the quality of her writing. She wouldn't celebrate her thirty-fifth birthday for another six months, but she worried about getting stuck writing fluff pieces when what she wanted to cover was hard news, meaningful stories. No news was bigger or harder than the story she wrote on the shooting, and she grabbed it for herself, not waiting for it to be assigned.

She sat back down in her chair and went to pick up the phone, but knew she wouldn't catch anyone at their desk for another half hour. Instead, she rubbed her temples and sighed. She should be on top of the world right now with such a big story and more to come. It was every reporter's dream to be in her position. But she felt empty. She fought a wave of dark helplessness that welled up from nowhere and started to crash down on her. Her eyes filled with tears as she hit the power button on her computer. She had to do something, anything, to prove to herself she could still function. She listened as the computer purred to life. It stopped to ask for her login number and password and she punched them in, bringing the main menu up on her screen. She clicked on the mail button and scanned the list of messages she'd been too busy to read yesterday. Three were from Karl Taylor, the paper's City Editor, relating to a bridge collapse, the mayor's affair with an aide, and the Charles Smith murder. She clicked on the last one. Taylor applauded her efforts on the first draft he'd seen and indicated he wanted to talk to her about how she got the story. She had a rough draft submitted before he'd even had a chance to assign it. She clicked through the rest of the e-mails, twenty-four of them in all, ranging from pressroom gossip to a sports reporter asking her to go out for drinks after work Friday. She shook her head and the pall of doom came for her again. She stared at the screen, unfocused. She began to feel clammy and her left hand shook involuntarily. She was sliding, sinking deeper into another nightmare when the computer's chime mercifully interrupted her. A text box popped up on the screen informing her she had a new message and queried her on whether she'd like to open it. She clicked the "Yes" button.

It had come from a FedEx Office Store. Her eyes narrowed and her breath caught as she read the subject heading: *I AM THE SHOOTER*.

She clicked on the message and began to read the email, not knowing if the real killer wrote the words or not…

I knew before I started this that I'd be demonized, called a monster or worse. I'm not, though. I'm a man, a very ordinary man. I don't have grand dreams. They're simple. I want to love one woman deeply and forever. To raise a family and to grow old with them near. I can't live normal, however. Not anymore. Asleep or awake I hear the screech of a heavy locomotive, its massive wheels locking up as the train crawls to a stop. I hear the hiss of the brakes. I don't see them, but I know they are loading the babies on, the way they used to shovel on coal years ago. Tens, hundreds, thousands, now millions of babies. I can't go on pretending I don't know about the mass murders...more than twenty million babies slaughtered in our country since the passing of Roe v. Wade. I need to do what I can, what I'm called to do.

I left a 30/30 scoped rifle on top of the building across from where I shot Smith behind his clinic. It wasn't mentioned in your article, so I figure the police kept that from you or you decided not to use it for some reason. I also left behind a small metal crucifix covered in blood. I'm only telling you these things so you know I really am the avenger and not some kook. I know what I'm doing won't be universally praised. The liberal media, including your newspaper, will likely lynch me publicly with your words long before the law catches up with me to do it for real.

Chapter Ten

A few blocks away, Cole and Ty sat in Cole's office. Both had gone home, caught some sleep, showered, and changed. After getting home last night, Ty kissed his wife and kids as they slept, and again as he tried to leave the house quietly that morning. Cole got even less time at home and none of the soft kisses.

Ty sipped from his large Yeti cup and Cole cradled a steaming, ceramic mug of coffee. He liked the warmth and the aroma of the coffee almost as much as he liked the taste and the way it nudged him awake. He also liked the fact that the brown, earthen mug he was holding had been made for him by his ex-wife when she'd taken a pottery class on a lark back when they were first married when things were much simpler and he knew love.

"What are you thinking about?" Ty asked.

"The case. What else?" Cole shot back, shaking his head and yawning. "Do we have anything else from DC or Chicago since last night?"

"Just that the blood was from a deer."

"Right. And I've been thinking about that. Who saves deer blood? The gun deer season only lasts nine days in Wisconsin and ended the weekend after Thanksgiving. Only a third of the roughly six hundred thousand hunters harvest a deer, but that would mean two hundred thousand suspects from the gun hunting season alone.

"Archers take another hundred thousand deer, and the archery season closed three weeks ago. Unless the killer's been planning this murder for some time, then maybe we should focus on men who took deer during the last couple weeks of the archery season. Most of the deer harvested with a bow are taken during the first few weeks of the season. Our list of hunters who took a deer during the last two weeks of the season wouldn't number more than a few hundred."

Cole sipped his coffee and sighed. "Nothing about this feels right. We should chase it down, but the killer could be trying to throw us off his scent. He might have been planning this for a long time. Maybe he's a poacher."

"I guess if you're willing to murder someone in cold blood you wouldn't have much trouble shooting a deer out of season," Ty conceded.

"Yeah, you can make that case, but I'm not sure our guy sees killing the abortionist as murder. It would probably bother him a lot more to kill a deer illegally than to kill a doctor whose main purpose in life is killing babies."

"Babies?" Ty said. "You make it sound like he's killing small children. I've been looking into this and ninety percent of the abortions in the U.S. take place before fourteen weeks' gestation. Even at the end of those fourteen weeks, the fetuses are less than three and one-half inches long and weigh an ounce and a half. It's not like they're viable human beings yet."

"That's how you see it, and a lot of other people, but our killer might not differentiate between a fetus, a full-term infant, or a toddler for that matter. Every one of them is an innocent young life to him, some just younger than others. I grew up Catholic, and that's not the only religion that preaches life begins at conception. When he looked through his scope at Dr. Smith, he didn't see a physician who helps women at a difficult point in their lives. He saw an evil person who's killed a lot of small children in the past, and who will kill more children in the future if he doesn't stop him. He sees himself as righteous…on the side of the angels. But killing a deer out of season? I don't get it. Where's the connection?"

Cole wrapped both hands around his coffee mug, enjoying the warmth that leached through it. He was leaning forward to take in the mild-flavored smell of the roasted beans when his desk phone rang. He hit the speaker button to pick up, preferring his hands free when he talked on the phone. "Cole Huebsch," he said.

"This is the executive assistant for Collin Jeffers, FBI Special Agent in Charge of the Chicago Field Office," the clipped female voice said. "Please hold for SAC Jeffers."

Ty pointed toward the door and raised an eyebrow, asking if he should leave. Cole huffed and shook his head. He might want a witness. There was a pause and he picked up his coffee and took a sip. Not piping hot, but still more than drinkable.

"Cole... This is Collin Jeffers. How are you doing?"

Cole had made his mind up to try to be civil. "Busy," he said. "Milwaukee's becoming an exciting little town."

"It's certainly grabbed a nation's attention. That's for sure."

There was another pause before Jeffers continued. "Listen, Cole. I know this sucks for you. We came into the Bureau at the same time and I'm heading up the Chicago office while you're basically in a Podunk suburb of Chicago. That's probably not the way you mapped out your career. And now that you finally get a big case, Gene calls and tells you he's giving it to me to run."

Cole shook his head and rolled his eyes when Jeffers started and caught himself clenching his sturdy coffee mug so hard he thought it might break. He tried not to let Jeffers get to him but the tone of the man's voice irked him nearly as much as his words.

"You still there?" Jeffers said.

Cole hit the phone's mute button and screamed, "Shit! Crap!" Then he unmuted the phone and said, "Collin. I'm here and I'm fine. No need to worry about my feelings."

"That's good, because we don't have the time or the luxury to worry about your feelings. I'm basically calling to tell you that. Plus, I'm calling to tell you that I want everything you get, when you get it. If you hold back anything in a desperate attempt to get your career off its dead-end path, I will fucking have you sacked. Am I clear?"

Ty's face grew crimson as he listened and he mouthed, "What the hell?"

Cole shrugged and shook his head again. "It's lovely of you to call," he said, looking to rile up Jeffers now. "You've always been an inspiration to me and the other sorry, run-of-the-mill agents in the Bureau."

"You want to be a smart ass now?" Jeffers said, raising his voice. "I wouldn't advise it. You don't have much of a career, but you do draw a paycheck. How would you like to lose it?"

"I'll try to do better, sir," Cole answered, with a smirk Jeffers could pick up over the phone. Cole was starting to enjoy the call.

Jeffers lowered his voice to a near whisper. "Make sure I get everything you come up with…immediately. Of course, that's assuming you come up with anything, which isn't all that likely."

Chapter Eleven

The Milwaukee Bureau's second-floor conference room was about the size of a larger office and the walls were simple drywall, painted white. In the center was a rectanglular, oak table that sat ten comfortably.

Cole and Ty sat at the table with two analysts. The Milwaukee field office covered all of Wisconsin and had satellite offices in Eau Claire, Green Bay, La Crosse, Madison, and Wausau. Cole had two assistant special agents in charge for the Milwaukee office, but Jeffers had appropriated them along with pretty much every agent who wasn't already hard at work on other important tasks.

Cole loosened his tie and undid the top button of his dress shirt. He'd shed his suit jacket back in his office and his shirtsleeves were rolled up below his elbows. Ty's tie was cinched crisply and he wore his suit coat buttoned.

Cole started, "I guess we could've held this meeting in my office. It's not a big gathering." He nodded to Li Song, the senior analyst, and said, "Tell us about the blood and the crucifix and what they might mean to our investigation."

Li returned the nod. She was thirty-four and had a law degree from the University of Michigan. She worked for three years in tax law at a big Detroit law firm before joining the Bureau. The FBI loved attorneys, accountants, and computer geeks. It didn't hurt if you were fluent in key foreign languages, but Li wasn't. Her ancestors emigrated from Hong Kong and settled in San Francisco, but Cantonese hadn't been spoken in the Song family in decades. Li settled into the FBI's Milwaukee Field Office without complaint. If you didn't know her, you might think her fragile. But you'd be wrong. She was lean because she ran distance and worked out fanatically. She loved judo and sparred three times a week. Her hair was raven black, mid-length, and pulled back in a ponytail. She pushed up the turquoise, tortoiseshell glasses that framed her eyes, one chestnut and one sky blue. She shared the rare condition of different colored irises with actresses Mila Kunis and Kate Bosworth. Most people never noticed, but once you did it was hard not to stare at first...they were striking and pulled you in. The first time Cole noticed she had said, "The condition is called heterochromia, and it's the only thing hetero about me." She looked directly at Cole now.

"What we're getting isn't coming from Chicago. It's coming from DC via a workaround set up by the Deputy Director, Gene Olson. He likely knew Jeffers would try to keep us in the dark."

"You mean, keep *me* in the dark," Cole sighed. "Whatever. As long as we get everything anybody else gets in a timely manner I don't want that to overly annoy anybody here. *Any* of us. We've got bigger things to worry about. Everybody from the President of the United States on down wants this solved yesterday. This is our town and we're going to do whatever we can to solve this as fast as possible."

Lane Becwar was twenty-nine and had been an analyst with the Milwaukee office less than three months. He was six feet tall in his wingtips and was athletic in a rangy kind of way. He lettered three years on a ranked Marquette lacrosse team while obtaining an accounting degree. He earned his MBA from Marquette in three years while working full-time in the local offices of one of the "Big Four" accounting firms. He headed to Quantico after passing his CPA exam. Lane had short but thick black hair, hazel eyes, and a nose maybe a size too big for his strong oval face.

"Are we going to share what we find with the Chicago SAC?" Lane asked.

"Roger that," Cole said. "Full transparency. I never said this would be easy. This killer is cold and smart, and I think it's certain he'll kill again if we don't stop him. We need all hands on deck. Gene will try to keep us informed, but if we don't get leads from Chicago in real time I'll go directly to DC at some point. Our egos could get people killed."

"It's not *our* egos we're concerned about," Li said, "it's Jeffers'. If he thought any more highly of himself, he'd appoint himself director of the Bureau."

"Duly noted," Cole said. "Now, let's focus." He took a sip of fresh, hot coffee. "What do we have?"

"The criminal psychologists at J. Edgar are having a field day with the deer blood," Li said, scanning the report again. She handed copies to each of them. "This isn't a run-of-the-mill murder and you can tell from the report it's giving them all a raging hard on."

"Raging hard on?" Cole interrupted. "Is that a technical FBI analyst term?"

Li looked up from the report and right at Cole. "Yes. Yes, it is."

"I can vouch for that," Lane said, grinning.

"Don't let her corrupt you, Lane," Cole said.

Li continued. "The eggheads in DC point out that in the Old Testament of the Bible, God required animal sacrifices to provide temporary covering of sins and to foreshadow God's sacrifice of his own son. They cite Hebrews 9:22 to strengthen their claim that animal sacrifice is an important scripture theme. '"Without the shedding of blood, there is no forgiveness.'

"Abel got on God's good side by sacrificing the firstborn of his flock. Noah sacrificed animals to God after the floods receded. You might say, 'Why kill innocent animals? Animals that did nothing wrong…hence the innocent part."

"But that's kind of the point," Cole said. "The animals died in place of the ones performing the sacrifice. Kind of like Jesus dying to save the rest of humanity even though he was sinless. Usually, the animals killed were lambs or goats, but a deer's not that different. They all have hooves."

"Split hooves," Li added.

"Otherwise known as *cloven* hooves," Lane said, holding up a page he'd been reading. "Cloven hooves sound spookier."

"Moving on," Cole said. "A deer could work as a handy sacrificial substitute for our killer's purposes. I mean, hell, we have almost one and a half million deer in our state."

"The guys at J. Edgar haven't lined up all the scientific similarities between goats, lambs, and our white-tailed deer yet, but you can bet they will to touch all the bases," Li said. "But they're all four-legged, have hooves, and eat grass. That's enough for me. And I'll bet it was also good enough for our shooter."

Cole stretched his legs under the table and reached his arms up toward the ceiling before lacing his fingers behind his head. "So, the shooter is telling us he sacrificed Dr. Smith? That doesn't make sense because in the shooter's mind Smith is anything but innocent."

"Maybe he sacrificed the deer to make amends for the killing of Smith," Ty said.

Cole shrugged. "Maybe, but I'm not sure he sees killing Dr. Smith as a sin. He might see it as a righteous act."

"Could be. But what harm would it do to hedge your bets?" Li asked.

"Or he could be messing with us," Ty said. "He could be trying to get us to chase this...to occupy our time following a lead that goes nowhere."

"While he plans the next murder," Cole added.

"If that's the case, his plan is working," Li said. "One thing this tells us for sure is that this guy is at least somewhat religious. He's read the Bible or heard enough passages over the years that he brought the blood into this. There's that."

"His leaving the little crucifix behind told us that already," Cole said. "The blood and the crucifix together add to the weight of it."

"Unless the cross was randomly lying up on that rooftop before the shooter got there," Ty said. "But the odds would be slim for that. Do we have anything else on the cross?"

Lane said, "For starters, we all need to get straight that it's not a cross, but a crucifix. There's a difference and it could be a critical difference. A crucifix is a cross with a depiction of Jesus on it, sometimes engraved but usually in relief like ours. Crucifixes are generally preferred by Roman Catholics, while crosses are preferred by Protestants."

"So the cross is an empty 'T' kind of thing until you have Jesus nailed to it and then it becomes a crucifix? I'm a cradle Catholic and I never knew that," Cole said.

"We analysts derive satisfaction from enlightening others," Li deadpanned.

"Yeah, well, continue enlightening then," Cole said, shaking his head.

Lane continued, "Our crucifix is roughly one inch tall and weighs about a gram. It's made in Italy out of zinc mostly, and has a crude clasp so it can be worn on a chain like a medallion."

"Next please tell us how rare a medallion like this is," Cole said.

"'Fraid not," Lane answered. "We found websites that sell fifty of these medals for fifteen ninety-nine. If you want to buy in larger bulk, you can get twenty-five hundred of these little heirlooms for five hundred and twenty-four dollars and ninety-nine cents."

"That's what… twenty-one cents apiece? No way," Cole said.

"Yes way," Li said. "The Bureau checked with a number of Catholic Archdioceses and a lot of Catholic churches across the country keep these medallions off their foyers where people enter. The crucifixes are sitting out and on the honor system. People can take however many they want and leave a donation in a box next to the medallions. It's a reminder of their faith and brings in a few shekels."

"We Catholics don't say 'shekels,'" Cole said. "I'm pretty sure that's the currency in Israel."

"Whatever," Li said. "It gets worse. It's not only Catholic *churches* that have these medallions lying around; other Catholic ministries like food pantries and homeless shelters often have them sitting out. Not every Catholic church and mission have crucifixes available and there are a couple of other styles and brands that are commonly used. But still… Anyway, Jeffers is having some of his team contact all the Catholic churches and ministries in Wisconsin to nail down which of them buy this exact medallion."

"Any chance a worker was up on the roof of the bakery and his crucifix medal broke and fell off days, weeks or months ago?" Ty asked. "I mean, how sturdy can they be if you can sell it for twenty-one cents and still make a profit? And if it's that cheap, you wouldn't spend much time looking for it even if you realized you lost it."

"Let's see what Jeffers' people come up with," Cole said. "If we can't catch this guy before he shoots someone else we'll be on the lookout for another crucifix at the next crime scene. I hope it doesn't come to that, but the killer could have left the crucifix as his calling card."

Lane's face scrunched up as he examined a photo of the crucifix blown up until it filled most of the paper. The image was grainy, but you could make out some detail. "This crucifix shows Christ's legs crossed and one nail through both feet. I've seen others where Christ's legs are straighter and a nail is in each foot. So, in our crucifix, there are only three nails total, like the Trinity, whereas others have four." He looked around the room. "Does the one nail in the feet versus two tell us anything?"

"Probably that we are now overthinking this," Cole answered, rubbing his temples. "But throw that at your DC buddies and see what they make of it."

Cole turned to Ty. "Your MPD brothers and sisters talked to a lot of folks yesterday: clinic staff, the bodyguard, bakery employees, shop owners, and bystanders all around the health center. Anything?"

"Not much. Everyone at the clinic was inside when the shot was fired. They were getting ready for the day. They had a couple of early follow-up appointments they hold for mostly professional women who need to get to work early. Those patients are seen first by a nurse. But the clinic wouldn't really have come alive for another half hour or so."

"Interesting choice of words," Cole interrupted.

"We did learn they perform over two thousand abortions at the clinic each year. Two of the staff have worked there more than ten years and nobody recalls violence or even threats at the clinic. The office manager said three old ladies protest outside the clinic once a week. Like clockwork. But that's it. The staff said the ladies are respectful; never say mean things. They've come to see the ladies as clinic mascots almost."

"Um, okay. I'm not sure what to make of that exactly," Cole said, "like pretty much everything else about this case."

Ty plowed ahead. "Not sure this helps, but the clerk said the clinic grossed three million last year. I would've never guessed that much. But health care is expensive."

"Lucrative, too, apparently," Cole mused. "And the bodyguard?"

"He's in a different kind of clinic today. Seeing his boss's head explode a couple of feet away messed this guy up pretty good. He would've been a nice choice for a bodyguard if he had to bowl a bunch of rowdy protesters out of the doctor's way to the clinic door, but not much help in stopping a bullet. He doesn't remember anything. No help to us either."

Cole nodded toward the middle of the table where the day's copy of the *Milwaukee Journal Sentinel* lay. "Anything of interest in the news accounts? On my way into the clinic yesterday morning I was almost run over by a woman with dark hair, mammoth sunglasses, and a reporter's notebook."

The black speakerphone in the middle of the table started chirping and Cole held his hand up for quiet as he hit the button to take the call. He half wondered if Jeffers was calling to chew on him some more. "Hello?"

"SAC Huebsch, this is Mary from the front desk. I have a gentleman on the line who says he's a lawyer representing the *Milwaukee Journal Sentinel.* He claims to have information concerning the physician's murder."

"Speak of the devil," Cole said, then followed with "Put him through, Mary." The phone chirped again, and Cole answered. "Huebsch here."

"Special Agent Huebsch, this is Frank Gumina. I'm an attorney representing the *Milwaukee Journal Sentinel.* I'm calling to tell you that someone proclaiming to be Dr. Smith's killer has emailed one of our reporters."

"Do you find it credible?"

"You tell me. He included some information in the email to back up his claim, information that he either fabricated or that you haven't made public. Specifically, he said he left his rifle on top of the nearby building from which he made his shot. And he said he also left a small, metal crucifix with blood on the roof as well. If you can confirm these things, then he's either the killer, or you have a leak. Which is it?"

Cole hit the phone's mute button and looked at his assembled team. "And now there's this…"

"Agent Huebsch? Are you still there?"

Cole unmuted the phone. "I'm here. And I need you to forward that email to me immediately. I'm also sending techs down to the *Journal* offices to trace the email's origin."

"So, you're confirming the email came from the killer?" The lawyer covered his phone and spoke quietly to someone else.

"I'm confirming nothing at this point. Just covering all the bases. And Gumina, please tell whomever's in the room with you, perhaps the publisher and editor, that interfering in this particular investigation will not go well for the paper itself or any individuals who don't cooperate fully."

"Well, now, there is such a thing as the Constitution and its first amendment. Freedom of speech and all that. You're probably sworn to protect such rights."

Cole knew the game well enough. "I have the number you're calling from. Expect a return call at that number in the next five minutes. You'll be speaking with lawyers from our D.C. offices. Work out a deal with them. In the meantime, I want two things. First, forward the alleged killer's email to me. Second, I want a face-to-face meeting with the reporter the killer reached out to. Have him meet me at the Calderone Club at seven p.m."

"Her. You mean have her meet you," the attorney corrected.

"Right." Cole clicked off.

Thirty minutes later, everyone had refreshed their beverages and read the killer's email. Reassembled around the conference room table, Cole asked for their thoughts.

Lane jumped in first. "DC's initial brief points out the guy, we're all assuming it's a guy of course, is fairly young. They think he might have screwed up and shared too much when he wrote that he wants to, ah..." he flipped through his notes, "when he wrote that he wants to 'raise a family... and to grow old with them near.' Everything the DC analysts say comes with caveats and stipulations, but they think that line from the email means the killer is likely between the ages of eighteen and forty."

"Or," Cole said, "he wants to make us believe that. But it certainly means something. Unless it doesn't. Anything else?"

Lane continued. "They're pretty sure the killer doesn't like abortions or the people that perform them. Not one little bit. The analysts are more certain of that than of the shooter's age."

"Li. Lane," Cole said, looking at each in turn. "You keep working hard and someday you'll be able to analyze an email that well."

He shook his head and stood up. "All right, everybody. Keep working this and share everything with all of us as well as with Chicago and DC as you learn more. Tonight I'll sit down and have a conversation with the *Journal Sentinel* reporter. Looks like our killer wants to be her pen friend."

Chapter Twelve

Cole waited for Michele Fields at the Calderone Club, an intimate Italian restaurant a block from the *Journal* Building. It was one of his favorite eateries. The soft lighting and even softer crooning of Sinatra, Martin, Como and company always relaxed him. The owner broke up the laid back and big band singing by mixing in popular songs from the late 60s and 70s. Cole was okay with that, too, since he'd hear songs his parents used to play when he was growing up. King Harvest's "Dancing In the Moonlight" was playing now.

The reporter was ten minutes late for their planned seven p.m. meeting and Cole had already finished a Motto Mosaic Pale Ale from the nearby Good City Brewing. It was fresh and delicious and maybe went down a little too quickly. Now he took his time with a glass of Kunde Estate Merlot. He swirled it, watching as the blood-red liquid repeatedly slid up the side of the clear bowl and then fell back onto itself, revealing its provocative legs. This was a ritual he did every time he drank a nice glass of red wine. In part it helped aerate the wine, bringing out the full fruit and oak hues of the quality Napa and Sonoma vintages he preferred. Maybe, he also thought, it was a simple nervous tic.

He stood up a minute or two later when Michele made her appearance. He knew nothing about the reporter when he asked for this meeting, other than the killer had reached out to her.

"Hi, Mrs. Fields. Thank you for coming. May I order you a drink?" He didn't have to be a special agent or a detective to figure out she was incredibly attractive. The way she moved as she made her way to his table told him she was self-assured, but there was also an almost indescribable hesitancy in her step. Maybe that was understandable given the events of the past two days.

"Yes, please," she said, smiling as she sat down. "I'll take a glass of sauvignon blanc. And please drop the Mrs. Fields. I'm not married and that moniker makes me feel like I should be whipping up a batch of cookies or something. Call me Michele. And one more thing, we need to split the bill. My paper won't pay for your meal, and it also prohibits me from accepting anything of value from anyone who might try to influence a story. That includes you."

"Fair enough," Cole said. After signaling their waiter and placing the reporter's wine order, he introduced himself as the FBI's Special Agent In Charge of the Milwaukee Field Office and told her he was working on solving Dr. Smith's murder. "Since the killer emailed you in response to your article, Ms. Fields, ah, Michele..." he corrected, "I think it's important that you and I maintain an open line of communication.

"I doubt today's story will be the last you write about the murder. I can feed you information, things that won't compromise our investigation. And you feed me any information you discover that could help us catch the killer. Also, our guys have already put a trace on your computer, so we can tell in near real-time where the killer's e-mails and phone calls originate from should he reach out to you again. If there's another killing or attempt, I have a warrant signed by a federal judge that lets me sit in front of your computer screen and read any message that comes in."

She leaned forward. She had on a simple navy blue pants suit with an ivory silk shirt that opened loosely at her throat. The flickering candlelight danced across her face and slender neck and Cole felt mesmerized. He had tried his best to come across as direct, impersonal, and maybe a bit intimidating. Now, he squirmed a little, uncertain he'd had the effect he'd sought.

"So," she said, straightening in her seat again, "you feed me. I feed you. And you read my emails and listen in on my calls. I'm not sure I like where our little relationship is headed," she said, taking the glass of white wine the waiter delivered and downing a third of it in one gulp. "Plus, there is that key verb that's part of any strong working relationship. It starts with a "T" and it stands for Trust. How do I trust that you will share information with me before you feed the pack of reporters that will surely be nipping at your heels, no, at your throat, throughout this mess?"

Cole leaned back in his chair and smiled at her. "I thought all good journalists were incredibly observant. Can't you look at me and tell I'm one of the good guys...that my word is my bond?" He tried to hide his smirk by taking a sip of the merlot.

"Yes, reporters are usually good diviners of truth. However, in your case, I'm dealing with the FBI. You guys are all about entrapment, disguise, and intrigue. I'm not sure you'll be straight with me." She said the last with no hint of humor.

"That disguise and intrigue stuff is more CIA than FBI. Beyond that, I don't know what else to say other than I'll share everything I can that won't compromise the investigation. Some of what I share you can attribute, and some will be off the record, that you can use as background. You'll have an incredible advantage over any other reporter covering this story."

"Even the hot Fox Newsgirls and the other TV starlets?" She smirked at him this time.

Cole paused, wondering if she knew about his ex-wife, before providing yet another awkward answer, "Ah, whomever. Yes."

The waiter came back to the table and took their orders. Cole asked for a starter of fried calamari followed by a t-bone steak smothered in mushrooms. Michele ordered zucchini sticks and chicken marsala.

"What do you know," Cole said. "Mushrooms are part of both our dinners. I think we've got some common ground to work from here."

"We're in an Italian restaurant," she said. "We've probably also got garlic as another common element. You could take that to mean mushrooms and garlic are the cornerstone of a wonderful new working relationship or realize instead that unless you stuck with the beer, wine, and maybe the Italian ice for dessert, that any two meals we ordered here would have those two things in common. But, nice effort on your part to create that trust thing. You'd do a better job of that by telling me what you've learned so far."

"Not a lot that will lead to anything quickly," Cole answered, shrugging his shoulders. "We found a rifle with a scope on top of the building that sits across the alley behind the clinic. We believe it's the weapon used to kill Dr. Smith. We also found a shell casing on the ground and a bullet in the chamber. The safety was in the off position and the gun would've fired again with a pull of the trigger. We're checking the gun and ammo for prints, but I don't hold out much hope. The serial number was visible and the gun was traced to a guy in Missouri. It looks like the guy is innocent though. The rifle was bought at a Waukesha gun show with what we believe to be a fake ID.

"We also found a small metal crucifix at the site. We think it was left by the killer, but there's no way we can be sure of that right now. Although that would be a heck of a coincidence if it wasn't. We also found deer blood at the scene."

"You know, I had all that. Everything but the deer blood," Michele admitted.

"Yes...well... We'd like to keep all of that...the rifle, the deer blood, and the crucifix, out of the media for the time being. I hope you agree that while it could add spice to your next story, it could be important in catching this guy. When we eventually corner the killer it could help us trip him up during an interrogation. He could let it slip and he'd have no way of explaining to us or a jury how he knew about any of those things without being the killer himself.

"That's about it though. We don't have much else to go on at this point," Cole concluded.

"Well, to start with, he has to be crazy, right? I mean, you don't just shoot another human being. This was done in broad daylight to a doctor who was serving the women of Milwaukee and other parts of the state as well." She cocked her head a bit, looking for encouragement or even assent.

"Yeah, I guess," Cole said, squeezing lemon juice over his calamari and then salting it. He dipped a morsel of the calamari with little tentacles into the marinara sauce provided. "Can we go off the record for a moment?"

"Sure."

"He probably is crazy. But he could also be sane and a very courageous person, at least in his own mind. You view the victim as 'a servant of women,' but maybe our shooter thinks killing two thousand unborn babies a year, half or more of whom would have someday grown up to be women if given the chance, is very different than being a godsend to women."

It was hard to tell in the dim light, but Cole thought the reporter's face flushed with emotion. She leaned back stiffly and her voice rose. "In your opinion then, this was a justifiable homicide, I suppose?"

"No. That's not my opinion. I'm saying that's how I think the shooter sees it. Given his email to you, it's probably even stronger than that. Today, abortion on demand, with few constraints, is protected by the law of the land, which includes me. But it wasn't that way until Roe v. Wade, and those laws could shift again in the future given the whims of our fellow citizens… that and a new Supreme Court Justice or two."

Michele was trying to hold her anger in check, but Cole saw a tremor ripple through her cheeks and he thought her wine glass might shatter, she gripped the bowl so tightly.

Cole took advantage of Michele's emotionally delayed response. "Did you know Jane Roe, Norma Leah McCorvey in real life, actually did a one-eighty and condemned abortion twenty-two years after winning her case? She called it wrong, murder, and said that U.S. women 'have literally been handed the right to slaughter their own children.' It took courage for her to do that."

Michele slammed her fist on the table, causing silverware to jump with a clatter. Other patrons turned to look. "Dr. Smith was the one with courage! He was the one who stood against the pro-life nut jobs. The killer is a coward. He shot Dr. Smith from a distance when he was unarmed by the way. And then he slunk off like a diseased rat. Every day the Dr. Smiths of the world drive and walk past the protesters, who yell vile obscenities at them and portray them as murderers…all so they can provide important health services to women who wouldn't otherwise have access to those services."

Cole followed a square of the medium-rare t-bone with two calamari circles. He hoped he wouldn't get indigestion, but he never did know when to back off a good argument. "Did you know that Dr. Smith also pretty much had to leave the practice of obstetrics?" he said. "His malpractice rate was the highest in the city and he turned to abortion full time as a career move. It turned out to be lucrative for him. We've been going over his books and Smith ran that clinic like a machine. He worked four days a week and averaged twelve abortions a day. He only worked forty-two weeks a year, taking an average of ten weeks of vacation, but he still managed roughly two thousand abortions annually. And his average charge per abortion was fifteen hundred dollars. If you go on his clinic's website you'll see that he takes American Express, Visa, Mastercard, even the Discover Card. You could buy your washing machine with your card in the morning and have your baby aborted with it in the afternoon, probably earn double points toward travel and prizes in the process. He didn't take personal checks, however. Dr. Smith was pulling in three million a year gross and, from what we can tell already, he couldn't have had more than nine hundred thousand in expenses at the clinic. So, Dr. Smith was clearing two point one million a year or better, pre-tax, by killing babies. That's professional baseball money. Maybe not Christian Yelich coin, but it beats the Major League Baseball minimum, which right now is about four hundred thousand a year. Those facts will likely never make their way into your paper I suspect.

"I don't think Smith was motivated by altruism or working for the common good," Cole concluded, reaching for a breadstick and snapping it in two. "He went into a business where he not only didn't get sued when a baby died on him, but they paid him handsomely to kill them. His was blood money, and he died a very rich man."

Michele stopped eating and looked hard into Cole's eyes again. "I can't believe what you're spewing here. How in the world can you do your best to put this criminal behind bars when you *sympathize* with him?" Her voice rose in both pitch and decibel level. "How can you stop him, take his life if necessary, when he's a hero to you?"

"He's no hero to me, but neither was Dr. Smith. I'll do my best to track down the killer the same way you'll write stories that tell both sides of those stories, I presume, even when the only side you're on is the pro-abortion, excuse me, the pro-choice side." He had an FBI tab with the proprietor and signed the chit the waiter proffered. He stood to leave, then, and held her gaze. "I'll do my best to get the killer, and you'll do your best to write balanced stories for the same reason...because those are our jobs. It's what we do." He turned and weaved through the tables and left the restaurant.

Michele sat at the table reflecting a few moments, swirling the last of the sauvignon blanc in her glass, when she realized Cole had paid for the meal. "Well, shit," she said to herself. Frank Sinatra was singing "I did it my way" faintly in the background as she drained the glass and got up to leave.

Chapter Thirteen

The shooter stared at the darkened computer monitor in the basement of his two-bedroom ranch, only semi-aware of his reflection. The house totaled less than a thousand square feet of living space, but it was plenty big enough for him. He lived alone since leaving his parents' home what now seemed a lifetime ago. That was when he'd run off and enlisted in the army. He had actually wanted to serve his country in a war people would later say should never have been fought. Looking back that was a dumb, even tragic, move. He might have been a little off when he and the other men in his company deplaned and walked into that wall of heat for the first time, but he was certifiably messed up by the time they sent him home. But how could he have known any better? He was a kid when he'd signed on to preserve and protect the American way of life. Then, like now, all he'd wanted to do was step up and be a man…to do the right thing. He thought maybe he had it right this time. He wasn't as fit as he'd been when he set off to fight all those years ago, but he was a helluva lot smarter.

He stretched his legs out under the counter his old tube-type monitor perched on. A thin veneer of blue indoor-outdoor carpeting covered the cement floor under his feet. The carpet had a blotchy green and blue pattern the guy at the store years ago had told him would hide dust and dirt. He turned his gaze down at the carpet and figured it would camouflage the mess pretty well if he hurled on it, too.

It turned out he didn't need to hide dirt. He kept the carpet and every inch of his little house meticulously clean. He liked things orderly and neat.

Maybe that's why he was still alone this far into his life. The shooter had lady friends along the way, as his mother would have called them. But he got uncomfortable when things moved past friendship or companionship and moved on toward something akin to intimacy. It made him feel claustrophobic. He was far more comfortable alone, even if it meant being lonely. It was safer. He often thought about children, and how he would've liked some of his own…maybe teach his boys how to hunt and fish like he'd learned from his father before his dad turned hard and mean. He hadn't really lied when he'd emailed that reporter that he wanted a wife and children. He just knew it wasn't in the cards for him. If that tidbit helped the Feds think their guy was a bit younger that was okay, too.

Mulling it over, he thought he was kidding both himself and the reporter. Over the years when kids got too close or clingy it made him anxious. It set him on edge as much, even if a bit differently, than when a woman did. He'd thought long and hard about his situation over the years, and had come to the conclusion that he revered women and children too much to allow himself to be a meaningful part of their lives. He put them on a pedestal, and he didn't feel worthy of them. He loved them unconditionally, even if from a distance. He was better off, and better able to protect them, he reasoned, if he was unencumbered.

The shooter shook himself from his stupor and sat up straight. He took a deep, settling breath and concentrated again. He shuffled through the stack of papers in front of him that represented his research on who was performing abortions, where they performed them, and where they lived. It wasn't easy to gather the information these days, but he'd found out a lot via the Internet when he first began planning this mission a month ago. He'd done his research in different cities, using computers available at public libraries or places like FedEx Office Stores. If the Feds had tracers on the sites he'd visited, they would have a difficult time following the breadcrumbs back to him.

Twenty years ago it would have been a snap to get the information he had worked hard on the sly to collect. Back in the late 1990s, a group of righteous lifers published a website called the *Nuremberg Files*. The site described abortion doctors as war criminals and called them out for their crimes against humanity. It ran photographs of the physicians along with their names, home addresses, and phone numbers. It would have made the shooter's job easier and he could have begun implementing his plan sooner. The site might still be available if it hadn't begun highlighting the names of abortion doctors who'd been wounded and striking out those who'd been killed. At that point, a U.S. Appeals Court decided the *Nuremberg Files* website was nothing more than a hit list. It ruled that the right to life and liberty trumped the first amendment and shut the site down in 2002.

His own typed hit list contained ten names, all arranged smartly on one page, starting at the top with Charles Smith, and continuing down, almost jumping off the white page in their bold 18-pt. Arial font. The Charles Smith entry had a hand-drawn pencil line through it. William Martin was in the number two slot. The Appleton, Wisconsin abortion provider had been pushed up on the shooter's list because a lefty pro-choice rag had recently included him in its listing of the "10 Best Abortion Doctors in America."

As he planned Dr. Martin's demise, the shooter shook his head and wondered aloud, "They're ranking these scumbags now? What's the world coming to?"

Chapter Fourteen

Cole descended the stairs that led from his apartment directly down to the attached indoor garage. He stepped lightly , not wanting to wake his elderly friend and landlady at the early hour. Halfway down the steps, however, he knew she was up already. He could smell the sweet, hickory scent of bacon and heard the faint sizzle and pop of it cooking on the stove through the heavy landing door.

"Cole?" she called from the kitchen. "Do you have time for breakfast?"

The landing led into the kitchen and he pushed open the door to find Alvina Newhouse standing at the stove in a plain yellow housedress. He went and gave her a gentle hug from behind.

"*Guten morgen,* Frau Newhouse." Cole said good morning in the tongue she spoke in her youth, handed down from the days when her great, great, great grandfather was building an empire around the beer recipes they brought with them from Bavaria in the mid-1800s. "Would I ever say no to your pancakes, Frau?"

She turned to face him and did an abbreviated curtsey in deference to her eighty-six-year-old knees. "*Danke schoen,*" she thanked him, smiling. "Even at this early hour, you can be a charmer." She was a little plump, but her full face was filled with even more kindness than wrinkles, and the soft, white hair that framed it reminded him of a halo.

He took a chair at the heavy oak table and she scraped three pan-sized cakes onto his plate from a black cast iron skillet.

"Are you trying to fatten me up?" he said, slathering on butter and pouring syrup over the pancakes 'til it flooded down the sides.

She made a clucking sound with her tongue and waved the spatula in front of him. "I'm hoping if I put some meat on your bones that I can finally marry you off. I could let my hair down a little if you weren't hanging around trying to watch over me all the time." She arched her eyebrows and smiled.

He finished his pancakes and half a pound of bacon within ten minutes and then allowed himself to share a moment drinking strong black coffee with Frau Newhouse. They didn't see much of each other during the week, but they ate dinner together nearly every Sunday evening. They rotated the cooking, but neither saw it as a chore. The Sundays were a ritual that started naturally, not long after he moved into the upper floor of her expansive house. The "castle mansion" as locals called it was built in 1891 of red brick and sandstone. It had been on the National Historic Register for more than forty years. Almost ten thousand square feet, it cost her family patriarch, August "Captain" Newhouse, one hundred and twenty-eight thousand dollars to build. In today's dollars, that sum would be closer to seventeen million.

Cole moved in eleven years ago, within a month of his wife's departure for the brighter lights of New York. Frau Newhouse had been looking for live-in protection after a break-in had scared her deeply, and Cole wanted to get away from the condo that he had shared with Janet. Everything about the modern apartment they had shared began to haunt him, reverberating silently but overwhelmingly that he had failed at his marriage.

"What do you think about, Cole?" Frau startled him.

"I was thinking about the day ahead. I've got a lot to do," he admitted.

She pointed to the front page of the newspaper that sat in the middle of the table. "Are you working on this case?" Her right index finger hovered directly over another story about the killing of Dr. Charles Smith.

He nodded. "I am."

"I don't think that doctor was a good man by any means, but he should not have been shot like that, like an animal. You need to find the person who killed him and put him in jail."

"Why, I couldn't have said it any better myself," Cole smiled.

"*Ya*. But be careful. This could get stickier than the syrup you have on your cheek," she said, rubbing it away with her rag.

Chapter Fifteen

It was still shy of six-thirty in the morning when Cole began backing out of the middle stall of the five-car garage. His hands were bare and the leather-wrapped steering wheel felt like it was made of pure ice. Even on winter's most bitter days, he didn't want to surrender to it by wearing gloves. This habit caused the cold, dry air to create little nicks and cracks in his fingers. He wore a suit, but no overcoat. He never wore a heavy coat over his suit coat, regardless of how low the outside temperature plunged. It made him feel constricted and he hated the extra bulk. So, he shivered and his butt felt cold on the frigid leather seat. He clenched his entire body in a quick isometric exercise designed to increase his blood flow, hit the button to start his heater, and turned the temp up to seventy-eight degrees with the fan on full throttle. At first, it would make things even frostier by blasting the cold air around the car's interior, but he knew in a few minutes the air would be toasty. The Dodge's heater was as reliable as Cole was. He reached down and flicked his seat warmer to high. He was looking backward and straining to see as exhaust billowed from his Charger, the vapor's life extended by the bitter cold. It hung in the air like ghostly apparitions that haunted the driveway as he maneuvered. He rolled into the quiet, dim street. As he shifted into Drive he looked up and saw that a faint moon was visible in the pre-dawn sky. For some reason that depressed him.

He turned on the radio and punched the button for "60s on 6" on the satellite radio. He brightened up when he heard one of his favorite Beatles songs playing. George Harrison, in one of his rare lead vocals, sang, *Do you want to know a secret?*

He thought of the newspaper on Frau's table and the reporter he met the night before. She was beautiful, confident, and smart. That was easy enough to see. But she was also vulnerable and skittish at times. A contradiction. He hadn't exactly won her over with his charm.

"*Whoa. Oh, shit*! he cursed, swerving to avoid a garbage can-sized pothole. The deep holes in the asphalt were caused by the intermittent freezing and thawing that wore on the roads and the people all winter long. Potholes could open up in a road overnight, at times only to be hidden by snow. If a wheel dropped into one, especially with any speed, you could wreck the tire and even a rim.

His visibility wasn't great. The car's windshield was streaked with dried mud and grime. He hit the windshield fluid button; the motor groaned, but no fluid shot out. The wipers came to life, however, smearing the mess even more. He was either out of wiper fluid or it was frozen solid. He pulled over to the curb, cursing himself. He got out and grabbed a big handful of snow. He threw it at his windshield and got back into the car, turning on his wipers again as he pulled back into the street. The snow cleared his windshield. He was nothing if not resourceful, he thought.

He followed an older pickup and the exhaust from the rusted-out Ford F-150 obscured his vision again. The sight reminded him, ironically, of muggy summer nights growing up in rural Wisconsin. He could envision riding his banana bike with a pack of kids behind the fogger that sprayed for mosquitoes. He felt the warmth of his parent's love then, bigger than any pothole, followed by the cold, hollow feeling of having lost them both without warning. He shook away the feeling.

He thought of the reporter again. If he was going to make progress in the case, he'd likely have to make headway in his relationship with her. He needed at least an uneasy truce, if not something more.

He swerved to miss another pothole, this one the size of a dorm room refrigerator. "Argh!" He let out his frustration and pulled the wheel hard right and into the Starbucks lot. He needed a Blonde before going after the brunette.

Chapter Sixteen

Michele stepped off the elevator into the midsection of the *Journal* building's second floor where most of the news staff worked. She was tired, but exhilarated at the same time. She was writing important stories. National stories.

She walked past the long row of cubicles with her head down, unfocused on the carpet, as she planned the day's interviews and potential stories out in her head. Still thirty feet or so from her cubicle she became aware of a presence. She looked ahead and saw Cole leaning back against her cubby.

She scanned the newsroom and saw they were alone in the large expanse. "What are you doing here?"

He stepped around the cubicle and picked up two grande Starbucks coffees and held one out to her. "I need to keep working on this relationship," he said. "I want to get this killer and get him bad. I need you to be clear that I don't have any mixed motivation in that area. I guessed you would take cream but no sugar. If I'm wrong you can have mine. It's black."

She showed the hint of a smile as she took the coffee. "Maybe your instincts are okay after all. You got the coffee right. I'd go for the sugar, too, but I can't afford the empty calories."

He returned the smile. "Normally, I would argue that point, but instead, I promise not to argue at all this morning. I'm going to do everything on my part to make this relationship work for as long as it has to, right up until we catch the killer." He pulled some typed sheets of paper out of a manila file folder and held them out to her.

"This is some of the background information we've compiled so far. First, the actual murder of abortion doctors is pretty rare. It's only happened four times in our nation's long history, five times when Smith is added. The last time it happened was back on May 31, 2009, when an abortion doctor in Wichita was shot and killed in the foyer of his Lutheran church. His wife was singing in the choir at the time. The people in the pews were quoted as saying they thought they heard a popping sound, like a child had brought a balloon into church and it burst. Unlike Dr. Smith, that guy had been in the high beams of the extreme pro-life groups for a long time. He took particular pride in offering late-term abortions. He'd been shot in both arms years earlier and had his clinic bombed and vandalized.

"Just like now, when the Wichita doctor was murdered, the U.S. Attorney General dispatched U.S. Marshalls to protect abortion doctors and clinics around the country. That's a lot of resources being deployed across the entire U.S. because of one bullet that was fired and no evidence yet that shows it to be anything other than an isolated event.

"Before Wichita, you have to go all the way back to the fall of 1998 when an abortion doctor was shot to death in his Amherst, New York home. He was killed by a single shot from a gunman with a high-powered rifle as he padded around his own house. He was shot through his kitchen window after he and his family returned home from their synagogue.

"Anti-abortion violence is mostly a U.S. pastime, but other countries including Canada have seen their share. Like the Amherst doctor, three abortion doctors in Canada were shot in late October or early November in their own homes. Those shootings took place between 1994 and 1997. Each time it was around dusk and they were shot with high-powered rifles. It's commonly believed to center around the Canadian observance of Remembrance Day. All three of the Canadian physicians who were shot survived the attacks."

"Hold on," Michele said, after taking a couple small sips of the coffee. "It's nice you brought me coffee and you're sharing information and all, but everything you've given me so far is right there for every reporter to find on Google. What can you tell me that I don't already know or can't find out on my own?"

Cole shrugged, conceding the point. "We already confirmed that the shooter left behind his rifle and a crucifix. We didn't share any of that with the general media and it pretty much proves your email pal is either the killer or an accomplice. Ballistics matched the slug we dug out of the exterior cinder block wall of the clinic with the 30/30 rifle we recovered from the roof of the two-story bakery across the street from the back of the building. Not that it matters, but it was a 170-grain soft pointed Winchester slug, the kind of ammunition you can pick up in most sporting goods stores without presenting any form of ID. The manufacturer sells millions of rounds a year across the country and overseas."

Cole noticed a photo on Michele's desk of a little girl maybe nine or ten years old, holding the tether to a large Holstein cow and smiling broadly. What looked to be her proud parents stood on either side of her. He looked up at Michele and asked, "Did you grow up on a dairy farm?"

She turned the photo face down on the desk. "Distracted easily, are we?"

"Right. So, the crucifix is somewhat interesting. It costs less than a quarter when bought in bulk and can be found in half the Catholic churches and missions worldwide. You've got a blown-up image of the crucifix in the sheaf of papers I gave you. MPD found the crucifix a few feet from where they found the rifle. We don't know yet if the shooter dropped it by mistake or to send us another message, but our betters in DC think it's a message and I tend to agree."

Michele nodded. "It's too symbolic and yet too random not to mean something." She was looking at him intently, and for the first time, Cole noticed how dark her brown eyes were and how long the lashes that protected them.

He took a sip of coffee. "We checked everything for prints, but it was all clean. The thing is, we did find the deer blood on both the shell casing and the cross. Right now we think the deer blood indicates Dr. Smith was sacrificed by the killer in a perverted Old Testament kind of way."

"What do you mean?"

"Either Smith was sacrificed for his sins, or the deer was sacrificed to make amends for the shooter's taking the life of Smith. We don't really know. But this early in an investigation, everything is important and none of this could be relevant. The shooter could be messing with us."

Michele unconsciously bit her upper lit gently and appraised Cole, wondering if he was sharing everything he had. He wouldn't be the first man to mislead her if he wasn't. "Any conclusions?"

"For now, all signs point to a religious zealot who, unfortunately for Dr. Smith and for us, seems to be able to hit what he aims at."

Chapter Seventeen

Christmas Eve (four weeks earlier)

The Sermon

"And he commanded us to preach unto the people, and to testify that it is he which was ordained of God to be the judge of quick and dead." — Acts 10:42

Father Bill Wagner spent the last moments of another Christmas Eve in the small rectory that sat next to the oldest existing stone church in the state of Wisconsin. The sturdy church had served the Roman Catholics of Prairie du Chien since 1836. At one time the little Mississippi River town was a bigger hub of commerce than Chicago, when Hercules Dousman became the state's first millionaire. Dousman began working for the Great American Fur Company some ten years before St. Gabriel's Church was finished, buying beaver and other pelts from both native and white trappers and shipping them east to his boss, John Jacob Astor. Both men grew rich without ever setting a trap. Dousman's son built Villa Louis; the mansion still stood on a rise a mile or so away from the church on St. Feriole Island, barely keeping dry during the river's worst floods, and drawing tourists from all over the Midwest and beyond throughout the year.

But the rectory was no mansion. It was a two-bedroom house clad in dull, dark red brick the color of dried blood. From the outside this night, with smoke puffing from the chimney and a warm light coming from the first-floor bedroom that Father Wagner called his study, the rectory looked cozy. But the priest wouldn't have described it that way if anyone had bothered to stop by.

The study had room for a small desk and chair, an old, wooden two-drawer file cabinet, and the big overstuffed distressed leather chair and ottoman he sat in now. Wagner had thrown on as many split lengths of birch and oak as he dared, and the tongues of fire leapt, popping and hissing straight up into the flue. But Wagner felt no warmth. Instead, he felt cold and alone.

Earlier he had celebrated Midnight Mass at nine p.m. It wasn't that many years ago that his parishioners had crowded the pews by eleven-thirty p.m. for a true Midnight Mass. If you came much after eleven you knew you'd be standing at the back of the church or along one of the side aisles. They would sing Christmas hymns for thirty minutes before the hour-long service even began. It seemed then that his people couldn't wait to greet the news of the swaddling savior. In recent years, though, the Midnight Mass had made the priest feel like Jesus himself in Mark's version of the Agony in the Garden. While he prayed and sweated blood, his disciples were sound asleep.

By ten p.m. on this evening, the last of the carols had been sung and the congregation streamed out of the proud old church like rivulets of water from a leaky bucket. The priest contemplated sticking around outside in the minus fifteen-degree night air to shake hands and wish everyone a Merry Christmas. But instead, he slipped out the back door of the vestibule. The chill crept into him then, and stayed with him as his shadow trailed him across the frozen lawn and into the side door of the rectory.

He went straight to the fridge and grabbed a bottle of Cave Ale, brewed in nearby Potosi. He opened it and drank from the bottle as he shuffled down the short, narrow hallway to his study, peeling off his coat and hat and hanging them on wooden hooks near the door. The leather chair groaned and creaked as his two hundred and fifty pounds settled in.

Two hours crept past and it was nearly midnight. Three ales and two Driftless Lagers stood empty alongside the chair. But empty bottles are neglected bottles. Wagner looked at the near-empty bottle of lager in his hand and gave hollow thanks to the owner of the town's only liquor store. The priest had let Nick Bower know when he first came to the parish that he relished the occasional beer. That was thirty-five years ago in July. Being a good Catholic, Bower began dropping off a six-pack of different beer each Saturday evening before he went back to his store after dinner. The years had been kind to Bower's store, and the priest's thirst grew along with the proprietor's business. Father Wagner's beer selection was now nearly as universal as his Church, and the two cases Bower slipped inside the priest's door every Saturday evening were always drained and the empties repacked when the proprietor returned the following week.

Wagner turned his vacant gaze to the small desk. It had been his father's. But his father died three months before Wagner was ordained. *He would have been proud that day I became a priest,* he thought. Then he teared up and lost the fight to hold back the moisture that suddenly filled his eyes and rolled down his face and onto his shirt. He wiped and rubbed his eyes with the palm of his hand, thinking, *but he would be ashamed of me now.* His dad had been a dairy farmer and Bill had helped him milk nearly one hundred Holsteins when he was a boy. They milked the cows by hand early in the morning and again before dinner. The son also helped tend to their hogs and chickens and the geese that ran free in the yard.

Together, they plowed the fields in early spring so mother earth would open up and receive their seeds of hay, oats, and corn. They nurtured the crops through the sunbaked summers and harvested them in the waning light of fall.

Every Christmas Eve, Billy and his parents attended Midnight Mass in the nearby town of Bloomington. By the time they made it back to the farm, the boy was asleep. His dad would wake him and the two of them would walk a few hundred yards, most years through drifted snow, to a small clearing surrounded by oak trees. His dad would lay down a tarp and throw two heavy sleeping bags in the middle. They would each climb into a bag and huddle together for warmth, lying on their backs and gazing up at the night sky.

Every year his dad would ask him about the wise men and how they'd followed the star. "Can you believe they followed the star for two years?" he'd say. "Can you believe they saw a bright star in the sky and knew they had to follow? They up and left their families and friends to welcome the Christ Child. You and I can hardly imagine the hardships they faced on their journey, Billy. They crossed mountains, and deserts so hot, they'd make hay-mowing season here seem like the cool of a mild spring. And they kept on until they found the baby. I don't begin to understand that kind of faith. I can only marvel at it."

Bill loved those pre-dawn Christmas mornings with his father. He would look up into the sky and see layer upon layer of stars overhead. Away from the light pollution of even a small town, the heavens were peeled bare and though a million suns shined for the boy and his father, always one stood out as the brightest. "Should we follow it, Billy?" his dad would ask. "Should we wake your mother and the three of us head out to find the new Christ Child?" They would laugh, then, and huddle closer. Sometimes Bill felt his dad wanted to light out after the star for real.

In the early hours of the Christmas morning six weeks after Bill turned seventeen, he and his father were in the clearing, their mom asleep in the nearby farmhouse. The boy told his dad that he felt called to follow the star, to become a priest. "But I know that can't be right," he said. He was an only child and there was no brother or sister waiting to take over the farm. His dad lay quietly and said nothing.

The boy woke late the next morning. His dad let him sleep in Christmas Day. That was the one morning each year his father milked the cows himself. His mom worked at the stove as he went out to see how his dad was doing. There in the middle of their gravel drive was a 4' X 8' sheet of plywood with "FARM FOR SALE" hand-lettered in red barn paint that was still wet.

He ran to the barn as his dad finished milking the last of the cows. His dad released the cow from its stanchion and gave it a tender but firm slap on its rear, sending the cow outside to join the rest of the herd. He had a contented smile on his face as Billy started to protest. "Dad, you can't sell the farm," he said. "It's all you and mom have ever worked for."

"We've spent our lives trying to put food in people's stomachs. But look around, son. People have more than enough to eat. Now we have a chance, through you, to feed men's souls. When it comes to food, we are a nation of plenty; but our souls are starving. I love you and I love Jesus." And the son knew there was no point arguing.

Father Wagner's head bobbed and he came back from the farm, his eyes blearily fixed on the desk again, the thin layer of veneer that covered it like a skin, was marred and nicked. He could picture his dad sitting at that desk, sorting through his few pieces of mail, or paying his larger stack of bills. The lower right-hand drawer of the desk had been his dad's "junk drawer," stuffed with rubber bands, dried-out pens, decks of cards for pinochle and euchre, string, and more. It was a treasure drawer for a young boy, but now it held only a loaded service revolver. A cold reminder that a young boy's dreams sometimes warp into an old man's nightmare.

Chapter Eighteen

Father Wagner sighed heavily and heaved himself out of the recliner. He went to the desk, bent over, and opened the lower right drawer. He picked up the gun in his right hand and nudged the drawer shut with his left foot. He shuffled back to the recliner and settled back into it.

He studied the gun through glazed eyes and with a brain dimmed by exhaustion and beer. The Smith and Wesson Model 19 felt heavy in his hand. Substantial, he thought. It was an old service revolver that Wagner had borrowed from one of his parishioners. Sheriff's Deputy Randall Hubbard served as an usher at nine-thirty Mass most Sunday mornings and helped out during holiday Masses, too. One day back in the fall, Wagner asked the deputy to stop by the rectory after Mass. The priest told Hubbard he thought he had seen someone outside the rectory from time to time, and that it made him feel uneasy. The deputy said he would make a point of driving by the rectory several times during the evening hours, even when he was off duty. But Wagner told the deputy he didn't want such a fuss made. "I would feel safer if I had a handgun, though. Just in case."

Hubbard had some misgivings, but the priest assured him he had grown up on a farm and was comfortable with firearms. Wagner also told the deputy that he would never shoot to kill, but that didn't necessarily help put the deputy's mind at ease. In the end, Hubbard couldn't deny his priest. He gave him the Model 19 he carried on duty his first couple of decades with the county, until the department issued semi-automatic weapons to its officers. The Model 19 was a great handgun. If there was a live round in the chamber when you pulled the trigger it would go off every time. "Dependable," was the word he used to describe it to Father Wagner.

Now, near midnight on Christmas Eve, Wagner sat in the chair and held the gun, the compact that carried six .357 magnum rounds in its cylinder. Light reflected off the polished nickel of the four-inch barrel, and the dark checked wood handgrip felt clumsy in Wagner's hand.

Wagner's mood was even darker than the walnut grip. He started to determine the best way to fatally shoot himself. If he put the gun under his chin and pointed it back a bit, would he feel much pain as he left this world? Or would it be more efficient and pain-free if he put the gun in his mouth, and "ate the gun" as people said? Would that give him a better chance of ending his miserable existence with as little pain as possible?

Warm tears of shame and despair streamed down his face. The room that felt so cold minutes ago now felt unbearably hot. *Maybe it's the entrance of hell I'm feeling,* he thought to himself. If he took his own life that is where he would go, according to everything the Church had taught him.

But part of him didn't believe in God anymore. In truth, most of him didn't. From where he sat right now, literally and figuratively, he didn't know if he could count a single fiber in his body that believed in God anymore. And that's what made him feel like such a failure. A charlatan. The beer dulled his pain a bit, but nights like this he was sure only the revolver could take away the pain completely and forever.

He lifted the gun up and held the barrel flush against his right temple. He figured this method was as good as any. The revolver had no safety. Every cylinder held a live cartridge. He made sure of that the day Hubbard gave him the gun. And it was reliable, firing a round every time you pulled the trigger. But he would only pull the trigger once. This would be no game of solitaire. No game of Russian roulette.

Chapter Nineteen

Father Wagner tried to hold the gun level, so the bullet would exit his left temple, as the life and death battle raged within him. He felt a tremor ripple through his forearm and wrist, and then a full-blown spasm in his hand that almost caused him to drop the gun. His arm felt heavy. Spittle gathered at his lips as he whimpered. He cried aloud, wild with fear, as he finally pulled the trigger and the hammer of the gun slapped down with a click.

No deafening noise. No pain. He closed his eyes tight and held the nose of the revolver tighter against his temple and screamed as he pulled the trigger again. *Click*. Nothing.

He moaned, then barely winced as he pulled the trigger robotically, again and again, with the same results. *Click. Click. Click. Click*. He was sweating profusely, drained and numb with confusion. He dropped the pistol and it landed with a muffled thud on the carpeted floor. Drenched in his own tears and sweat, but not in his own blood, he held his head in both hands and sobbed. Frustration, grief, and relief all tore at him from different directions. He was a fraud, such a coward and utter failure that he couldn't even kill himself.

Tremors wracked his body and he shook violently. He looked up as if to the heavens, for the first time in years, his face contorting to a mask of pure anger. In a quavering, breaking voice he screamed, "What is your will? What would you have me do?"

His chest heaved in and out and he struggled for air as he waited for a response he was sure would not come. It was quiet then, with only his labored breathing breaking the stillness. He waited, and when he was certain no answer was coming, his eyes fell upon the parish calendar on the wall above his desk. It was open to December. On the page above the dates was a large colored print of the nativity scene; the baby Jesus in a manger surrounded by Mary, Joseph, the wise men, and shepherds. A radiant light shown through the clouds above and spotlighted the infant. As Wagner looked through watery eyes at the print, he wanted to believe in the birth and the rebirth that the scene promised. New life for the world and for himself. At that moment a loud pop came from the fireplace, trapped steam escaping from a burning log. And the room began to brighten. A stream of light came through a crack in the closed drapes and fell on the calendar, bathing the baby Jesus and his followers in a soft, sweet radiance.

An immense weight lifted off the priest then, and a lightness descended upon him. Maybe it was from above or maybe from within. It didn't matter. Either way, he felt more like that kid again on those Christmas Eves long ago, snuggled in a sleeping bag under the stars with his dad, marveling at the majesty of the heavens above. "Father," he said, invoking the name of his dad and of his Lord and Master at the same time, "forgive me. I love you. Thy will be done."

He got out of the chair and retrieved the gun. He took out the shells one by one and dropped them in the bottom desk drawer along with the gun. If the Lord had not prevented the gun from firing, he would not have been given this chance at redemption. He thanked Him for His grace.

Father Wagner would have done well to also thank Deputy Hubbard, whose uneasiness had caused him to remove the gun's firing pin before loaning it to the priest.

Chapter Twenty

Father Wagner went to the bathroom and splashed cold water on his face. He examined himself in the mirror as he patted himself dry. Though he looked dog-tired, Wagner saw a light reflected in his eyes that he had believed had burned out long ago. He poured himself a glass of water and drank it down before walking back to his study. He sat down at his desk and pulled out a pad of paper and a pen. He felt almost giddy, recalling the scene in Charles Dickens's *A Christmas Carol*, where a reformed Ebenezer Scrooge awakens to a new day and the possibility of a new life. He felt like emulating Scrooge and throwing open a window to shout his joy to the world, but he held back. If any of his parishioners were out at this hour they would think he was crazy, drunk, or both. Instead, he knew he needed to somehow capture the moment in case it was fleeting. But he didn't know what to do next.

He picked up the Bible that had sat unopened on a corner of the desk, gathering dust for months, and randomly flipped it open. He landed in the New Testament, Act nine of the Acts of the Apostles. It was the story of Saul and his conversion on the road to Damascus.

The priest read aloud, "And suddenly a light shone around him from heaven. Then he fell to the ground and heard a voice saying to him, 'Saul, Saul, why are you persecuting me so?'

"And Saul said, "Who are you, Lord?

"Then the Lord said, "I am Jesus, whom you are persecuting.'

"So he, trembling and astonished said, "Lord, what do you want me to do?"

Wagner gasped. Those were essentially the same words he had used moments before, during what he now realized was his own conversion. The Lord had saved him for a purpose. But what was it? He picked up the pen and stared at the lined yellow paper before him. He didn't know quite where or how to start. But the Lord had led him this far. He allowed his eyes to roam again and they were drawn immediately back to the calendar. The light streamed from the window and highlighted the baby Jesus. And then, in great clarity, he knew. He was to herald the coming of the Lord and to stand up for not just Christ, but for all infants. Why, if unrestricted abortion had been the law of the land in Nazareth or Bethlehem two thousand-plus years ago when Mary was ripe with child, would Jesus have even been born? He started writing his Christmas sermon then and it poured out of him.

Chapter Twenty-One

Christmas morning arrived and Father Wagner awoke feeling more alive than he had in years. He actually sang carols in the shower. He ate toast, drank a small glass of tomato juice, and read the *La Crosse Tribune, Dubuque Telegraph Herald,* and *Wisconsin State Journal,* the dailies that covered Prairie du Chien and its surroundings. He finished dressing, tugged the heavy coat on, and went out into the cold. His thermometer read minus sixteen, but if you added in the wind chill factor, it felt more like thirty-five below. Wagner went out in front of the Church and began greeting the early arrivers for Mass, nearly forty minutes before the ten a.m. service would begin. They shook his hand and said their "Merry Christmases," but the regulars looked at him with equal parts wariness and skepticism. Wagner never greeted his flock outside of Church before a Mass. But here, on the coldest and busiest of mornings for a priest, he stayed there shaking hands and bellowing a hearty "Merry Christmas" until almost nine fifty, when he hurried around to the back of the church and entered the sacristy.

He slipped a new white robe over his street clothes. The bright alb was worn at Christmas, Easter, and other feasts by Catholic priests as a sign they were rejoicing. He tied the alb at his waist with the girdle, a sign of his chastity. Over his shoulders he draped the white stole that was given to him at his ordination. The stole was a reminder of the days when slaves wore towels around their necks, and when bending or kneeling would wipe their master's feet or those of his guests. It was to remind the priest that he, too, was a servant of Christ and his people. Not since the day he celebrated his first Mass as a priest had this simple act of dressing felt so pure and honest to the priest. Finally, Wagner layered on his chasuble, a white, sleeveless garment. While donning his vestments he recited a series of prayers, asking the Lord for virtue, purity, and restoration. Never had the words been so meaningful to the priest.

As he pulled the last of his vestments on and finished his prayers, he stood content. He took a deep breath and exhaled long and slow. From the sacristy, he heard the last of the Christmas carols. A young college boy home on vacation tested the limits of his strong tenor voice, singing, *"O night, O holy night, O night divine!"* As the young man beautifully held the last note, the priest went out to be with his flock.

The processional and the first part of the Mass were a blur to the priest, but he had never led his congregation with such surety and confidence before. To the mesmerized parishioners who watched in awe, Father Wagner's body and his voice seemed to float, but with an energy and strength none in the pews had witnessed previously. Two loyal and long-standing members of the parish council delivered the traditional Christmas readings. All at once, it was time for the sermon.

Father Wagner stood tall and looked out over the congregation. His notes were spread before him on the lectern, but he didn't so much as glance at them. Parishioners who sat in the pews faithfully six days a week were wedged close to family, friends, and strangers who came this one day of the year. On this day, Father Wagner was open to things that rarely, if ever, caught his eye when he said the Mass. His church was beautiful. Breathtaking even. The fourteen Stations of the Cross lined the twenty-foot high walls of the church, each a large carved work of art with Christ's suffering and sacrifice depicted in bold relief. Towering stained-glass windows that threw a warm rainbow of hues throughout the church separated the Stations of the Cross.

A large crucifix hung from the wall of the sanctuary behind him, and twin eighteen-foot-tall Frasier firs flanked Christ on the Cross, replacing the criminals who'd been crucified with him for real more than two thousand years ago. The Christmas trees were each lit with more than five thousand warm mini-lights, and their glow bathed the entire sanctuary. The stone altar rose above a lush bed of large, vibrant poinsettia plants. The bright crimson flowers climbed up the front and sides of the altar with leaping red flames of color. A nativity scene, hand-carved by a devout parishioner over one hundred and fifty years ago, was nestled in the middle of the poinsettias. The baby Jesus lay in a makeshift crib, while Mary and Joseph flanked him, kneeling in prayer, watched over by shepherds, angels, and animals alike.

The fragrance of incense mingled with the smell of burning candles. A comforting warmth filled the church.

While his own flock fidgeted in their pews in anticipation, Father Wagner felt a rare calm. The church was quiet. No coughing. No babies crying. There was a shared sense of anticipation. The entire congregation felt something unusual coming, but none knew what it might be.

Wagner was unhurried. He looked up and to his left at a large statue of Joseph the Carpenter, the simple, selfless man who raised Jesus as his own son. It reminded Father Wagner of his own father and his eyes shown a little brighter. When Father looked to his right, he saw a statue of the Blessed Virgin Mary protectively holding the baby Jesus to her breast. Instead of looking out over the crowd, Mary looked lovingly down at her child. *Our savior,* Wagner thought. *How fitting.*

Chapter Twenty-Two

"Good morning," Wagner began, the small microphone clipped to his robe carrying his words clearly to all in attendance.

"Good morning, Father," came the joined response of the congregation.

Wagner smiled and stepped out from behind the pulpit. He walked down the steps and stood in the center aisle. Husbands stole glances at wives and neighbors at friends. Eyebrows rose. Another twist. Father Wagner never left the lectern. He stayed there, hunched over, avoiding eye contact, reading word for word tired sermons written decades before. But here he was now, standing tall. Beaming. No notes in hand.

"I should say that it's a great morning," Wagner continued. "This is the day we celebrate the coming of our Lord, God, and Savior. It's a great day indeed!"

He looked around the church and tried to really see every person seated before him. "I want to start this morning with an apology. In the past I've spent the bulk of each Christmas sermon chastising those who come to Church only one or two times a year, criticizing you for a lack of either faith or commitment." He paused and shook his head. "What a waste. How wrong I was. How terribly wrong. Please, forgive me. Today, instead, I welcome all of you who haven't been with us for a while. Like the prodigal son, we rejoice in your return. If we can rekindle a small spark inside you, that would be amazing. But if you are only here to share this hour, then thank you for that blessing. I love you. Welcome home!"

In the pews, glances were stolen quickly left and right again.

Father Wagner smiled. "I know," he said, "you're all wondering what the heck has gotten into me. I don't blame you. I've been with this parish thirty-five years. That's a long time for a priest to be with one parish in our faith." He chuckled and said, "I don't know if it's because no other parish wanted me or if I was simply forgotten. My first five years I tried to be the best priest I could be. I hope you believe that. But, little by little since then, I gave up. I regret the fact that for these past decades I've been coasting at best. Somewhere along the way, I started feeling sorry for myself. I put in the least amount of effort I could. That's no way to be a good priest, a good shepherd. Frankly, it's no way to be a good man, a good father, a good son, or even a good neighbor or friend. But that's a topic for another homily.

"Last night, on Christmas Eve, I was given the most perfect gift imaginable." Wagner began walking slowly down the aisle, turning to touch a parishioner's shoulder or arm or to look directly into their eyes. He looked up and over the congregation and said, "Last night Christ appeared to me and gave me new life!"

A murmur arose from the crowd. But Wagner's words were strong and clear and he let them sink in. He nodded with surety, "I said, last night Christ appeared to me and gave me new life."

He was striding as he made his way to the back of the church. He shook his head animatedly and raised his hands and looked up at the choir in the balcony above and said, "I know, right? That's unbelievable. Most of you believe God sent his angels to talk to a poor shepherd boy, or you wouldn't be sitting in your pew today. But the thought of Christ himself appearing before your own stumblebum of a pastor? No way! Heck, you probably think Christ would appear before a donkey before he would seek me out. Right?"

Some in attendance snickered. Some laughed nervously. But Wagner turned quickly serious. He lowered his voice but everyone heard him clearly. "I would have thought the same thing, until Christ came to me last night. Until he came to me and gave me new life! God sent his only son to us more than twenty centuries ago to save us from our sins." He looked around again, nodding, and said, "And he sent him to me last night for the same purpose."

He paused and looked around before continuing. "He came to me and asked that I bring you a message this morning about abortion. And His message is a strong reminder that abortion is murder, pure and simple." The spell that was being conjured wasn't broken, but hairline cracks and more appeared. A different murmur arose and a woman in the middle of a pew stood up and glared at Wagner before worming her way out of the pew and down the outside aisle and out of the church. A few more people, young and old, men and women, alone and in couples, excused themselves to their neighbors and left the church, most shaking their heads in dismay. The priest watched them go with a sad, but determined, look on his face.

"This isn't an easy topic, but I have no choice but to bring it up," Wagner said after the echo of his parishioners' heels receded and one of the big doors at the back of the church closed shut. "And for those of you along the walls, I can announce that a few more seats just opened up." His attempt at humor only heightened the tension and anticipation.

The priest started to walk again and stopped. "I know that abortion might seem like an odd topic for Christmas morning, confrontational even, but Jesus called me to discuss the issue today. And when the Lord speaks to you, he can be very compelling. Before I finish, I hope you will agree that there could be no better day for this talk.

"Think of all the ways that Jesus could have appeared to us initially, and remember that he came not as an adult, but as an infant. The Christ Child. He wasn't born in a palace. He wasn't invincible. He came to us as a poor, helpless baby. Was that by accident, or part of God's grand plan? I think probably the latter. And could you imagine if God tried to send his son to us in this day and age only to have him aborted before he could save His people?

He surveyed the crowd and changed gears. "Ever notice how neat and tidy abortion clinics are portrayed by the media? Spic and Span. They adopt names like 'Women's Health Clinics' or 'Family Planning Centers.' But these sterile clinics don't exist to plan families, but to downsize them…in the most inhumane ways imaginable.

"Everybody in these clinics wears white, bringing to mind holiness and not the evil that takes place there. The doctors wear clean, crisp white medical coats, like the doctors who dedicate their lives to healing. In nearly every respect these death clinics are set up to look, feel, and even have the antiseptic smell of any other physician's office. But remember that Jesus is often thought of as a healer, as a physician. Remember him helping the blind to see and the lame to walk? That's a far cry from what happens at an abortion clinic. The abortion clinics are a carefully orchestrated charade meant to confuse all of us, but especially fragile young women. They try to show that abortion is not just okay, but the embodiment of goodness. But abortionists aren't healers. Instead, they take lives. That's their job description. Their sole purpose."

Wagner kept walking the center aisle of the church, touching as many people as he could. They were listening intently. "I need each of you to look deeper. I suspect if you looked more closely at the clinic walls, the white would fade and you'd see them consumed by blue and orange flames. And your nose would burn from the pungent odor of sulfur.

"And if you looked even closer, squinting your eyes a bit, you might see the charlatan of a doctor a bit differently. His white coat would vanish in a cloud of ash and a monster would be revealed...one so hideous and evil that you would quickly look away, screaming in terror. And as this demon went about his nasty work of tearing a baby from its mother's womb and shredding it with its claws, it might throw its head back and unleash a shrill victory cry in a tongue that wasn't of this world. But you would know what the demon shouted as surely as if it came from someone in a neighboring pew today in the most impeccable English. You would know the blasphemy. The demon would cry out, 'Victory is mine. I have claimed another of your innocents!'

"Who is this abortion doctor?" Father Wagner asked, nearly spitting the word 'doctor' out with distaste.

"He is the devil. Satan. Beelzebub. He is the Prince of Darkness," he shouted, "and he goes by the name of Dr. Smith or Dr. Jones, but always he is the Evil One!"

Father Wagner lowered his voice to normal and sighed. "The media tells us abortions are down across the country. If that's true, then God help us. Because the truth is that one million babies are still slaughtered here every single year. One in three women in America will have at least one abortion during her lifetime. And one in every five pregnancies in our twisted society is aborted! One in five! Think about that." He waited, letting the numbers sink in. He nodded his head to one side of the aisle and then the other. Look around the church today at all the women here and imagine that one out of every five who might be pregnant will take their own baby's life.

"If you believe abortion is wrong as I do, as the Church teaches, then you are in the minority. Two-thirds of the men and women in the United States today say they support Roe v. Wade.

"Do I blame the women who turn to abortion? No. I don't. To me, it's akin to a person whose body is overtaken by a demon, and who needs an exorcism." He stopped and looked around. "Is that a poor analogy? I don't think so. If you look at the media and entertainment industries these days, they've turned into twenty-four-hour marketing campaigns for abortion and other abominations. Hollywood starlets, their breasts hanging out of the small bands of cloth they call dresses, tell talk show hosts how easy and natural abortion is. They sit there with their legs bare to their crotches and describe abortion as routine. Like popping an aspirin or sipping Champagne. They make it attractive. They seduce our young into thinking that abortion is the most natural thing in the world.

"The same celebrities who lead marches on our city streets because we kill animals for sustenance, march down those same city streets with pickets advocating for, and even celebrating, the heinous murder of our children."

Wagner's voice rose again and hardened as he continued. "And make no mistake, abortion is an industry. It's a for-profit industry with armies of highly paid lobbyists. It's an industry where evil people get wealthy carving up the lives of the most innocent and vulnerable of God's creatures!"

He paused and scanned the crowd again. "Who will stop this? I think to myself that I am old. I'm a tired old priest from a small town who has mostly lost the respect of those he was called to serve. I have a hard time believing that God is really calling me to wage this fight. It seems overwhelming and an insurmountable challenge."

Father Wagner looked down, contemplating, and in a clear, quiet voice he said, "But if not me, then who?" Looking up again and more loudly he said, "If not us, then who?" And after a pause, his voice echoed off the stone walls of his church, "And if not now, then when?"

He turned around as he shouted even louder, "Who will help me shoulder this burden? Who will stand with me? Who is ready to take a stand for our children? Who among you will carry that cross?"

Two-thirds of the congregation clapped wildly, while the other third looked on in stunned silence. Some of those still in attendance, who were strongly on the pro-choice side of the abortion debate, were unsettled and upset with Father Wagner. Only a few of these began to quietly reconsider their position. Some in the middle shifted to the pro-life side. And some of those who were firmly on the pro-life side when they walked into church that morning became die-hards. A few were now off the scale.

The priest shook his head then, like waking from a reverie. He rubbed his eyes and looked out over the crowd. He saw John Lawler and Grant Grae standing tall in their pews on either side of the church and he smiled.

"John. Grant. Bless you. You can sit down. When I asked 'Who will stand with me,' I was speaking rhetorically. But I love your enthusiasm." He chuckled and most in the audience let out a laugh that released some of the tension that had built over the course of the sermon.

"I know this wasn't an easy homily to hear," Wagner said. "Especially on such a Holy Day of celebration. But please think about what I said and what each of us is called to do about it. Sometimes things seem so big, so entrenched, that we feel helpless. We give up. But the stakes here are much too high to throw up our hands in meek surrender. One child, like the Christ Child whose coming we celebrate today, is worth fighting to save. One million a year? I'd say we have no choice but to get involved.

"On this day as you celebrate the birth of Christ with your own children, think of how blessed you are…and what you can do to save other children created in God's likeness. Thank you all. I love you more than ever. Amen."

Chapter Twenty-Three

The Fast

"Therefore also now, saith the LORD, turn ye even to me with all your heart, and with fasting, and with weeping, and with mourning..." —Joel 2:12

John Lawler sat in the lobby of the small, three-story painted-white brick building on Blackhawk Avenue that served as Prairie du Chien's City Hall. He'd been there three days and the city employees worried about him. The former mayor was eighty-six. His thin, white hair was cropped so close to his scalp it mirrored the three-day stubble that covered his chin and sagging cheeks. His eyes were slate gray and had a depth to them that spoke of wisdom. His heavily lined face showed the wear and tear of hard battles with prostate cancer and a heart attack, combined with deep laugh lines carved by raising four children to adulthood in the best possible way.

The oldest of Lawler's four children burst through the doors of City Hall just then. Matthew was at his father's side in six long strides. "Dad! What the hell are you doing here in your pajamas?" he said, looking down at his father snuggled into a sleeping bag on the floor. "The mayor said you've been here haunting the place for days."

"I'm on a hunger strike," the old man said in a quiet, dignified voice. He wasn't used to one of his kids towering over him with his voice raised. He felt somewhat intimidated, but wasn't about to show it.

"Against what, for Pete's sakes?" Matthew demanded loudly. All around them, in the rooms that faced the lobby, people could hear at least the son's side of the conversation. Some of those people listening had worked for the old man and loved him greatly.

The father's voice was steady and firm, but low. "I'm not eating again until people in this country stop killing their babies. I'm fasting until we outlaw abortions."

"What? Does this have anything to do with that Christmas sermon Father Wagner gave?" The son was worried. When his father made up his mind about something, when he felt he was right on something important, he wasn't easily deterred. If he was serious about this, then he'd just told his eldest son that he was going to kill himself, slowly, here in the lobby of City Hall.

Matthew slid down the wall and slumped into a sitting position near his father's head. His voice lost its bravado and came out soft and scared. "Please, Dad," he whispered, "come home with me. You've got kids and a wife who need you and love you. Grandkids, too. If you won't reconsider for me, then do it for Mom. Have you thought about how this will affect her?"

"It was her idea," his father said, a broad smile lighting his face. "I told her I wanted to do something, to tilt at one more windmill before I die, and she suggested this. She said, 'If it worked for men like Gandhi and Cesar Chavez, then why not me? And why not now?' She's wonderful. Almost seventy years I've been with her, and she still surprises me. Oh, how I love her, and you kids. You've been my greatest gifts."

Matthew shook his head. "I appreciate your commitment, Dad. But I can't let you go through with it. The mayor has called a special meeting of the common council tonight, and I'll be there to tell them that your sons and daughters want you home, even if you have to be dragged out of here in handcuffs by Prairie's finest." He started to get to his feet, but his dad caught his shirt in surprisingly strong fingers and pulled his son back down to him. He leaned in close.

"Listen, son," he began, tears pooling in his eyes, "I've tried to do the best I could for you. There's no book that teaches a young man how to be a perfect dad, but I did my best. The one thing I always wanted you to know was that I would love you…come hell or high water…forever. Like with your mom, in good times and in bad. People with better educations than mine call it unconditional love. Well, that's the only kind my parents taught me, and the only kind I ever wanted you to know."

"But, Dad. I can't walk out of here and come back in a few weeks to bury you. That's not love."

"I'm not asking you to turn your back on me, Matty. I want you to go to that meeting tonight and fight for me. You're the best damn lawyer in La Crosse. Make sure they don't forget that! Tell them your dad's not crazy, and that his entire family stands behind him. Tell them there's still something called free speech in this country and something else called civil disobedience. Tell them your old man's willing to die trying to save the lives of kids who haven't even been born yet. And get Grant Grae from the *Courier Press* there; make sure he gets it all down. We may not change any laws before I die, Matty, but we could sure raise some awareness on this issue. We need to move this sick business into the bright light of the truth. I don't think it will survive that, not in the end."

His father held Matthew's hand and spoke to him in a voice swirling with emotions. "All my life I've wanted to be there when you and the rest of my family needed me," he said, squeezing the hand more tightly. "Now, I'm depending on you to be there for me."

His son broke down and grabbed his dad, burying his face in his father's pajama top, staining it with his tears.

Chapter Twenty-Four

Dr. William Martin held his wife close, swaying to the music with his eyes closed. They circled the softly lit dance floor as Nat King Cole sang "Too Young," a haunting ballad about young love enduring. He whispered into his wife's ear, "They're playing our song," and felt her return smile on his neck.

Bill Martin and Heather Lawrence had married right out of high school, against the advice of parents and friends. They made it through college with a load of debt, and Heather worked full-time in marketing while Bill ground through four years of medical school and another four-year residency. He built a thriving obstetrics and gynecologic practice in Wisconsin's Fox Valley and took over the reins of the area's lone family planning clinic when the former president and medical director retired and nobody else stepped forward. Heather became a stay-at-home mom after the birth of their first child, and now they had three amazing girls, ages fourteen, eleven, and five. Nikki, their youngest, was an unplanned blessing. After scraping by in their early years together, the Martins were finally set financially, too.

"That's a big smile on your face," Heather said, now moving to a Perry Como song with her husband.

Bill looked at her and laughed. "Guilty," he admitted. "I'm happy we raised over a hundred thousand to help fund adoptions tonight, but maybe more so because I'm dancing with the most beautiful girl at the ball."

He pulled her even closer, and they both felt his cell vibrate in the inside pocket of his tux. "Probably another woman trying to cut in," Heather said with a fake pout, as Bill held her in one arm and eased his phone out. "You wouldn't leave me for another woman just to help her have a baby now, would you?" she chided.

He tried to look serious. "It's worse than that," he said, scanning the text. "It's three women. They're very young, and they want to know if we'll blow this Popsicle stand and come watch a movie with them."

She laughed. "They'd have to stay up past their bedtime. You okay with that?"

He pulled her off the dance floor laughing louder. "What could it hurt?"

Chapter Twenty-Five

The shooter shivered violently inside his down parka as he tried to steady his crosshairs on the granite island inside Dr. William Martin's expansive kitchen window. He'd been scoping the kitchen almost an hour from the relative seclusion of the fence that ran along the north lot line in the physician's massive yard, which was buffered by thick hardwoods beyond. *He must have seven to ten isolated acres here,* the shooter thought, with the land in back of the house tumbling down into Lake Winnebago. At nearly a hundred and eighty thousand acres, Winnebago was the largest lake encompassed completely within the state. The shooter huddled against the lower branches of a twenty-foot blue spruce, the tallest specimen in the yard that surrounded the grand two-story Tudor home.

The shooter felt it inevitable that the physician would come to the kitchen for a beer, wine, soda, water...some beverage. Or maybe he'd grab an after-dinner snack. If he stopped at the island, the shooter planned to abruptly end his night, and his life.

Another hour passed and the physician still hadn't visited the kitchen. During that time the shooter held the doctor's wife, a young daughter, and even his golden retriever in his crosshairs. The golden had a nasty habit of "counter cruising," the shooter noticed. Two or three times during the shooter's vigil, the big dog had actually put his front paws up on the island, hefted his big head over, and sniffed around for scraps. His luck this night hadn't been any better than the shooter's.

His shivering came more frequently now, and he knew he'd have to abandon his stakeout if the doctor didn't show soon. He softly cursed the parka's manufacturer. It was billed as an "arctic survival parka" and was supposed to keep him comfortable at minus forty degrees Fahrenheit. It was slightly below zero now, with a scant breeze that made the wind chill a bit worse. But the shooter knew the rating was based on "moderate to light" activity levels, and that trying to remain absolutely still for hours on end didn't fit that description.

His feet worried him the most. They'd been fine when he'd been walking and his blood was pumping faster, but they got ice cold soon after he settled into his vigil. Then they went numb inside the winter pack boots he wore. He tried to wiggle his toes inside the boots periodically, but he couldn't tell if they were even moving. There had been no feeling at all the past ten minutes, and that unsettled him.

He thought again about calling it quits for the night and trudging back in failure to his vehicle. If he shivered while squeezing the trigger, the tremor would likely throw off his shot and probably allow his quarry to escape. He didn't want that. This wasn't meant to be the proverbial shot across the bow. He grunted softly and started to stiffly rise to his knees when the doctor made his appearance, padding through the kitchen on the other side of the glass.

The shooter settled somewhat painfully back in and did some quick isometric exercises, trying to flex his muscles tightly from his feet all the way up to his neck, anything to increase his blood flow without creating noticeable movement. He was fairly certain the doctor couldn't see him. Even seventy yards closer, he'd probably be invisible to the doctor inside the well-lit kitchen.

The doctor came to the island. He'd gone to the fridge, out of view of the shooter's position, and he now laid out bread, lunchmeat, and cheese. *Probably some fancy Boar's Head meat and maybe some smoked Gouda to layer on top,* the shooter thought while bringing his rifle up into position. He tried to find the doctor in the scope, but he was gone.

He lowered the gun a bit, and the doctor shuffled in view again with a plate, a rounded loaf of artisan bread, a jar of mayo, a large knife, and a glass of milk. Like the surgeon he was, he cut two chunks of bread and dipped the knife into the mayo, and began spreading.

The shooter brought the gun to his shoulder as the doctor screwed the lid on the jar and walked back out of view again. He couldn't believe how fast the doctor had made his sandwich. He likely had one shot at this now, when the doctor stopped back at the island to pick up his sandwich and milk. The doctor did just that, steadying the rather full glass of milk before preparing to move back into the adjoining room.

Steady kills. The shooter thought of the old hunter's axiom as he pulled the trigger. The window exploded inward and the doctor toppled behind the island. The shooter levered another round into the chamber. He wanted to get out of there, but he also wanted to see if he'd put the doctor down for good. He expected to see the wife and kids race into the kitchen and to hear screaming and general pandemonium. Instead, it was eerily quiet.

He readied to leave when the doctor's right hand came up onto the island counter. He hefted himself up and leaned into the counter for support, blood streaming down the left side of his face. He may or may not have been fatally injured, but he was confused. He turned slowly.

"Shit." The shooter brought the gun back to his shoulder. The doctor took an unsteady, shuffling step toward some help that was out of view. The shooter stopped shivering now. Fear of failure and adrenaline heated his blood and he held firm in the center of the doctor's head as he gently squeezed the trigger. The gun kicked and the shooter wasn't able to see the doctor go down. He was certain he must have hit him hard, but he couldn't be sure.

He saw movement behind the island again and slammed another shell into the chamber. He brought the scope up and looked through it in time to see the retriever's big head and front paws on the counter. The dog stretched forward and inhaled the doctor's sandwich in two large gulps. That was all the evidence the shooter needed. He set the rifle down, leaning it against the boughs of the evergreen he'd set up in front of. He slipped a small crucifix from his pocket and dropped it in the snow by his feet. He retrieved a red catsup bottle from inside his parka and squirted deer blood in the direction he'd dropped the crucifix. Then he turned and headed down the fence line and back to his car.

When he reached the Blazer he got in, fired it up, and took off down the street. He planned to take the back roads home and was in no hurry, not wanting to attract attention.

He hit the power button on his radio and his old compilation CD came on. Ray Charles crooned, "You don't know me."

The killer dialed the temp in the car up to seventy-five degrees and as soon as he felt heat returning to the car, he turned the fans on full blast. He adjusted the vents so that hot air blew down by his feet, and he tried not to let the Blazer swerve as he tugged off his boots and damp socks as he drove. His feet felt like chunks of ice and were numb as he replayed the kill and drove.

It was a sloppy kill. That bothered him. He was never a sniper, but he'd grown up hunting whitetail, taking at least one each season since he was twelve. He prided himself on being a good shot. He wouldn't win any ribbons in a marksmanship competition at a thousand yards against the pretty boys from the Marines or Special Forces. But he goddamn well ought to be able to make a clean shot from seventy yards out, even through thick-pane glass.

He stewed as he drove and the pain in his feet grew in intensity as they thawed out. First, he felt tiny pricks of feeling in his feet, but these grew steadily into agony. The pain got so bad he wouldn't have been able to drive if it weren't for cruise control. He was wallowing in the sloppiness of his second kill and the pain in his feet when Johnny Cash's gravelly voice and hard-driving acoustic guitar came on the radio.

For a moment he forgot the pain in his feet as the wisdom of Cash's "The Man Comes Around" washed over him.

Maybe it was better the kill was sloppy, he thought. *Was it ever clean when a doctor murdered an innocent ? Hell, no. It was pure evil. Black as sin.*

And despite the awesome pain in his feet, he started tapping his aching toes along with the music.

Chapter Twenty-Six

On the other side of the Martin residence, the rest of the family was watching a movie in their large media room. Heather was off in a corner, curled up on a comfy, modern leather chair. She had a Scottish blanket over her legs and was halfway through Tina deBellegarde's latest cozy mystery novel. The volume on the eighty-inch HD TV was too high, but she didn't mind. She loved the fact that her three girls were lying on the floor together, watching an old Disney classic.

She was brought back to the present when she felt her feet being nudged. She lowered her Kindle and looked over the top of her reading glasses, looking down at their eight-year-old golden retriever. Though full-grown, Moose still acted like a puppy and demanded more of her attention than her kids. She leaned forward and scratched the top of his head and the outside of his ears. His tongue was out and he looked content. She was about to lean back into her chair when she saw Moose's paw prints smeared across the off-white carpet.

Her brow furrowed. She slid the throw off her legs and stood up, puzzled. She followed the tracks through the dimly lit room and down a long hallway floor made of rich cherry wood. The tracks were still wet on the wood and she shook her head as she followed them, Moose padding at her side. She felt a chill breeze and hugged herself. She called out, "Bill?" as she neared the brighter glow of the kitchen. "What in the world are you making? Moose is tracking all over the house!"

She stepped into the kitchen as she finished the sentence, and it hung in the air as her mouth dropped open. Her husband lay sprawled on the floor against the island, blood staining the wall and pooling on the floor.

The girls were huddled together in the media room while Belle tried to talk the town's mob out of going after the Beast. Their mom's keening, a loud, long wail of grief, drowned out the movie soundtrack, and all three girls ran for the kitchen.

Chapter Twenty-Seven

Cole walked into the Martin kitchen just over an hour and a half later. The Oshkosh EMS squad and the local police made it to the house within twenty minutes of the shooting. There wasn't much the paramedics could do, but the police started making all the necessary calls. Cole was one of the first on their list. When he got a call at ten p.m. or later like this, given his social life, it was never good news. He picked up Detective Igou at a North Side park and ride and they made the eighty-five-mile drive north up I-41 to the doctor's home on the banks of Lake Winnebago in an hour.

Cole stopped and looked around the kitchen. Blood covered nearly a third of the hand-painted ceramic tiled floor. The doctor had fallen to his knees and then slumped against the bottom of the island, his face pressed against the thirty-bottle wine cooler. It looked uncomfortable , but Cole guessed the doctor didn't care at this point.

He was told the doctor's wife and three children were in the house at the time of the shooting and that they'd all been taken to St. Elizabeth's Hospital in Appleton. They were being treated for shock. Cole was grateful he didn't have to face the family.

Ty came in the back door and motioned for Cole, who stepped carefully around the body and the blood and walked over to hear what his friend had to say.

"This guy *definitely* wants to get caught," he said. Ty's voice was almost a whisper, but Cole saw the excitement in his eyes. "He not only dropped another rifle, he left a pile of cigarette butts, which means plenty of DNA.

They're on the way to the state crime lab in Madtown. We're also running the serial number of the gun, so we'll track down the last guy who bought it. It's another 30/30 and looks like it could be a twin of the first murder weapon."

"Any sign of blood or a crucifix?"

Ty nodded. "They found plenty of blood sprayed in the snow by the shooter's nest. No crucifix yet, but there's a lot of snow cover. I told the crime scene guys to be on the lookout for one. And to keep quiet, too. I'd bet anything they'll find another crucifix. It's like part of his signature."

"Well, then, our boy's consistent at least."

"Why do you think the guy leaves his gun behind at the scene? I don't get it. It's not something you see all the time."

"He does it because he's smart," Cole said. "After he shot Smith he had to walk down a couple flights of stairs in a building in the middle of a fair-sized city during daylight hours. If someone heard a shot and saw a guy carrying a long object, they might get suspicious. Maybe he gets confronted, or maybe someone gets a reasonably good description they can pass on to us. Either way, the killer loses.

"If he's pulled over a couple blocks from the scene, or his house is searched later, the last thing he wants someone to find is the murder weapon. If they don't, he's clean. The same thing with this murder," he continued. "Here he had a quarter-mile hike back to the road and a drive to who knows where. Same story. Why risk getting caught in possession of a murder weapon that you can buy at a gun show for two hundred and fifty bucks, give or take a couple twenties?"

"What do you make of the cigarette butts?"

Cole shook his head. "I know I'm tired, but it makes no sense to me," he said. "Why leave a pile of butts here, DNA all over, when the killer didn't leave any butts behind when he shot Smith in Milwaukee? From the reports we got from that scene, it seems like he had to wait a while before taking that shot, too. So why no butts there?"

Ty leaned in closer. "Does this mean we have multiple killers? A smoker and a non-smoker? And what if there are more…a group of pro-life deer hunters who decide to take a stand against abortion and take the law into their own hands?"

"We can't discount that we could have multiple shooters on our hands, especially now, especially after this. But that doesn't fit for me. I can almost see the shooter in my head now and my gut tells me he killed both Smith and Martin. Not scientific, I know. And I can't explain the cigarette butts. Like I said, I don't get it."

Cole shook his head again and cursed under his breath. Then he looked directly at Ty and nodded. "But we will get it. You can bet your ass we'll get it."

Chapter Twenty-Eight

Michele lay on her back. Naked. Not cold or warm. Unfeeling. Through a haze she sensed someone moving rhythmically above her. Muffled sounds, like those made by a boar in heat, whispered to her darkly. Something inside her told her to scream, but she didn't remember how. The hazy figure kept moving above her as her world went from gray to black.

She opened her eyes and looked around. Outside now, she walked in the darkness wearing only a threadbare cotton nightgown. She knew she should be cold, but she wasn't. Her heart raced as tentacles of fog or smoke reached out for her as she walked toward a soft yellow glow of light in the distance.

She heard a hissing sound as she walked. She tried to stop and go back, but she couldn't turn away from the light and the noise. Something drew her forward. Something unholy.

She came to the edge of the light and dimly made out the form of a huge, ink-black steam locomotive. It wasn't moving, but it trembled with life somehow. "Shhhhhhhhhh...." Steam escaped, swirling from the engine and slithering through the dark toward her.

Michele looked further down the length of the train. Massive black boxcars snaked behind the engine as far as she could see, hundreds of them. Their doors were open and shadowy men in dark clothes bustled about, up and down the line. They scraped the cement, she thought. They were shoveling. They scraped the concrete with big steel coal shovels, the blades glinting in the faint light. The filthy men scraped the concrete until their shovels were full and then tossed their loads into the open boxcars. The contents landed with a soft clang at times and other times with a sickly, wet sound; the sound a rubber boot makes when it's pulled from muck or warm manure.

Michele couldn't make out what was being shoveled. The light was too low and the haze too thick. She needed to know so she walked closer. A breeze rippled her nightgown and the fog was swept away. Suddenly she could see clearly. They were babies. Some alive. Some dead. The scene before her bloomed from blacks and grays to pinks and dark, violent reds...

Michele screamed. She struggled to wake up and threw her sweat-soaked sheet and comforter away from her as the iPhone on her nightstand played Don Henley's "Dirty Laundry."

She was disoriented, breathing raggedly. Tears streaked down her face while Henley kept singing...

"Can we film the operation?

Is the head dead yet?

You know, the boys in the newsroom got a running bet..."

She picked up the phone and saw the large ghostly-white three a.m., as she swiped her finger across its face to answer the call. She stammered, "Heh, hello."

"Michele. It's Cole. Cole Huebsch. I'm really sorry to call so late, or so early, but another doctor's been killed."

"What?"

"I said, another abortion doctor has been shot and killed. Dr. William Martin. He ran the Family Planning Health Center in Appleton. He was shot at his home."

"Cole, hold on." She reached over and turned on the lamp on the nightstand and grabbed the legal pad and pen she kept there. She switched the phone to speaker, turned the volume all the way up, and set it down on the nightstand. "Can you hear me?" she asked.

"Yeah. I can hear you."

"Okay. Then go on," she said. "I want to take some notes."

Cole kept his voice low as he drove back toward Milwaukee going eighty-five down I-41. He'd already filled in his team and Gene Olson, and Li Song volunteered to alert the Chicago office. Now Cole drove the lonely stretch of highway as Ty snored softly in the passenger seat.

"The killer used a 30/30, same as with the Smith murder. But this time he shot the doctor through his kitchen window. Dr. Martin bled out on his own kitchen floor. His wife and daughters all saw him lying in a pool of his own blood. His head was a pulpy mess. I don't know how they ever overcome that." His words came out choppy and got louder as he explained what he'd seen. He caught himself and looked at Ty, still sleeping beside him.

"Do you think it's the same killer?" Michele asked, trying to get control of herself. She set down her legal pad and sat up, hugging her legs close to her, trying to shake the images and sounds from her own nightmare.

"There's no way to tell for sure yet if it's the same shooter, but we know it's related to the Smith murder. We found blood where the shooter waited for his shot. We'll know tomorrow, but I'm pretty sure it'll be deer blood again. We haven't found a crucifix yet, but we're betting we will. There's a foot of snow on the ground up there, so they'll need to bring in a metal detector."

Michele was still groggy. "The killer went inside and left blood there?"

"No. He sprayed it at the base of a tree. The spot from where he took the shots. That's also the area our guys are concentrating their efforts to find a crucifix or any other evidence."

Michele shook her head and ran both hands through her hair. "Wait. Did you say shots? As in plural? Was anyone else injured besides Dr. Martin?"

"Yes. There were at least two shots from what we can tell and, no, the doctor was the only one shot. The shooter's first attempt apparently didn't kill Martin. Part of his head was taken off, but the techs on the scene believe he made it to his feet after getting hit. He likely had no idea what had happened, but he staggered to his feet and the killer knocked most of the rest of his head off with the second shot."

A weariness crept into Cole's voice and it cracked. "I know we don't agree on the amount of honor that exists in the profession these physicians shared." He paused, almost stopping. He continued partly because he was overtired and the conversation would help keep him awake. Mostly, he just wanted her to understand. "My wife and I tried so hard to have children.

But it didn't work out for us. Physically, we were incapable of producing kids. And that created a wedge that became a rift that grew into a chasm so big neither of us could cross it to find each other again."

He took a hand off the wheel to wipe tears from his eyes and stole another glance at Ty sleeping. "I started having dreams of being a father the first night I proposed to Janet. I know that sounds stupid or crazy, but that's the way it was for me. Maybe part of that is because I lost my own mom and dad so young. Now I'm at a point in my life where I just don't see myself ever having children. Those dreams are dead, and it hurts me to see so many viable lives unwanted and discarded."

He clenched his teeth. "But nobody deserves to die the way Dr. Martin did. I've seen a lot of crime scenes before, but I've...I've never witnessed anything like that. I can't shake the thought that his three little girls all saw him like that. I can't shake it."

Michele thought he might be crying and she felt the weight of his burden. Even though she was struggling with her own emotional baggage, instinctively she wanted to help shoulder his.

"The wife and kids were innocents as much as any unborn child and their loved one was brutally murdered almost in front of their eyes," Cole said. "To have them walk into all the gore... I keep asking myself, how does anyone pick up and move on from that?"

Michele didn't know if she should be reporting or consoling. She had only seen Cole as strong and tough. But she felt his vulnerability now as much as she felt her own. She picked up her phone and held it in both hands. "I'm sorry." It felt inadequate, but she didn't know what else to say.

"I'm the one who should apologize. You don't need to hear me spill my guts, feeling sorry for myself like some newly minted agent."

A strained, unexpected grin appeared on Michele's face. "Newly minted agent? Who talks like that?"

Cole laughed, glad she teased him and tried to take his mind off what he'd seen. "Actually, those are the Bureau's words, not mine."

"I'm pretty sure you're not minty fresh anymore, Special Agent Huebsch. And I'm glad you let your guard down with me. You said when we started this that we would be helping each other. There's no reason I can't help you here."

After she spoke the last sentence she wondered how it sounded, and what she even meant by it. She knew she needed to get to work on the story, but she didn't want the moment to end.

"One other thing," he said. "When you get off the phone, google 'Slepian murders.' The Martin murder is similar to the murder of Dr. Barnett Slepian back in 1998. It looks like our shooter planned this killing by ripping a page out of sniper Charles Kopp's playbook. See you in the morning."

"It's already morning," she reminded him. "Meet me at the *Journal* Building at six-thirty, the State Street entrance. I'll let you in."

"That, that sounds good." Before she could hang up, Cole said, "Wait, please." He tried to collect his thoughts. "Thank you for letting me talk about how this hit me. It helped. I can be robotic at times and not always the most sensitive. Someone close to me used to point that out. I've been in tough spots before, but nothing like this. I'm just trying to say that I appreciate it. Thank you."

After they said goodbye, Michele looked at her phone, wondering what the hell was going on.

Chapter Twenty-Nine

The shooter rolled over in his double bed and looked at his alarm clock. Six twenty a.m. glowed blood red. He rolled onto his back, cradled his hands on the pillow behind his head, and stared unfocused at his bedroom ceiling.

It had taken him four hours to drive home after shooting Dr. Martin. He'd avoided the Interstates and kept to two-lane U.S. and county roads the whole way back. He passed through at least a dozen towns on the way, and none of them had populations approaching even a thousand residents, either sleeping or awake.

He had driven through that last two hours of Friday and the first two hours of Saturday without attracting undue attention. Even in the most rural areas, some people were out and about on Friday nights and in the wee hours of a new Saturday.

The shooter made liberal use of his cruise control, even passing through the towns, and kept his speed between the posted limits and three to five miles-per-hour over. While he had a backstory prepared, he had no interest in being pulled over for going too slow or for being in too much of a hurry.

Ten p.m. to two a.m., from Friday night into Saturday morning was considered prime time for Wisconsin law enforcement, from state troopers to county sheriffs to local PDs, to hand out DUIs. Drinking to excess was a hobby for too many people in the state, and it didn't slow down much, even during the dead of winter.

He'd gotten home okay, but the last hour or so after the thrill of the kill had worn off, he had fought hard to keep from falling asleep at the wheel and hurting himself or anyone else still on the road. Luckily, there were no long stretches of straight road, but even the curvy, hilly roads he'd driven had nearly lulled him to sleep.

He drove under his carport and shut down the Blazer, leaning forward and resting his head on the steering wheel. He gave a soft thanks to God for helping him successfully eliminate Martin, and for shepherding him home safe and undiscovered. He got out of the car and made his way into the house, his frost-bitten feet barking with every step. Inside, he emptied his pockets on the tiny kitchen table. He didn't turn on any lights. Harsh, white light from a streetlamp spilled through the plastic kitchen blinds and lit up the laminated countertop. The dim glow from a night light in the lone bathroom lit the way to his bedroom.

He stood stiffly in his room and peeled off his clothes. When he was down to his boxers and t-shirt, he lifted the thin sheet and bedspread and slid under them, sure he would fall asleep instantly.

Instead, he slept fitfully. Exhausted as he was, when he closed his eyes he saw Dr. Martin clinging to his kitchen island, his head half gone, staring back at him with an accusing eye. The shooter was reasonably sure he hadn't seen that through his scope, and he tried to push the image away. When he shook the image off, a worse one, of Martin's wife and girls, replaced it. In his research, the shooter had seen Google images of Martin and his wife. Dressed up at galas benefitting causes like breast cancer research and their local hospital. He couldn't tell if they were in love, but they seemed happy in the images.

He rolled over and pushed those thoughts away only to have them replaced by images of three smiling, innocent girls. He never actually saw photos of the girls, but he'd seen one through his scope the night before. She was carefree when she flitted into the kitchen. He saw all three of the girls clearly as he lay there now...laughing, bouncing curls of blonde hair, shining eyes, pretty white teeth, angelic. And then he heard their screams.

At six-thirty a.m., he got up and knelt at the side of his bed, even more exhausted than when he'd lain down. His knees ached immediately from being mashed against the hard oak floors. He looked at the crucifix above his bed, last year's brittle fronds from Palm Sunday draped over it. The dark wooden cross bore a pale ceramic Christ in acute agony, with dark blood seeping from wounds on his hands, feet, side, and head. The shooter identified with the suffering Christ. He was in agony himself. Shooting Dr. Smith had been easier somehow. Even from a couple hundred yards away, Smith seemed showy. Smug. Dr. Martin was more of a Jekyll/Hyde type...a monster in his clinic maybe, but a family man and a philanthropist at the same time.

The shooter felt Martin's remaining eye, surrounded by gristle and gore, boring into him. Damning him. Overwhelming exhaustion and self-loathing overcame him and the shooter buried his head in the bedspread, muffling his sobs. He lifted back up at the crucifix, conflicting tears of shame, fear, and anguish streaming from his eyes in rivulets that dripped onto his shirt.

For the first time since Christmas, he doubted himself and his call to protect the children. "Help me, Lord!" he blubbered. "Give me some sign!"

It was quiet save for his sobs and ragged breathing. No flash of light. No loud bang. No winged messenger sent from above. But after a while, somewhere through the fog in his mind, six words came to him, tissue soft at first, but building in clarity and volume. "Vengeance is mine saith the Lord. Vengeance is mine saith the Lord. VENGEANCE IS MINE SAITH THE LORD!"

The shooter trembled, excited. He recognized the words from the Bible's Old Testament. But he was confused. Was God telling him to leave any vengeance to Him? Did he want the shooter to stop his one-man crusade? To turn himself in?

But the same voice began softly in his head again. The shooter cocked his head a bit, staring at the crucifix as he strained to make out the new words. They repeated over and over, indistinguishable at first but growing louder and louder until the shooter lifted up shakily from his aching knees.

"THY WILL BE DONE! THY WILL BE DONE! THY WILL BE DONE!" he shouted along with the voice. He collapsed back onto his bed then and slept dreamlessly until dinnertime.

Chapter Thirty

Michele couldn't sleep after talking with Cole, so she got out of bed, pulled on her robe, and padded barefoot to her kitchen. Her coffee maker was set to go and she hit the button that started the grinder inside. It whined in protest as she pulled her laptop out of the large bag she carried everywhere during the day.

By the time her laptop was up and running, the smell of brewing coffee reached her nose and her lips turned up in the hint of a smile, her first of the morning. It smelled so good. She googled "Slepian murder" and started taking notes, toggling back and forth between a Wikipedia page, old *New York Times* stories, and the article she'd started in a Word document.

James Kopp murdered Barnett Slepian on October 23, 1998, in Roxbury Park, New York, an affluent suburb outside Buffalo. Dr. Slepian was fifty-one years old. He'd endured years of picketing and harassment and moved his family into the new home two years before in hopes of avoiding protesters.

The day he was killed, he had returned home after attending a memorial service for his father at Synagogue. Kopp shot him through the kitchen window with a high-powered rifle as Slepian was preparing soup. The bullet struck him in the chest, shattered his spine, and tore his aorta. It barely missed the head of one of his sons as it exited. All four of his sons were at home. They saw the carnage and heard their father's anguished cries for help. His wife was there, too. Slepian died two hours later.

Michele stopped typing and hung her head. She was tired and emotionally raw. She could feel the horror, the pain, and the shock of the Slepian family, and it brought back the trauma Cole described at the Martin residence. She ran her hands through her hair and focused on the keyboard in front of her. She was determined to convey those feelings as clearly as she could to her readers, without letting them cripple her.

Slepian's murder was the fifth in a series of anti-abortion sniper shootings that took place in Canada and western New York from 1994 to 1998. A sniper used a high-powered rifle in each of the attacks, firing through a window of the doctors' homes. Slepian was the only fatality. Of the others, the first was shot in the leg, the second in the right elbow, and the fourth in the shoulder. The shot on the third doctor missed, but he was injured by flying glass. Only two of the five ever performed abortions again.

All five shootings occurred within a few weeks of November 11, which is honored as Veterans Day in both countries. November 11 is also known as Remembrance Day in Canada, and some anti-abortion activists call it "Remember the Unborn Children Day."

A spokeswoman for Buffalo GYN Women's Services, the private clinic where Dr. Slepian performed abortions, said in a news account at the time that they'd received a warning from authorities at the clinic Friday morning reminding them about the four-year pattern of attacks. The fax was sent to Dr. Slepian at his private office in Amherst. "He was aware of the threat," she said.

Michele's breath hitched as she read the FBI's account of the murder. The gunman who shot Dr. Slepian hid in a strip of woods behind his house, then fired a single shot from a high-powered rifle. It was eerily like Martin's murder a few hours ago.

The FBI worked the shootings with Canadian law enforcement and chased Kopp across Mexico, Ireland, and, finally, France, where he was captured in March 2001 and extradited. He was convicted of second-degree murder and was serving a twenty-five-years-to-life term in prison.

Michele finished her story with a quote attributed to Dr. Slepian. "Abortion is undeniably the taking of a human life. It is not pretty. It is not easy. And in a perfect world, it would not be necessary."

I couldn't agree more with that last sentence, she thought, as she sent the story to her editors.

Chapter Thirty-One

Michele stood in the *Journal* building's high-ceilinged lobby and peered out its State Street entrance, her nose almost touching the glass. Her breath created a saucer-sized circle of frost, and she ignored the crazy impulse to scribble "Hello" with her finger. A uniformed security guard read the paper's early edition at a large round desk twenty feet from her, as the minute hand on the clock behind him twitched past six twenty-five. The sun wouldn't poke its head above the horizon for another hour and Michele couldn't see beyond the amber cone of light cast by the sconce mounted on the building's exterior. The rustling of newspaper caused her to look back at the guard and she thought about the guts of the new story she'd written and the sources she planned to contact during the day. When she turned back, her breath caught; a man with a crooked smile stared at her, his face pressed close to the glass. His red, wrinkled face was partially shielded by stringy white hair stuffed under a dark and dirty wool watch cap. He wore a stained black pea coat buttoned to his neck and reminded Michele of the men in her dream who scraped the concrete with their shovels. She shrank back from the door and heard the guard getting out of his chair.

Cole came into view and tapped the man's shoulder. When he had his attention he gave him a bill from his wallet, and the man shuffled into the gloom. Cole noticed Michele's hands shake as she opened the door, and he signed in with the guard while she hit the button to call the elevator. They got off on the second floor and walked down the main aisle toward her cubicle. Halfway there a tall man roughly Michele's age stepped into the aisle from his own cubicle. He stretched an arm out and leaned against a cubicle wall, blocking them. He looked directly at Michele. "Hey, girl, who's your friend?"

Cole saw her stiffen, before gathering herself and ducking under his outstretched arm. She made a beeline for her desk.

Cole studied the man as the guy watched Michele's escape. He was roughly six foot four and wore sharply creased dress slacks and a form-fitting black cashmere v-neck sweater that showed off his powerful build. He had thick, wavy black hair. When he turned back to Cole, his dark brown eyes bore into him, and dimples to match the cleft in his chin appeared to create a fake smile. "Apparently, she needs some caffeine," he said. "I'm Dan Rippa. Sports reporter. I cover the Bucks and Brewers and do a TV show on Channel 4." He held out his hand. Cole shook it, half expecting the reporter to try to crush his; he obviously had feelings for Michele.

"I'm Cole Huebsch. FBI." Rippa stiffened, but kept working the smile. He nodded, "Nice to meet you," and stepped out of the way.

Two and a half hours later Cole and Michele sat at Michele's cubicle nursing their third cup of coffee each. They'd read and re-read Michele's draft on the second shooting. Cole had to admit she captured the brutality of the scene and the dissonance between the happy family before the killing and the shattered, chaotic scene that followed.

They didn't know if the killer would try to reach out to her again, but they were ready if he did.

Michele leaned back in her ergonomically correct task chair and stretched, trying to knock the cobwebs from her head. She felt bone tired. Cole struggled to stay atop the exercise ball Michele kept at her cubicle for "stealing" exercise time when she could. He turned from the screen and looked at her. A hint of perfume, soft notes of roses and vanilla, reached him and he caught himself leaning imperceptibly closer. He righted himself on the ball.

Her eyes darted his way and she met his gaze. "What?" she said. "I know I haven't dropped a donut on my blouse, because you didn't bring donuts," she accused.

He shook his head, smiling. "No, it's nothing like that. You haven't dribbled coffee either." He averted his eyes downward for a moment, but raised them to lock back onto hers. "I was admiring how well you're holding up under the pressure. This is a huge story with deadlines you can't prepare for. You hammer out the story late into the night and early the next morning, absolutely nailing it, and then you sit here looking refreshed, ready to take on the new day and whatever it throws at you. That's all," he said, turning back to the computer screen.

"Are you convinced he's going to email me again?"

"Nothing's certain, but I think so. He's only struck twice so far but he already seems to find some comfort in establishing a pattern. Leaving behind the gun, blood, and crucifix are all examples of that. Emailing you again would fit."

"Wait, you said you found another crucifix?"

"Right by the blood. Maybe a foot or so away. It was hidden under the snow. The killer's not precise in placing the things he leaves behind, but it's clear he wants us to find them.

"We found cigarette butts on the ground where the shooter hid before and while taking the shot," Cole continued. "We should find DNA and it could break the case, but this seems like something else that's just too easy."

Michele's eyes opened wider. "Does this mean we have two killers? A smoker and a non-smoker?"

"Jeffers sees it that way. He's the Chicago SAC and the guy who's leading this investigation. Ty likes that angle, too. But it doesn't feel right. The more people involved in these killings, the more likely we would have gotten at least one solid tip by now. But we've got nothing."

"How many cigarette butts did you find?"

"Five."

"Do you have any idea how long the shooter was behind the house before killing Dr. Martin and leaving?"

"Our best estimate is that the killer was in his hide between one and four hours."

Michele winked. "I guess the shooter could have become a chain smoker in the week between his killing Dr. Smith and last night. I mean, taking a life could give someone the jitters and cause them to pick up a bad habit, right?"

"I know," Cole smirked. "It doesn't make sense. You and I haven't taken up smoking in the past week and we've been under our share of stress. Plus, we've got some of that sleep deprivation thing going on, too."

"So, you agree with Jeffers and Ty that we likely have multiple shooters?"

"Actually, no," Cole answered, grimacing after taking a sip of his coffee which had grown bitter and cold. "Like I said, it doesn't feel right."

Cole looked at the coffee cup absently. "He wasn't a bad guy, you know?"

Michele squinted at him. "What?"

"Dr. Martin. He wasn't a bad guy," Cole said, looking at Michele with his head cast down. "He was near the top of his class in medical school and did his obstetrics residency at Northwestern. He built a thriving OB practice in Appleton. About ten years ago he also took over the operations of a clinic there because he felt like there were no good family planning options for women in that part of the state. He and his wife also founded a non-profit adoption service in the Fox Valley. Not a bad man at all."

Michele studied him. "You're starting to surprise me, Huebsch," she said. "It almost sounds like you admire Dr. Martin."

Cole smiled, and then glanced at Michele's computer screen, noticing that it was after nine a.m. "It doesn't look like the shooter's going to reach out to you on a schedule. I'd better get back to the office and see if anything new has come in."

"Can we catch up later?"

"How would it work if I come back here around seven tonight? I could pick up something for us to eat on the way over. We could debrief over tacos."

"Tacos? Mmmm," Michele smiled. "Maybe you're not all bad after all."

Chapter Thirty-Two

By ten-thirty a.m., Cole was seated at the small round table in his office. Besides his desk and the two chairs facing it, the table with four matching chairs was the only furniture in the room. On the walls, he had a large whiteboard and a forty-inch flat-screen TV that had been installed by a predecessor, along with a framed autographed poster of Olympic wrestling champion Dan Gable. A pair of Cole's old wrestling shoes hung from a peg behind his desk. He'd worn those shoes when he won his NCAA championship, and he'd had them autographed right after the meet with a borrowed black Sharpie. The guy who signed his name on them was Cael Sanderson, another U.S. Olympic wrestling champ and the only wrestler to win every one of his NCAA matches. A large, round, battery-powered clock ticked audibly as it kept time from its place above the door, its longest hand vibrating visibly as it ticked off every second. A huge, wildly colorful painting of Kurt Cobain took up most of another wall and captured the attention of everyone who entered Cole's office for the first time.

A fresh cup of coffee sat in front of Cole. He reached for it as he looked around the table at Ty, Lane, and Li and shook his head. "Jesus. How pathetic is this? We're trying to nail a serial killer and our entire team could fit in a damn closet."

"I'm not completely sure," Li said, "but I'm pretty sure you suggesting we all go into the closet is out of bounds HR-wise."

"Yup," Lane added. " You suggesting it is creepy, and I'm feeling a little uncomfortable myself, here."

Ty watched the interplay with amusement.

"Really," Cole said. "If you want to talk about discomfort and the closet then I can go to said closet and grab the nine-iron I keep in there. Then we can talk about discomfort." He tried to sound gruff, but it wasn't working.

Lane turned to Ty. "He gets a bit testy at times when he's close to breaking a big case."

"So true," Li nodded. "He gets like Joe Joe the Circus Boy…a little wacko."

"Okay. Christ. Stop already. I'm your SAC, for God's sake. Listen, I know you guys are trying to be cute, but there's so much wrong with it. First, I'm not the least bit testy. If I start to feel that way, I make sure it's hidden beneath my calm exterior. Picture the M&M and the chocolate underneath the hard candy shell. Only I've got the calm shell over the mostly calm genius inner layer. Second, we are nowhere near breaking this case. Instead, we're spinning our wheels. Let's try to get some traction here. Li, what do you have?"

She stood to point at the whiteboard behind her. Before she explained the diagram there, she looked at Cole over her reading glasses. "Don't forget you started the conversation by talking about how dinky our team is that's trying to solve such a big case. But you *are* forgetting that Jeffers has a veritable battalion of agents working this, including most of ours. And that's not mentioning our DC colleagues. Most of the Bureau's assets are being brought to bear on this case."

She turned to the board again. "So, as I was beginning to say, while you were having your breakfast date with the reporter…Lane, Ty, and I pulled together what we have so far."

"Stop! Stop!" Cole burst out, almost knocking over his coffee. "Breakfast date? We were waiting for the killer to reach out to her. Now, please, for Christ's sake…focus!"

"Ah, Cole…" Ty said, keeping his voice flat. "In the ten minutes since we've sat down, you've used the names God, Jesus, and Christ multiple times. Does it help you figure out the bad guy by getting into character like that? I'm hoping to learn how you do this." He was smiling now, too.

"Atta boy, Ty. Welcome to the team," Li said.

Lane leaned close to Ty and added, "Well played, sir."

"Li, please, let's keep going," Cole pleaded. "You're killing me, pun intended."

"Okay." She turned to the board. "We've got enough geographic data points now to look at this spatially. I've drawn a crude map of the State of Wisconsin here and…"

"Crude doesn't begin to do that monstrosity justice," Cole interrupted. "Horrible would be a better descriptor. Or kindergartenish if that's a word."

"Which I'm pretty sure it's not," Li said.

"Pre-schoolish?" Ty offered.

"I hate to say it, Li, but Cole and Ty are right," Lane said. "Crude doesn't begin to describe how bad your map outline is." He held up his left hand with his fingers splayed apart. "It looks like a toddler traced his hand to make a squiggly figure of a turkey for Thanksgiving."

"Exactly what I was thinking. Good analysis, Lane. Way to earn that government paycheck," Cole said, smiling.

Li raised her eyebrows and gave Ty and Lane a "Whose side are you on?" look.

Ty laughed out loud. "Tell him what we've got, Li."

"Hmph. Okay," she said, turning to the board yet again. "This blue dot is in Milwaukee, where the Smith murder took place. The second blue dot is outside Oshkosh, a two-hour drive, mostly due north of Milwaukee. That's where Martin was killed. The gun used to kill Smith was purchased in Waukesha a couple weeks ago. I've marked that with a red dot. Waukesha is a thirty-minute drive west of Milwaukee, give or take, depending on traffic. We learned this morning that the gun used to kill Dr. Martin was purchased within five hours of the purchase of the first murder weapon. But this rifle was bought used at a VFW Post in La Crosse. I put another red dot on La Crosse, which is a little under a three-hour drive west from Oshkosh and a little over a three-hour drive mostly west from Milwaukee. I've connected all four dots and you can see we've got pretty much a triangle."

"A crude triangle," Cole interjected.

"Very crude," Lane nodded.

"To continue," Li said, "if you shade the inside of the triangle, you get a good sense that you can get from any one point to another in just over three hours. It's a concentrated area. And outside Milwaukee and Madison, it's not densely populated."

"So, you're saying we've narrowed our suspect list down to the three million or so people who live within that triangle?" Cole asked.

"Not funny," she said. "Then you take out all the women and kids, the non-hunters, etc., and keep peeling away the layers of the onion until there's one left."

"That's still a big onion," Cole said.

Lane jumped in. "So far DC has focused the hunt on Wisconsin and the states surrounding it. Let's be glad that Li didn't try to draw Minnesota, Iowa, Illinois, and Michigan. That would've been a disaster."

"An unmitigated disaster," Cole agreed.

Chapter Thirty-Three

They broke to catch up on emails and to see if anything new had come in from Chicago or DC. Cole also checked up on the other cases his office was working. The FBI handled terrorism, white-collar crime, organized crime, public corruption, cybercrime, violent crime, and civil rights issues. Wisconsin had seen a fair amount of each in Cole's time in the Milwaukee office and he'd had the opportunity to work them all. The murder of the abortion physicians was seen as a violent crime, domestic terrorism, and a civil rights issue. No other branches of law enforcement were questioning their jurisdiction, first because it was clear, but mostly because of all the non-stop, unwanted attention the case was getting from politicians and the media.

Nobody had taken time for breakfast or lunch, so they grabbed what they could and brought it back to Cole's table as the clock ticked past two-thirty p.m. Cole looked up at the clock and thought the hands were moving even more erratically than normal. "Someone tell me how the purchase of the rifle in La Crosse went down," he said.

Lane swallowed a mouthful of sub and answered. "This was about five hours after the purchase at the gun show in Waukesha. An old vet had a 30/30 Marlin he'd used to hunt deer since he was twelve. He had to give up hunting because his hearing was bad and the bark of the rifle, even with muffs, wasn't helping any. The gun held good memories and he didn't want to give it up, but he finally realized that someone else might be able to create new memories with it so he put it up for sale. His son helped him post an online ad and a daughter made up some flyers with the old vet's number printed a bunch of times on the bottom where someone could tear one off if they were interested. Those flyers were posted at the VFW Post and at a couple grocery stores in the area. A guy called the vet and they agreed to meet at the VFW Post to make the transaction.

"The buyer came in, stooped over and shuffling, said he wanted the rifle for his nephew. He wore an old army jacket like our buyer in Waukesha, but no wheelchair. He had a bushy beard like some of the professional baseball players have today…or like the guys have on the Smith Bros. cough drop boxes."

"The guys? You mean, the Smith brothers?" Cole teased.

"Exactly," Lane continued. "Anyway, the buyer wore big, black plastic glasses that hid most of his face and he had a hoodie up over a battered Menards baseball cap. The seller didn't even ask for ID."

"Wait, back up," Cole said. "The guy was wearing a Menards hat?"

"Yeah. It's a home improvement store." He flipped through his notes.

"I know it's a home improvement store, but if the killer's not jerking us around, then this reinforces the decision to keep the focus of our investigation on the Midwest."

"That's right," Lane said, referring to the sheet in front of him. "Menards started in Eau Claire, Wisconsin, and operates three hundred stores out of fourteen states, all in the midwest. It competes well against Home Depot and Lowe's.

"Anyway, our seller at the VFW took two hundred and fifty in cash from the buyer and offered to buy the guy a cold one. But the buyer said he couldn't stay and left. The only thing the seller thought was odd about the whole transaction is that a guy would turn down a free beer."

"It is un-American," Cole said, rolling his eyes. He had a corner office and the largest expanse of windows faced mostly east toward Lake Michigan. Ty shielded his eyes from the sunlight that now flooded the room from the northwest. Cole got up from the table and closed the blinds. It protected Ty's eyes from the harsh light, but the room suddenly lost a little of its warmth. "Let's keep pushing," he said.

"Tell him about the boot prints outside Martin's house," Ty suggested.

Li took over. "The killer walked through a lot of snow to get from his vehicle to the house and back. The boots must have been new or close to it because there was no wear on the rubber tread." She passed around photos taken at the scene of some of the crispest indentations. You could clearly see the mirror image of 'L.L. Bean' where the heel joined the instep.

"Our guys matched the tread to L.L. Bean's Snow Boots," Li continued. "They've got thick felt liners and they're rated down to minus forty-five degrees Fahrenheit with moderate activity and to plus ten degrees with light activity."

"I won't ever forget the night of the Martin murder and it was right around zero. Not much wind," Cole said. "With those boots, the killer would've only needed to do some simple isometrics. Hell, just wiggling his toes every so often would keep him reasonably comfy. What size were the boots?"

Li pursed her lips as she reviewed her notes. "Size seven…in a women's."

"Women's? Size seven? No way," Cole said, shaking his head.

"Yes, way. The width is typically the same, but there's about a size and a half difference between women's sizes and men's in terms of length, so if the shooter is a man it would be more like a size five and one half in a men's size."

Cole kept shaking his head and slumped in his chair a bit. "You're telling me our killer is a tiny woman?"

"Doubtful. Serial killers don't usually have vaginas," Li said. "The men's and women's boots in this line are identical in appearance, like a lot of higher-end Pac boots. They've got heavy rubber soles and nice leather uppers. The killer must have small feet and bought the women's because they fit better. The average man's shoe size is between nine and a half and eleven. A man's five and a half would be pretty small. There's not a perfect correlation between shoe size and height, but our D.C. guys estimate the shooter is somewhere between five foot and five four."

"Weight?" Cole asked.

"On the way in, he weighed roughly one sixty-five," Li said. "Keep in mind he was carrying his rifle and likely wearing a lot of heavy clothes. His rifle alone weighed eight pounds. On the way out he weighed closer to a hundred and fifty-seven pounds. The math works."

"So, we have a guy who stands a little over five feet and weighs one fifty or so in street clothes and without clunky boots," Cole said. "That narrows the field. We've got a short guy who's either chubby or a powerlifter. Let's hope chubby. Anything on the cigarette butts ?"

"No. And that's odd, too," Ty said. "On a case this big we should have had the results back within twenty-four hours. It reminds me a lot of the deer blood at first, where they didn't believe what they were seeing and so they double and triple checked before sharing the results. It's got that feel to it. They know as well as we do that a positive DNA match could potentially solve this thing, and yet they're being cautious. You know Jeffers and DC are both leaning on the lab to turn around those results."

"Please tell me we have something else?" Cole asked.

Before the others could answer Cole's phone vibrated. He held up a finger, asking for a moment. He looked at his screen and didn't recognize the number, but he answered anyway. "Cole Huebsch, here."

"Cole, this is Michele. You might want to turn on channel twelve, or channels four, five, or six for that matter. All the local stations are covering a protest at the Women's Health Clinic. I'm here, too. Things look like they could get out of hand."

Chapter Thirty-Four

January is the coldest month in Milwaukee. Twice in the city's long history, it had seen record lows of minus twenty-six degrees without adjusting for wind chill. The average January high in the city was still below freezing at twenty-eight degrees, and the average low for the month was thirteen.

Outside the Milwaukee Women's Health Center this afternoon, the sun had scaled the top of a crystal blue sky and by two p.m., it had started its slide down to meet the earth to the west. It was twenty-six degrees. With no wind to speak of, it felt comfortable to the three ladies bundled up on the sidewalk. Before Dr. Smith's murder, there hadn't been much commotion outside the Center. In fact, there hadn't been any major demonstrations at the clinic in a decade, and on most days there weren't any protestors at all. The three ladies who stood outside the clinic now showed up most Wednesdays, but it was more of a social thing for them these days rather than out of any fervent hope they could stop what went on inside the building. Annie, seventy-six, was a Catholic, and Betty, eighty-two, a Lutheran. Grace, seventy-nine, was non-denominational, but she believed in "a greater power" and thought She wouldn't think kindly of abortion or those who performed them. The one sign they had between them was propped up on the snowbank in front of them. It read, "Jesus loves you and your baby, too!" They thought that said it all.

Today Grace brought coffee and Annie six of her homemade sticky buns. They had been at their post since the clinic opened at nine a.m., and had started noshing their afternoon bun rations when four vehicles pulled up and twenty college-aged kids piled out and set up on the sidewalk ten feet down from the ladies. They were laughing and talking excitedly, happy to be outside rather than in class. Their UW-Milwaukee sociology teacher had made this trip a class requirement and it was the only class all year at which she would take attendance. She had also offered extra credit to those who brought their own picket signs and had promised an "A" grade for the semester for the student whose sign she deemed best. The attributes she'd judge the signs on were how hard the messages hit and how clever she found them. The kids waved their picket signs aloft and then pushed the base of the signs into the snowbank so they faced the ladies and the street as well.

They read, "KEEP YOUR ROSARIES OUT OF MY OVARIES!!" "GET YOUR POLITICS OUT OF MY PUSSY!!" "THIS IS BEAVER COUNTRY. RESPECT THE BEAVER!" "NO MORE COAT HANGERS!!" "VIVA LA VULVA!" "MY VAGINA IS MAD AS HELL AND SHE IS NOT GOING TO TAKE IT ANYMORE!!"

Annie, Betty, and Grace looked at each other nervously. They didn't know what to make of their visitors. Then a TV van rolled up with the CBS logo emblazoned on the side. Almost before it stopped, a young reporter jumped out with a microphone and the driver hopped out, lugging a large camera. They walked toward the picketers. Annie pointed down the street and said, "Look!" Vans with the ABC, NBC, and Fox logos were now all nose to bumper at the curb. The sound of their doors opening and slamming carried over the crisp air.

A new red Honda Accord Hybrid drove ahead of the other cars, parking right next to a matching red fire hydrant. The sociology teacher got out and went around to the back of the vehicle. She wore a sleek Sorel parka with faux fur trim around the hood. Oversized cat-eye Ray-Bans hid most of her face, but to those students nearby, her smirk was evident.

She opened the trunk and yanked out a picket sign of her own. As she walked to where the students were congregated, they saw her sign and started hooting and clapping. She turned it around to face the three ladies and stabbed the base into the snowbank. The sign read, "IF I WANTED THE GOVERNMENT IN MY WOMB, I'D FUCK A SENATOR!"

Betty had a small wedge of sticky bun frozen halfway to her mouth, which was agape. All she could do was look at the signs, the defiant teacher, and her pack of kids and say, “Oh, my…”

Michele watched it all from her car. She put her notebook in her bag and drove away from the circus.

Chapter Thirty-Five

Cole flipped through the channels and had seen enough. Every local TV affiliate was covering the clinic protests and within an hour the story would likely be picked up by all their national news anchors. This was a fresh angle to an already huge story. "Well," he said to the group around him, "if you thought the pressure was on, you ain't seen nothin' yet."

He was about to turn off the TV when the CBS affiliate he had landed on broke in with an announcement. They were going live to a press conference outside Milwaukee's FBI headquarters.

"What the hell?" Cole said. "Did any of you know about this?" Ty, Lane, and Li shook their heads in unison.

They were glued to the TV as the station switched to another young reporter. He wore a charcoal gray dress coat and held the microphone to his face with a black leather-gloved hand. The cameraman came in tight as the reporter said, "We're here outside the FBI headquarters in St. Francis. The FBI's Special Agent in Charge, Collin P. Jeffers, is about to address the media regarding the recent murders of two prominent Wisconsin physicians."

"Collin P. Jeffers," Cole spat out. "I'm guessing the 'P' stands for prick." He got up and paced. The main entrance to their headquarters was on the other side of the building, so he couldn't see Jeffers and the media outside his windows. But he could see them clearly enough on the TV screen.

Jeffers stepped into the nest of microphones extended in front of him. There was no wind and his swept-back jet-black hair was perfect. His dark chestnut-colored eyes were steady. His cheeks were a ruddy complexion because of the chill, but it gave him a healthy, active look. The fading sun hit his face and lent him a certain radiance.

"He's not unattractive," Li offered.

"And he looks competent. Authoritative even," Ty answered.

"Traitors," Cole muttered, his eyes glued to the TV.

"This will be brief," Jeffers said evenly and clearly. "So far, two Wisconsin physicians have been murdered in separate incidents, three days apart. One took place here in Milwaukee in broad daylight, and one under the cover of night outside Oshkosh. In both instances, a physician was ruthlessly cut down, murdered, by a cowardly sniper. I am here to tell you that we are following a number of solid leads and that we will catch these cowards, these murderers, shortly. I can't say more because it could compromise our investigation. So, that's it. No questions." He nodded to the reporters, turned, and headed into the building.

Viewers could hear the shouted questions from the reporters. "Agent Jeffers, are you confirming there are multiple killers?" "How close are you to solving these murders?" "What else can you tell us?" But the questions hung in the air unanswered, like so much frosty vapor.

The camera swung back to the reporter who looked straight in the lens and the eyes of the viewers and said, "That's all for now from Milwaukee's FBI Headquarters here in St. Francis. Stayed tuned for more on this breaking news story."

Chapter Thirty-Six

A minute later, Jeffers barged into Cole's office. He went behind the desk, pushed the chair back, and stood looking down at the four people sitting at the table.

"I want to know what you're up to, and what, if any, progress you've made in this investigation so far," he demanded. "Do you have any idea how much pressure there is on me to solve this...*yesterday*?" His voice rose. "These killers are in your backyard. Mocking you! They're killing law-abiding physicians and then laughing about how inept you are."

Cole stood so he was on the same eye-level as Jeffers. "How can you be sure we have multiple murderers? You think there's a big conspiracy with multiple people involved? Wouldn't that make it harder to keep a lid on what's going on?"

"Of course it would," Jeffers sneered. "But how many people were involved in the planning and execution of the 9/11 attacks, and how well did that leak out?"

"It doesn't feel right," Cole said.

"Again with your feelings! I told you before I don't give a hot fuck about your feelings," Jeffers yelled. "Your feelings and hunches be damned. You don't have shit."

Cole looked at Jeffers and said softly but clearly so everyone in the room could hear. "If you're still pissed at me because I broke your arm when we were at the Academy all those years ago, I said I was sorry. You need to get over it."

"I don't even know what you're talking about," Jeffers said, reddening.

"Well, if you're mad about my wife slapping your face when you hit on her a few years back, you shouldn't hold that against me, even if she did break your nose."

"You mean, your ex-wife, and she didn't break my nose," Jeffers said. "Let me say that if you and your little crew here don't come up with something soon, then I will pull these three onto my team and you'll be sitting here playing with yourself."

Jeffers picked up Cole's desk chair and threw it against the closest wall, one of the legs punching a hole in the drywall. It hung from the wall before slipping out and clattering to the carpeted floor. Then he stormed out.

"He gives interesting pep talks," Ty said.

Cole said, "We were all just visited by the Ghost of Christmases yet to come. Either we change our ways now or we will be like SAC Ass Clown a few years down the road. It's a scary thought."

Nobody spoke for a moment before Li broke the awkward silence. "There's a lot of pressure to solve these murders," she said, turning serious. "The abortion industry is already seeing a chilling effect. It's widespread and growing. A few clinics across the country shut down operations after Dr. Smith was murdered. Those clinics did it as a precautionary measure to protect their staff. But there was still hope that this was a one-off. We haven't gone public with the shooter's email to the reporter, so there was unwarranted optimism among his peers that Dr. Smith pissed someone off personally, owed gambling debts, whatever. Since Dr. Martin was killed those hopes have been literally shot to hell. We're getting reports that more than a third of the abortion clinics in the U.S. have temporarily stopped offering services. There's a resolve among many of the abortion physicians, but a lot of others aren't showing up for work these days. It's especially true in the Midwest. The clinic physicians and staff expect us to keep them safe, and we're failing them. The other thing that's happened since the first physician was murdered is the no-show rate is climbing. Before the murders started, last-minute abortion cancellations were about ten to fifteen percent. Now they're approaching forty percent. So, fewer clinics are offering abortions and more women are skipping their appointments at the clinics that are still open because they're afraid. It's a double whammy."

"And that's why two murders across our state are driving the president, all the pro-choice politicians, and our DC brass bat shit crazy," Lane said. "Meanwhile, seventy-two people get shot and twelve killed a little south of here in Chicago on a bad weekend and they hardly notice."

"Nobody said life was fair," Cole said, concluding the meeting.

Chapter Thirty-Seven

Michele sat in her dim cubicle, returning emails. Most of the other reporters had gone home for the night and it was quiet, save for the soft hum of cars driving by outside. The big room was lit softly, with halos cast by scattered desk lamps.

Michele thought back to her visit with Cole that morning. She was pretty sure he had looked at her with more than simple professional interest. She thought maybe he was attracted to her and felt his admiration for her was real. But she didn't know what to make of it. She was too busy right now to make time for a relationship, and she sure as hell wasn't ready for any kind of romance. She started to wonder if she was imagining his feelings for her when she heard him coming down her aisle.

He held up a large brown bag as he came toward her. "I stopped at BelAir Cantina on the way. I got an order of guac and chips and six soft-shell tacos. I got half Zihuatanejo shrimp and half fresh avocado and bacon and was hoping we could share. I wish I could tell you I had a pitcher of margaritas with me, but you'll have to settle for bottled water."

She stepped out and took the bag from him, starting to unpack its contents. "The shrimp tacos are my favorite, but the avocado and bacon are right up there. Did you do some digging or was this your gut telling you what I might like?"

"It was definitely my gut," Cole admitted with a broad smile. "I figured if my gut liked those tacos, then there was a decent chance your gut might like them, too. Sounds like I was right."

"You were indeed, SAC Huebsch. And I'm starved. I haven't eaten since grabbing a yogurt for breakfast." She was laying the food out and grabbing napkins from her desk when her computer chimed, telling her a message had arrived in her inbox. She caught Cole's eye before leaning forward. She hesitated before clicking okay to accept the message, knowing even before she did that it was likely from the killer.

The subject line read *I Wish You Could Understand*! Both she and Cole held their breath as they read the words that followed.

I read your story and your editor's opinion piece on Dr. Martin's death last night. You still don't understand! Whatever happened to 'fair and balanced' reporting and the old 'two sides to every story' proposition? You and your paper described my actions last night as 'harsh and brutal'. Those words should have been used to describe Dr. Martin's life's work, but not his death. Nature IS harsh and brutal at times. When a tornado scours a path through a small, close-knit town or a hurricane washes away the lives and the refuse of a large, impersonal city. Those things are as harsh as they are brutal. Not my act! You also bemoaned his death as tragic. What was REALLY tragic is that Dr. Martin callously murdered a thousand infants a year for more than a decade! It's tragic or worse that nobody raised a voice or a hand before now to stop him. It's also incredible that you wrote that his life was cut short. Martin was fifty one. He terminated lives in the womb. Those were lives cut short! Not every life is sacred, Ms. Fields, and the world is a safer, more beautiful place this morning than it was yesterday. I wish you could see my view of things.

Michele looked over at Cole. "Why does he reach out to me? Is he trying to get caught?"

Cole rubbed his eyes and lowered his head, shaking it as he stared down at the floor and talked to himself as much as Michele. "He reaches out to you because you caught his eye with that first story you wrote on Dr. Smith's murder; you put the spotlight on him. You know we'll likely have the location of where the email originated from, probably within the next five minutes. From his first email we could tell he wasn't some techno-geek who knows how to encrypt his messages to throw us off his scent," he said. "It's more likely he walked into a public place, unnoticed, and sent off his message and left again. It's easy enough to do. We'll check for surveillance cameras, but a lot of places don't have them. The ones that do usually have them aimed at the cash registers. Even when they're pointing at the seating areas, it's easy enough to avoid them if a perp wears a cap and keeps his head down or turned away from them.

"Some on our team believe he wants to get caught, but I don't see it. He does come across as conflicted, like he knows killing these physicians is horribly wrong, but somehow better than the alternative of letting them continue on. I'm no profiler, but I think he wants you, and the hundreds of thousands of subscribers who read your stories, to believe he's not a villain. He believes he's following a call that's larger than he is and larger than his personal needs are. That's the best I can do with this right now," he concluded, getting unsteadily up from the exercise ball to leave.

"Will he kill again?" Michele asked.

He looked into her eyes and held them. "It's only a matter of when, unless we can stop him, of course. The killer is on a mission. He won't stop until the abortions do or until he's dead.

"One more thing, off the record," Cole said, as he lingered beside Michele's desk. "Again, I'm not a profiler, but I read through this last email again. It looks to me like the killer is from a small town, probably a rural area. I'm sure the eggheads at the Hoover Building in DC will have their own thoughts about it, but that much jumps out at me based on his description of the small versus big cities. I guess we'll see."

He noticed Michele's lips move as she re-read the killer's email. She looked up. "I see what you mean. The part where the killer writes, "'When a tornado scours a path through a small, close-knit town or a hurricane washes away the lives and the refuse of a large, impersonal city.'"

"Yeah, the small town is close-knit and the big city is impersonal. I may be reaching though and he could be trying to throw us further off his scent."

Chapter Thirty-Eight

The killer picked up a number two lead pencil and drew a line through Dr. William Martin's name on his carefully drafted hit list. *Twenty percent of the way done*, he thought. He sat in the glow of his tube computer monitor and the yellowish, fluorescent overhead light and wondered what he would do when he ran a line through number ten. Would he draw up another list, or retire undefeated? He pushed the thought away. If he was honest with himself, he knew he'd be lucky to kill one or two more abortion doctors before they put him away, either in a tiny cell or a pine box. He wasn't looking forward to either option, but he was committed to his mission.

The basement was cramped and dingy. This was no walkout. The only natural light entered from two casement windows no bigger than porthole windows on a small boat. Even that light was filtered by the hardened grit etched on the windows' exterior. But the killer felt comfortable. He was waging an anonymous, one-man war and the basement was his command bunker.

He tried wriggling his toes but wasn't sure if they all cooperated. He swallowed four Advil an hour before, but his feet still hurt. He pushed his chair back and pulled off his clean athletic socks. At least they'd been clean an hour ago when he put them on. Even in the scant light, the killer could make out the red and purple toes, lighter toward the outside of his feet and a darker plum by his big toes. Grape-like blisters grew on every toe, making them appear distorted and misshapen. Some had torn and popped and stained his socks.

His feet had gone from numb, to prickly, to excruciatingly painful on his ride back from Oshkosh. The pain lessened a little as the hours crawled by, but he was taking a lot more Advil than the label recommended. He doubted he'd be around long enough to hurt his kidneys or other organs, though. Not with every law enforcement agency in the country hunting him. He knew they had their own list, and he was at the top or close. He wondered about the work ahead of him. He knew that more walking would further damage his feet, but didn't see that he had a choice.

He scooched back over to the counter and looked at his list again. Number three was Dr. Aarav Sadana. It felt a little odd to him, deciding who would die and who might be spared. He felt like he was playing God, but then he reassured himself that he was only doing God's will. Like Father Wagner, he was nothing more than an instrument of the Lord.

He drew a star by Sadana. He didn't have a clue how to pronounce the physician's first name, but he was pretty sure he had the last name down. "Mañana, Sadana," he whispered.

Chapter Thirty-Nine

It was nine p.m., and mostly dark in the FBI building. Cole went back to the headquarters in St. Francis after reading the killer's email with Michele. He sat in his office looking absently at the clearance section of the Jos. A. Bank website. He liked his Brooks Brothers suits, but even on sale, they could be pricey. Ty told him they had some great sales at "the Bank" every so often, so Cole had been checking it out. The men's clothier had multiple lines of suits, dress shirts, and accessories, in varying quality and price points. Their "Reserve" collection was their top-grade, and Cole was amazed to find their clothing fluctuated wildly in price one day to the next. He was looking at a Reserve navy blue pinstripe suit that sold for twelve hundred two days ago but was now on sale for one hundred ninety-nine in the retailer's clearance section. They had a tailored fit in his forty-two regular so he clicked "add to bag." He was typing in his Visa information when Ty knocked on the door and poked his head in.

Cole looked up and said, "You should be home, Ty. But let me guess. We don't have a DNA match on the cigarettes. Right?"

"Oh, no," Ty said. "We have matches to go with the cigarettes."

"Cute. Anything interesting?"

"To put it mildly."

Cole punched in the submit payment button. "Tell me what you have."

"We've got two matches from the cigarettes. They found enough DNA on one to run it and matched it to a seventeen-year-old gang member named Johnny Smith. He likes to be called 'SW' as in Smith and Wesson. For a juvie, he's been pretty active. His priors include multiple auto thefts and an attempted armed robbery. SW is a rising member of the Raging Disciples, and his older brother, Jimmy, ran it until we put him away last summer. Didn't you lead that?"

"Yeah. That was righteous," Cole nodded, remembering. "That was the result of eight months of hard, smart work by our regional gang task force. The DEA let us lead, but they played a big role along with MPD and other police departments. And it wasn't only Jimmy Smith we took down. We put away twelve of his disciples on multiple counts of drugs and weapons charges."

"Twelve disciples?"

"I know. Karma's a bitch. We nailed them for some pretty heavy stuff. It should disrupt them for quite a while. We got Jimmy on two counts of murder and he's off the streets for good. He liked to pull the trigger himself in any dispute. He wanted to intimidate personally rather than try to keep clean. And it bit him."

"I heard Jimmy got sent to the Supermax Prison in Boscobel. Not easy time," Ty said.

"Hardly," Cole said, nodding. "You know they renamed it the Wisconsin Secure Program Facility?"

"Really? Why'd they do that?"

"To make it sound more PC," Cole said. "But it's still Supermax to me. Five hundred and nine cells and every one of 'em is an isolation cell. No pictures. No TV. No possessions period. Those poor bastards spend twenty-two hours a day in a cell the size of a parking stall or a nice-sized walk-in closet. With zero human contact. If you weren't bat-shit crazy before you went in, you sure as hell would be when you came out. On the rare occasion they get a visitor, they only get to see them on a video screen."

"You don't see me crying over Jimmy's fate," Ty said. "You guys made a good bust and Jimmy probably killed a lot more guys that you nailed him for."

Cole was quiet, lost in thought, before he said, "You really think Jimmy's little brother, SW, shot Martin? Waited more than an hour to take him out with a scoped rifle? There's so much wrong with that, starting with the fact he'd be jumping up from the minors to the big leagues when it comes to crime."

"Every boy becomes a man sometime," Ty said. "Maybe this was his time to step up somehow."

"But gang members aren't into long-distance sniping," Cole said. "Their weapons of choice are easy-to-conceal pistols. I think Smith and Wesson is actually one of the most common, along with the cheap Hi-Point pistols. You can get a new Hi-Point for a hundred and sixty bucks. The movies show all the gang bangers with Glocks, but they're not that common given they start at six bills or so. A cheap gun kills just as dead as an expensive one."

He continued. "Guys like Jimmy and his brother don't snipe one precise shot at a time; they spray. And they're not trying to kill someone anonymously from a distance. It's up close and personal. If someone needs killing in their eyes, then they not only need to kill them but make it known they did it. They kill to intimidate rivals. And they're typically not planned. They're spur of the moment. Shit happens and they react. No gang member I know of would be able to sit against that pine for a couple hours waiting for the shot. If the Raging Disciples were involved they'd kick in the front door and riddle everybody in the house with 9 mm bullets. This is messed up."

Cole ran his hand absently through his hair and leaned back, letting out a big sigh. "You said there were two matches. Can I assume the second one came from another member of the Disciples?"

"No, you cannot." Ty gave Cole a look that said, 'you're not gonna believe this.' "It gets even weirder. The second DNA match from the cigarettes came from Agnes Jones. What we have on Agnes so far is that she's a seventy-eight-year-old woman who hails from Nekoosa, which is northwest of here a couple of hours. It's pretty close to Wisconsin Rapids."

"Nekoosa... Nekoosa..." Cole searched his mind. "Oh, yeah. That's where the Bandon Dunes guys built their Sand Valley Golf complex. They've got three golf courses up and running, and two are world-class. I've got to get up there next spring before the rates peak."

"Meanwhile, back at the ranch. It turns out Agnes is a drunk. She was in the system because she's been convicted on six counts of DUI. The last one she almost killed a mom and her baby daughter when she drove the wrong way on I-90…at three in the afternoon."

"So we have a seventeen-year-old gang banger, hiding with a seventy-eight-year-old drunk lady for over two hours before one of them pops the good doctor. And there's only one set of boot prints coming in and going out," Cole said. "With this case, anything's possible, though. So maybe the elderly drunk also snorts some kind of dust that allows her to fly. Anything else?"

"Just that two of the other cigarette butts had DNA, but neither matched anyone in the system," Ty said.

"Which doesn't mean they haven't committed a crime or been charged with one," Cole reminded him. "It simply tells us they've never been arrested for a crime that carries possible jail time. Otherwise, we'd have swabbed their mouths or collected a little blood with a finger prick and they'd be in the system. I can't wait to see what Jeffers and our pals at the Hoover building make of all this."

Chapter Forty

Cole's cell phone woke him and he looked foggily at his alarm clock as he stretched to answer. The big red numbers read three-thirty. He grabbed the phone off his nightstand and took in a lung full of air before answering. His breath rushed out in a sigh. "Hello."

"Hey. Are you awake?" It was Michele.

He sat up . "I am now. Five seconds ago the answer would have been no. When I heard the phone and saw my alarm clock, I figured it was someone calling with bad news. Now, I'm hoping you're calling to say you missed me."

"Or," she said laughing, "I might have found something that's worth looking into."

"What have you got?"

"Well, I couldn't sleep. This whole thing is both scary and exciting for me. This is the kind of career-making opportunity that never comes along for most journalists, and I'm at the center of it. Anyway, I got sick of tossing and turning and went to my computer to look for any recent articles on abortion clinics, abortion violence, whatever. I came upon a story that ran the first week of January, written by the editor of a small, twice-weekly newspaper in Prairie du Chien.

"I'm familiar with Prairie. I grew up there. But what about the story piqued your interest?"

"Your hometown? Interesting. The article's about an old-timer there who won't leave City Hall. He's a former mayor who's waging a hunger strike until the country halts all abortions. The editor believes the guy will see this through to the end...meaning his death. The editor worked at the *Journal Sentinel* a number of years ago, and I recall some of the veterans speaking highly of him."

"That does seem odd. When is the last time anyone in the U.S. stopped eating for any cause? It's more of a Gandhi thing. The way we like our food, it almost seems un-American. And when did Wisconsin become the focal point of a movement to stop abortions? We represent less than two percent of the country's population, and yet we've got two people in our state who are trying to stop them, one with a rifle and the other with his stomach."

"Actually, we have three people in the state trying to stop abortions, but the last one is more subtle, and he's in Prairie du Chien, too."

"What are you talking about?" She had his full attention now. Like most lawmen, he didn't believe in coincidences. He was also wondering how his hometown played into everything.

Michele answered, "The editor of the paper that ran the story about the mayor's hunger strike? He runs a counter at the top right of every paper he prints that shows how many babies have been aborted since Roe v. Wade. It kind of reminds me of how McDonald's used to show how many burgers they'd sold. It makes me sick."

"When did the editor start running that counter?"

"The best I can tell, around the first of the year," Michele said. "I think we should go to Prairie du Chien and interview the guy who's fasting, and then talk with the newspaper editor. If there's something that links those two, it could also provide a link to the shooter."

"Are you after my job?" Cole asked. "Seriously, it's a great idea. The best anyone has come up with yet. Meet me at Mitchell Field tomorrow morning at seven. Go to the chartered flights area. It's on Howell. You turn a little before you get to the main terminal. And it won't take us three hours," he finished. "More like one. See you in the morning."

"Cole, you mean *this* morning, right?"

He looked at his alarm clock again and groaned. "Right. In three hours. See you then." He ended the call and reset his alarm. He tried to go back to sleep, but couldn't stop thinking about heading 'home' after more than twenty years away.

Chapter Forty-One

By seven, Cole and Michele were strapped into the second row of seats in a seven-passenger King Air turboprop. The pilot sat alone, manning the controls ahead of them.

It was a cold, crisp, clear morning, with the sun making another rare mid-winter appearance in the southern half of Wisconsin. The reliable Pratt and Whitney engine purred while supplying the four-bladed propellers on either side of the cozy cabin with over one thousand horsepower. Other than the steady thrum of the engine, they sat in silence on their flight west as the sun rose behind them, chasing them across the state.

Michele and Cole confessed before takeoff that they were afraid they might get airsick in the plane, but after ten minutes of flight time both dug into the large banana nut muffins and strong coffee the pilot brought on board.

The land below them changed as they cruised from flat to rolling hills. As they flew on they could see the Mississippi River Valley in front of them. Prairie du Chien was tucked neatly into that valley, nestled between the Mighty Mississippi on the west and steep hills with hard, solemn bluffs to the east. Just to the south of the town, the Wisconsin River bled into the Mississippi. Both rivers looked to be frozen solid with snow cover hiding the thin spots in the ice that claimed a victim or two every winter.

They banked over the big river and flew back into the wind. Now they were headed due east and from their elevated vantage point, the sunrise was majestic. With the snow a reflective blanket below them, the few scattered clouds were backlit by red, orange, yellow, and purple hues that boiled and shifted as the sun climbed to meet them.

They were gawking at the multi-colored sky when the plane landed with a gentle thump. It shuddered as it slowed, taxiing down the runway to the nondescript terminal building. The pilot pulled up next to the building and two men came out. He slipped down the aisle and opened the door to drop down the flight of steps.

As Cole and Michele stepped off the plane and onto the tarmac, they were met with a firm handshake and a hearty "Welcome to Prairie du Chien. I'm Larry Gates, the airport manager." Gates was a shade over six foot tall and even without the parka he wore, you would have noticed he was broad in the shoulders.

The second man was closer to five seven and with or without his Gortex winter uniform coat with its POW*MIA patch, you could tell he was slim. He stuck out his hand and said, "Good morning. I'm Deputy Randy Hubbard. I've been asked to chauffeur you around while you're in our town."

"Mr. Gates. Deputy Hubbard. Meet Michele Fields. She's a reporter for the *Milwaukee Journal Sentinel* who is collaborating with the FBI on a case at this time," Cole said. "I'm FBI Special Agent Cole Huebsch, Prairie du Chien's prodigal son."

Gates had only lived in Prairie du Chien for three years, but the deputy remembered him. "Like most everyone else around here, I followed your wrestling career." Hubbard shifted, looked at Michele, and said, "Wrestling isn't the biggest sport around, but when one of ours wins state championships, let alone a college championship, we kind of all take pride in that." He turned and Michele and Cole followed him as he shuffled along toward his car. He was wearing thick, cushioned black orthopedic shoes spit-shined so well they could pass for a pair just pulled from their original shoebox. Cole put him at somewhere between his mid and deep sixties.

They wedged into the backseat as Deputy Hubbard turned the key and the powerful V8 engine roared to life. The deputy had only been waiting for their plane a few minutes and the engine was still warm. He pulled up to the lot exit. There was no gate, but he had to wait to pull onto Highway 18. A big, blue, New Holland tractor was lumbering south on the road. It was followed by an oversized wagon loaded with hay and a train of cars anxious to pass. Hubbard idled a moment, waiting for a break in the cars. The tick-tick-tick of the left turn signal carried to the backseat. Hubbard looked over his shoulder at Michele. "Our southern city limit sign is a few blocks from here," he said. "We've got a 'Welcome to Prairie du Chien' sign there that was donated by the Jaycees a while back. The sign also says, 'Home of NCAA Champ Cole Huebsch.' We've got a sign just like it donated by the Kiwanis with the same message about Cole that sits on the highway as you come into town from the north, too. I thought you might like to know that."

"That is good to know," she said. She looked at Cole as she said it, her eyes filled with mischief. Hubbard turned around to face the road, and the parade of cars was still trailing behind the tractor and blocking their exit. He put on his lights without the siren and the cars held up for him. Hubbard drove out of the airport lot. He took a left on US 18 and Cole saw a familiar sight. The Black Angus supper club was still open for business. It had been a mainstay in Prairie du Chien for decades and he and his parents had celebrated anniversaries, birthdays, and some of his scholastic and athletic achievements there. Further on they passed a Piggly Wiggly and a Tractor Supply store where a Walmart used to be. They passed the Cinema where he'd watched every action movie that came out when he was growing up. A lot of businesses flashed by the windows that he remembered well and just as many he didn't. They passed the Dairy Queen and he thought about warm summer nights when he and an army of kids from the neighborhood would descend there for a cone, a Dilly Bar, or a slush, but mostly to hang out and laugh.

Michele nudged Cole in the ribs with her elbow. "You still with me?" He turned to her and noticed the sunlight playing across her face.

"Yeah. It's been a long time since I've been back and it feels both familiar and distant," he said. "In some ways, it feels like home, but I also couldn't feel more like a stranger. I've got so many memories from here, and the majority are great. But there's an almost overwhelming sadness that I feel here, too." He realized he was opening up and stopped, "I'm sorry. I'm sure I sound mixed up. I need to keep my head in the game."

She touched his arm. "Don't be sorry. I'm glad you shared that. I can't imagine losing both parents suddenly and I don't know how I'd react, even years later. Coming back here is causing you to feel certain things… good and bad. By admitting that, you can better deal with it and focus on the investigation."

"A reporter *and* a licensed psychologist," Cole teased. "Let's hope you're right."

They followed Highway 18 north for less than three miles before Hubbard took the second roundabout left onto Blackhawk Avenue. In most river towns, Blackhawk Avenue would have been called Main Street. It was lined with brick retail shops, a couple of sturdy banks, a diner, a cafe, and a pizzeria. There wasn't a single chain on the nine or so blocks that led west to the near east side of the Mississippi. They pulled up in front of the city municipal building and Cole noted that the entire drive from the airport had taken no more than five minutes. He felt like half of his lifetime had run through his mind on that short drive.

Michele was struck by how empty the street was in front of City Hall. No CNN or NBC crews shoving each other aside to get an exclusive. "I wonder if anyone else besides the local editor has interviewed this hunger strike guy yet," she asked as they got out of the car and started into the building, the deputy holding the door for them.

"I doubt it," Cole said. "La Crosse has a small airport and it's only an hour upriver. Madison is only two hours east. But to get decent flights from New York, DC, or Atlanta you have to go through Milwaukee or Minneapolis. Milwaukee's a three-hour drive from here and the Twin Cities take a half-hour longer. So, travel's a pain. Plus, I don't think there's any place to get sushi in this town."

They went inside and sized Lawler up as they drew closer. He was slumped against the wall and looked weak, but he held himself with an undeniable dignity. His eyes were bright, and Cole saw in them wisdom and courage. Two men sat on either side of Lawler, and it was obvious they were sizing up the two strangers as well.

Cole bent down and offered his hand to Lawler. "John Lawler, I presume.

I'm FBI Special Agent Cole Huebsch, and this is Michele Fields, a reporter with the *Milwaukee Journal Sentinel*. Michele shook the older man's hand as well and she and Cole straightened up at the same time.

"We're investigating two separate murders of physicians that are probably linked," Cole said. "We'd like to ask you a few questions, if you don't mind."

The bigger guy on Lawler's right started to say something, but Lawler grabbed the man's hand and he stopped himself. "This is my son, Matt," he said. "Matt's a lawyer so he tends to try to protect my interests. And this is my son, Luke," he said, nodding to the man on his left.

"I don't suppose you have another one at home goes by the name of Mark, do you?" Cole said, smiling. "It would come in handy when, say, you wanted to put together a golf foursome, or maybe write a bunch of gospels."

"Matter of fact I do have a son named Mark, but none of my boys, or girls for that matter, live at home anymore."

"Okay," Cole said, shifting gears. "Tell us why you decided to conduct your hunger strike, and when you made the decision to start ?"

"I decided to fast to raise awareness of the abortion issue, and it came to me on Christmas Day. I picked City Hall because I used to work here. Plus, it's a public place."

Matt Lawler interjected, "Tell the agent about the Christmas sermon."

Cole caught Michele's eye. They both turned back to the elder Lawler.

"Some of the people around here are calling me a martyr. *Me!* Imagine that. It's not true, though. Not even close. If I was twenty or thirty and healthy I don't believe I'd have the courage to sit here and starve to death. It's easier for an old man like me who's lived a long life filled with blessings."

Luke put his hand lightly on his dad's shoulder. "Dad, tell them about the Christmas sermon."

"I guess that did ignite this flame in me," John Lawler admitted. He smiled and nodded as he recalled it. "When Father Wagner lit into all of us Christmas morning and challenged us to stand up for the children, for life's innocents...well, it was as inspiring as it was unexpected. I couldn't ignore it.

"And it wasn't Father Wagner speaking to us. I believe it was God himself.

I've sat through Father Wagner's masses for three decades, and the only time he's moved me before was to indigestion. I thought he'd checked out a long time ago, if he was ever really with us. But this was something else... something beautiful...glorious even. God used Father Wagner to call me to action. I've no doubt about it."

Cole's gaze moved from Matt to Luke. "Were you with your dad when this took place?"

Matt spoke first. "It was Christmas morning. We always go to Christmas Mass as a family. And it happened like Dad said. I'm a lawyer and I've seen a lot of amazing openings and closings at trial, but even I have to admit, that homily was pretty compelling."

"It was amazing, actually," Luke added. "The whole place seemed to get brighter and brighter as Father Wagner talked, and I swear at one point, the old stone walls of the church were shaking."

"Usually, you can hear babies crying during the sermon, you get distracted by people fidgeting in their pews or the rustling of hymnals or church bulletins," Matt said. "But that morning, all you heard and saw was Father Wagner. He completely commanded his audience."

"When he finished his sermon, Father Wagner asked those gathered, 'Who is ready to take a stand for our children? Who among you will carry that cross?'" John Lawler said. "It's funny, because I swear Father Wagner whispered it to me. He spoke softly but it carried to these old, sorry ears of mine. I stood up in my pew, right then."

"Did anyone else stand?" Michele asked.

The elder Lawler nodded. "Grant Grae was a little ahead of us on the other side of the aisle. He didn't look around to see who else might stand. He just stood tall."

"He's the editor of the town's newspaper, right?" Michele asked.

"Yup. He's the editor of the Prairie du Chien *Courier Press*," Lawler answered. "He's also its publisher, ace reporter, chief photographer, and leading ad salesman. He's also a good human being."

"Anyone else stand up that you remember?" Cole asked.

Lawler shook his head and his sons did, too. "Nobody else stood up that we could see, but we were three-fourths of the way toward the front of the church. We wouldn't have seen anyone standing behind us."

"Anything else about the sermon or the Mass that stands out? Anything else you think we should know about?" Cole asked, handing them each his card with his contact information.

Nobody offered anything more.

"Please, call me if something comes to mind," Cole said. "I appreciate your help." He looked directly at the elder Lawler and said, " I also want you to know that I respect what you're doing here."

Cole shook John and Matt's hands and then grabbed Luke's. Luke looked at Cole closely, and he held the handshake an extra beat.

"Cole? Cole Huebsch?" he said. "I remember you now. I graduated from high school the year before you started. But I used to come back and wrestle with the team during Christmas breaks when I was home from college. I never saw a guy improve as fast as you. You were impressive."

Luke turned to Michele. "This guy won three state championships for Prairie High. Only two other kids from town ever won a single one. He won an NCAA championship, too. He was a one-of-a-kind stud."

"A one-of-a-kind stud," Michele said, looking at Cole and holding back a laugh.

Cole was blushing. "Thanks for the kind words, Luke. Working with older guys like you helped me get better."

John Lawler squinted at Cole anew and a warm smile lit up his gaunt face. "I see it now. You're Larry and Vicki Huebsch's son. You look a lot like your father. Your parents were two of the nicest people I ever met. And twenty-five years after they started their life together, they were even more in love than the day they got married. That's a rarity. And they loved you, too. They let everybody know it, in the best possible ways. To this day, I'm sorry for your loss."

"Thanks," Cole stammered. He teared up, a reminder of why he hadn't returned since his parents' funeral. "Thanks to each of you for your help. Have a good day."

He led Michele down the hall and escaped into the sunlight.

Chapter Forty-Two

Three minutes after walking out of City Hall, Cole, Michele, and Deputy Hubbard pushed through the glass door of the Prairie du Chien *Courier Press*. The paper covered local news and sports and published every Tuesday and Thursday. They also published a weekly shopping supplement that was distributed to area homes and businesses and printed flyers, brochures, business cards, and other projects to bring in extra revenue.

A squat receptionist's desk sat just inside the door; the woman hunting and pecking on the keyboard there didn't see them come in.

Cole looked around. Framed articles that ran in the paper over the years covered most of the wall space. He noticed a story with a large photo of President Jimmy Carter's visit to town. He leaned closer and saw the date: August 19, 1979. He felt a nudge in his side. Michele had a smile on her face and pointed to a framed article with a photo that showed Cole with both hands in the air. It was taken after he won his third straight high school wrestling championship. Cole grinned. It looked like he was three feet off the ground. The large headline blared, *Cole Huebsch Three-Peat!*

"The young stud himself," Michele whispered. "I thought the Chicago Bulls coined the three-peat thing."

"In so many ways I was ahead of my time," he whispered back.

The receptionist caught movement or a snippet of the hushed conversation and looked up. "I'm sorry. I didn't hear you come in. I'm Barb McDougal. I'm the receptionist and the gossip columnist, and I put together the classified section of the paper...although that's dwindled to almost nothing since Craigslist and copycat sites popped up on the internet."

"I'll try not to keep you," Cole said, stepping forward. He introduced himself and Michele and said, "We're looking for the editor, Grant Grae."

"You're in luck. Just go through the door behind me and you'll find his office immediately on the left. If he's not there, he's in the conference room, well, kitchen, right across the hall. Or he could be in the pressroom, which is through the doors beyond that. There's not many places he can hide or that you can get lost." She waved them back.

Cole pulled the door open and stepped into a narrow hall. He took a couple steps further and leaned into the open doorway on the left. The guy he figured for Grant Grae sat at a beautiful oak roll-top desk, which made the cramped office more appealing. Grae looked up to face the door and inquired, "Can I help you?"

Cole stepped into the office and introduced himself and Michele to the editor. Deputy Hubbard nodded at Grae and the editor responded with a friendly, "Morning, Deputy."

Two small chairs faced the desk and Grae gestured for his guests to take a seat. "Randy, if you're staying, you can grab a chair from out front."

"I'll wait in the hall." He stepped out and left the door ajar.

Michele sat down, but Cole stayed on his feet. He studied Grae. The editor had deep brown eyes that returned his gaze. He had a slender nose and full lips, but the features that caught most people's attention were his bushy eyebrows and unruly but full head of hair. They were as white as the scratchpad he'd been scribbling on before being interrupted. Cole guessed Grae was in his early sixties. With the editor sitting down it was hard to tell his exact height, but he was definitely on the shorter side.

Cole turned and inspected the massive shoulder mounts of the whitetail deer that dominated two of Grae's four office walls. He pointed to the first one and asked, "My God, is this the thirty-point buck the Yupers sing about every year on the radio during hunting season?" The base of the antlers was wider than Cole's wrists and huge; irregular tines jutted out every which way from the wide rack.

"Michael actually has thirty-six points, according to his *Boone and Crockett* score. He's got close to a twenty-five-inch inside spread. I took him the first year I moved to Prairie ten years ago. I wanted to get out of Milwaukee and find a place I could still write and educate, but where it was easier to hunt and fish."

"You name the deer you kill?" Michele asked.

"Before I ever shoot them," he answered. "I scouted each of those two for months before the hunting season. I got to know their habits so well we were on a first-name basis. The other one's name is Gabriel, or Gabe for short."

"Well, Mike's the biggest atypical I've ever seen, and I've registered my own share of bucks harvested in the woods around here," Cole said, impressed. "Gabe's a monster, too, and I've never seen a twelve-point rack that symmetrical. Each side is a mirror image of the other."

"That's why I mounted him," Grae said. "I grew up a meat hunter and never saw the need to have 'trophies' made of my hunting successes. But after harvesting Michael, I knew I had to get him mounted. I wanted to share the beauty."

"You said 'harvested,'" Michele said, "almost like you picked a bushel of apples or corn. You shot the deer, right?"

"Well, sure. I shot both these fine animals," he answered. "But I speak for a lot of hunters when I say there's a spiritual side to the sport. When I shoot a deer and field dress it, I'm not thinking, 'Yippee, I killed a deer.' I'm actually taking a moment to thank God for allowing me to take the deer for food. It's kind of hard to explain to a non-hunter."

"I get it," Cole said. "I got that same feeling every time I harvested a deer, or any animal for that matter."

"After Michael, I figured I'd never have another deer mounted in my life, but when I shot Gabe and saw how perfect the rack was, well, I had to get it done. I don't make a lot of money here, but I don't have a lot of expenses either. So what the heck."

Cole nodded to a tall metal cabinet behind the editor. "That a gun cabinet?"

"It is. I keep a shotgun and a rifle in there. Locked up. It's not for protection," he said. "I keep them here in case I get the chance to sneak out early. Since I'm not only the editor and publisher but also the owner, that happens from time to time. But you didn't come here to talk hunting I imagine."

Cole sat down and looked directly at Grae. "You're right, we came to talk about a couple of murders. Right now you're a person of interest." He decided to be blunt to make sure he got Grae's attention.

Grae cocked his head. "What murders are you talking about, and how could I possibly be involved?"

Michele watched the interaction between the two. "Two physicians were killed in our state in the past few days. The first was murdered outside his clinic in Milwaukee by a sniper with a deer-hunting rifle." Cole purposely let his eyes drift, first to Gabe and then Michael peering down at them from above. He looked again at Grae. "The second physician was shot by the same type of rifle while making a sandwich in his own kitchen. His wife and three daughters were in the house and all of them saw what 170-grain bullets can do to a man's head.

"I read the stories," Grae said. He turned to Michele before adding, "And you're a damn good writer by the way."

"Thank you," she said, without emotion.

"But you haven't told me why you're interested in me," Grae said. "The fact that I started running a counter in my newspaper that roughly calculates how many babies have been murdered through abortion since Roe v. Wade doesn't make me the killer. I'm not going to sit here and lie to a federal agent and say that I don't have mixed emotions about the killings, but I didn't murder anyone or aid and abet either. Like a lot of people, I secretly admire the thought that these abortionists are being held accountable, but I can't imagine taking a human life myself."

Cole could tell Michele was getting frustrated and was about to take the editor to task for somewhat condoning the murders. He reached over discreetly and touched the back of her hand, but Michele pulled away.

"It seems like too much of a coincidence," Cole said. "A guy starts killing abortion physicians roughly the same time another starts a hunger strike against abortions. And at the same time, the editor of a newspaper starts running a recurring banner that estimates how many pregnancies have been terminated since Roe v. Wade was decided. The hunger striker and editor both happen to live in the same town with a population under six thousand. We just left John Lawler. He's staging his hunger strike two blocks from here. What are the odds?"

"Then we walk in here and you have two deer hanging on your walls," Michele said.

"And they're not any deer mounts either," Cole pushed. "Ninety-nine percent of the hunters who pick up a gun and walk through the woods never see a deer as magnificent as these , much less shoot one. And you've got two. That means you're patient enough to scout the deer over a number of weeks, clever enough to come up with a good plan, and stealthy enough to sneak up on them when almost nobody else could. Maybe most importantly, you had to be calm under pressure. Where most hunters' hearts would be pumping a mile a minute you would have slowed yours down. And then you'd have to be able to make the kill shots. All of that combined makes you a person of interest, make that a person of great interest."

Grae shrugged and let out a sigh. "Okay, I get that. I'm obviously not shy about how I feel about abortion. To me, it's the taking of a life, pure and simple. But I didn't shoot anyone. I can't shoot a fly off a deer's ass from three hundred yards out either, but I typically don't miss what I aim at. You're right that I scout and plan meticulously. And I don't take careless shots. Period. I'm patient and wait until I have a good kill shot. Every animal I've ever shot at has ended up in the freezer. I'm damn proud of that. I've never wounded a deer and had to wonder if it ended up dying a hard, slow death later."

He looked up at Michael and Gabriel with a satisfied smile on his face. "These two didn't end up on my wall because I'm the best shot in the state. I took both of these beautiful animals inside of seventy-five yards, because I did the work and had a pretty good idea of where they'd be at day's end."

"Tell us about Father Wagner's sermon," Michele said. "Did it move you in any way?"

"It got me off my dead ass, both figuratively and literally," Grae answered.

"I sleepwalk through most sermons and through most of life if I'm honest with myself. But Father's sermon on Christmas Day was a wake-up call. When he asked who would stand with him, I jumped up. I don't even really remember doing it, but I was out of my seat immediately. I felt silly when I realized Father didn't mean we should literally stand up, but I didn't regret standing up that day and I don't now. If anything, I regret not acting sooner."

"Have you lost any readers?" Michele asked. "I'm wondering if people who disagree with your view on abortion, who think it's a woman's decision and not a man's, would cancel their subscriptions."

"Fact is, we lost more than a third of our readers and about the same percentage of advertisers after I ran my editorial explaining my stance and started including the abortion counter. But both readers and advertisers are coming back already. We'll have some holdouts, but nobody covers small-town news the way a paper like ours does. You want to see your kid's name in the paper for sinking the winning free throw or winning the spelling bee? Around here you need to subscribe to the *Courier Press*. And if you want to reach those readers, you advertise here."

"So you have a monopoly?" Michele asked.

"I wouldn't say a monopoly. For most of us putting out these papers...we do it as a labor of love. It's more of a calling than a job. I make half what I made at the *Journal Sentinel*, but I'd make the switch again. I always figured you could have Pulitzer quality reporting at a small paper like ours. But you have to be in it for reasons other than money."

"I carried a Springfield bolt-action 30-06 when I hunted deer," Cole said, redirecting the conversation. "It was a hand-me-down from my grandpa and I loved that gun. I used the 165-grain Remington ammo. It was a little heavier than the 150-grain load but I had it in my head I wanted the stopping power of more lead. Did you use a 30-06 to bag these two?" He nodded at the big mounts.

"It's funny," Grae said. "I prefer more stopping power, too. I use the 170-grain bullet. But I like a lighter rifle when I'm tromping through the woods. So, the answer to your question is no. I've never hunted with a 30-06. I took both Michael and Gabe with my Marlin 30-30 lever action."

Chapter Forty-Three

Cole and Michele sat by a window at a table for two at Simply, the quaint café on Blackhawk Avenue, across the street from the *Courier Press* building. It was a little after eleven a.m., and they were on the early side for the lunch crowd.

Simply had a deal where you could pick two of three main items; a half sandwich, a half salad, and a cup of soup for less than nine dollars. Cole selected the half grilled chicken Po'Boy sandwich with a cup of gumbo, and Michele ordered half a cranberry walnut salad with a cup of vegetable soup. A good portion of kettle chips came with their meals and Michele told Cole to help himself to hers. Cole sipped a black coffee while Michele nursed a caffé mocha.

A mixture of coffee, chocolate, herbs, and spices scented the air around them. The café was warm and Cole liked the feel of the sturdy maple chair he sat in. He felt grounded. It felt natural, sharing the intimate setting with Michele.

"I like this town," she said, sipping her mocha and enjoying the little jolt the double espresso brought her. She licked her lips to savor the rich flavors of chocolate and sweet milk. "Quaint comes to mind, but it's somehow better than that. It's hard to put into words, but I get the feeling that people care about one another here. Everyone feels connected to each other and to the town somehow. You don't often find that in cities like Milwaukee or the suburbs that surround them."

"The downside is you never have any anonymity unless you get out of town. Everyone knows your business," Cole said.

"Well, then, I guess if you live here you'd want to be a decent human being," Michele said, smiling through the steam of her mocha.

They sat in silence, savoring a moment's respite from thoughts of the murder. Cole looked across the street at the newspaper building. "My parents used to own that place."

Michele looked at him, cocking her head. "Hmm?"

He nodded out the window in the direction of the *Courier Press*. "My parents owned the building that houses the newspaper now. When I was growing up they ran a supper club there called Geisler's Blue Heaven. It looked a lot different then...especially on the inside. My grandpa's last name was Geisler, and he started the restaurant."

Michele could see he was drifting back in time, struggling with his emotions, but she was glad he wasn't hiding it from her. "Do you have good memories of the place?"

He smiled as he looked across the street. "Yeah, I do," he said. "But it's not easy owning a restaurant. My mom and dad put in long hours, six days a week. Mom waited tables and Dad tended bar. I spent a lot of time there growing up. I started helping out when I was five I think, washing dishes in the kitchen alongside my grandpa. I'd stack dirty dishes and plates in these big racks and they'd go through the automatic machine. I'd do that for hours and he'd give me a dollar. I thought I was rich.

"When I got older, I bussed tables. Everyone who worked there watched out for me. We only had one car and later, when I came home on a break from college, I'd want to take the car. My parents would let me, but the one attached string was that I'd have to pick my dad up at work after I'd closed down the bars. When I went inside the Blue Heaven to get him, he'd usually be cleaning up or restocking the coolers behind the bar. He'd give me some quarters to feed the jukebox and I'd play oldies like *Cab Driver* and *I left my heart in San Francisco*. We'd sing along until he was finished and could lock up. They sacrificed a lot for me."

"Seems like you should come back here more often," Michele suggested.

"Maybe," Cole said. "I've been thinking a lot about that since you made the connection to Prairie du Chien last night. This town and the people here shaped me in so many ways…but it's hard. It's hard because things here remind me of my parents; how much I lost and how suddenly I lost them. Like most kids, I took my parents for granted and I've missed them so much for so long now…"

They suffered an awkward moment, neither knowing what to say when Cole changed the subject. "So, what do you make of our conversations with Lawler and Grae?"

"I think that sermon pushed a button with at least a few people in attendance at that Christmas Mass. It set things in motion. Lawler stood up at the end of the sermon and after talking with his wife, he headed down to City Hall and started a hunger strike. That doesn't happen every day. Grae stood up at the same Mass and now he's running that counter in his paper. He believes in the righteousness of what he's doing and did it knowing it would cost him readers and advertisers. He said they're coming back, but he wrote his editorial and began providing his running total of abortions thinking it would cost him financially…maybe some friends as well. As much as I believe they're both wrong, I admire their conviction. One is willing to sacrifice his life and the other was willing to sacrifice his livelihood. And the sermon seems to have been the catalyst that set them both off."

"I think you're right," Cole said. "It's too much of a coincidence to not see it that way. Obviously, the elder Lawler isn't the shooter, and his boys are too big to be considered suspects given the boot prints we found after the Martin murder. But do you think Grae could have committed the murders?"

Michele looked at him smugly. "I'm not on your payroll, you know. Shouldn't you be answering *my* questions?"

"You should be flattered that a decorated FBI agent is interested in your perspective," Cole said with a smile, taking a sip of coffee. "I noticed when Grae stood up to shake hands goodbye, that he was shorter than you, but not by much. So, let's put him at five-six or seven. Determining height from shoe size is iffy at best, but that would put him outside the outer end height-wise of our range of probability based on the boot prints we made. He obviously has the skill and the motivation though, and he admitted to owning a 30/30 and favors the same 170-grain bullet our killer's used. So he can't be ruled out. I'm going to see what kind of alibi he has for both of the murders and the rifle purchases. Chances are he won't have a solid alibi for all those, but he should have an alibi for at least one."

"What does your gut tell you?" she asked. "You don't have much of one, but you think with it more than anyone I know." She was staring at him.

"Thank you?" he said. "I'm not sure how to respond to that. You need to trust your instincts, but you also need to vet them. I don't know where intuition comes from, but it pulls from all the things that we don't see, hear, or feel in a clear and obvious way. We pick up on subtle cues and hints and our 'gut' helps put those pieces of the puzzle together until we have a clearer picture. My gut has served me pretty well over the years."

"So FBI Special Agent Cole Huebsch, what is your gut telling you right now about Grae?"

"Frankly, he's our best suspect. A lot of signs point to him. He's got the ability and a motive, but I like him more as a person than a suspect. I tended to believe him when he said he hasn't killed anyone. So my gut tells me we check him out but keep looking."

"What's next?"

"We need to talk to Father Wagner. I don't know if he'll remember me, but I sat through hundreds of his sermons growing up. I want a copy of his Christmas sermon and I want to get that in the hands of our analysts. I also want to see what he knows, and to rule him out as a suspect."

Michele's eyebrows shot up. "You think the priest could have killed the physicians?"

"Right now he's as good a suspect as any. When he called out to his parishioners it sounded like he asked, 'Who will stand *with* me?' He included himself in the fight. And he was standing when he asked the question. So far we haven't heard of anyone else who stood up besides Lawler and Grae when Wagner called the congregation out. Someone could have stayed seated and felt the conviction to act, though, so there's still a lot we need to know.

"I also want to find out everyone who was in church for that Mass on Christmas morning. I want to know every butt in every pew. If you and

I are right that Wagner's sermon was the match that set off the fireworks that have come from this, then we've narrowed down our suspect list to a few hundred. By the time we rule out women, kids, and larger guys, we could get our suspect list down to a couple dozen or less. That would be real progress."

"If we're right about the sermon being the key to the whole thing."

"Of course, there is that," Cole answered, finishing his sandwich.

Michele reached into her purse and retrieved her iPhone. The screen was covered in texts. She scrolled through them as Cole flagged down their waitress and gave her his credit card. He could tell Michele was getting nervous and excited. She unlocked the phone and sent out two quick messages and looked up as Cole signed the merchant copy of their receipt.

"I need to get to the airport," Michele said, jumping up and sending her napkin flying. "The *Journal* is sending me to New York to do an interview on Fox News about the murders. They've chartered a small plane that will take me to the Twin Cities and I'll fly nonstop from there to LaGuardia. They expect me on the air live in the studio tonight. My editor said I can expense a new outfit once I get to Manhattan if I need to. This is crazy." She let out a whoop that caught the attention of everyone in the café.

"Whoa. Slow down. We should have expected this," Cole said. He reached across the table and took one of her hands in his, looking directly into her eyes. "Please, try not to give away too much. Don't share anything about the sermon or this town if you don't have to."

"Okay," she said cautiously. "I'd really like to do a story on John Lawler's hunger strike, though. I realize someone might connect the dots like we did, but I'd be careful not to mention the sermon or the local editor's abortion update. Tonight, I'd also like to mention that the killer emailed me. Would you be okay with that? It would allow me to bring something new to the table and I wouldn't provide anything that could get in the way of the investigation."

"I can live with that," he agreed. "If you can omit the crucifix, deer blood, rifle type, cigarette butts, etc., we should be all right. That still leaves you with a lot to talk about."

"What if I run out of things to say?" She smiled.

"Then look the camera in the eye with that beautiful smile of yours," he said, knowing as the words came tumbling out that he was taking a chance.

Michele winced when he said *beautiful* and she pulled her hand away from his distractedly.

Cole cursed himself for losing his professionalism. "'I'm sorry," he said. "I was trying to be funny and helpful and I was neither. I didn't mean to come across as an ass."

"No. It's okay," Michele said, confused. "I'm kind of messed up and I have a lot going on right now."

"Well," Cole said, using his phone to summon a ride for her from Deputy Hubbard, "again, I really am sorry. Let me see what I can do to get you on a plane bound for New York."

Chapter Forty-Four

Larry Gates, the Prairie du Chien airport manager, was waiting for Michele when Hubbard dropped her off. He led her to a four-seat Cessna single-prop idling just off the runway.

"Your paper called and they prepaid for a charter to get you to Minneapolis pronto," Gates almost shouted. "I'm sorry I don't have anything bigger, but you'll be safe with Ed."

Gates opened the plane's passenger door and introduced her to Ed Pedretti. The pilot's old PDC baseball cap covered a mop of long, unruly gray hair that pooled at his shoulders. The look gave Michele the impression the pilot liked to fly with the windows down. "Afternoon, ma'am," Pedretti said with a broad grin.

While helping find her seatbelt, Gates said, "This airplane was built back in the late fifties, but Ed keeps it running well. And he's been flying it up and down the Mississippi Valley for close to forty years." He shut her door tight and shouted loud enough for Pedretti to hear, "*Mostly* without incident!" Pedretti shook his head and fed the Cessna gas. Michele thought she could hear Gates' laughter even as they picked up speed and raced west down the runway.

They followed the Mississippi River two hundred miles north to the Minneapolis-St. Paul International Airport. Ed's little Cessna got Michele there in just over an hour, which beat the three and a half hours it would have taken her on winding roads in a car. She hopped off at the Humphrey terminal and caught a ride to the Lindbergh terminal. From there she boarded a Delta flight to LaGuardia.

The paper had sprung for a first-class ticket so Michele could be one of the first to deplane when they landed. She was seated in the second row and kept her seatbelt on even after the big Airbus reached its cruising altitude fifteen minutes earlier. She took a deep breath and tried to relax. But she was too excited. The morning and afternoon had been a whirlwind, with the rest of her day looking to be the same. She couldn't help but think about the difference between riding first class in the Airbus and her ride with Ed in the front of the Cessna. Both were a first for her and exhilarating in their own ways.

Her publisher and editors were wild about getting one of the paper's reporters in the national spotlight. Usually talking heads from the likes of the *New York* or *LA Times, Washington Post,* or *Wall Street Journal* sat across from the network anchors and shared their opinions. This was heady stuff for a *Journal Sentinel* reporter. From her seat by the window, she looked down at the neon blue sky below. Brilliant white clouds mushroomed like puffs of cotton candy, with wisps breaking free and floating away.

She was nervous and hoped she would come across well under the harsh studio lights. She knew millions of pairs of eyes would be watching her from all across the country and distant spots on the globe. It was daunting. Realistically she knew that her looks qualified her for television news, but she'd always been in love with the written word. Before finishing high school she read every book from America's best-known authors like Hemingway, Twain, Steinbeck, and London. English authors like Jane Austen and Mary Shelley inspired her as well. Her favorite single book had been Harper Lee's *To Kill a Mockingbird. Still could be,* she thought with a smile.

Michele knew that in any in-person conversation, the majority of what gets communicated isn't through the words used, but in nonverbal cues like tone of voice and body language. When she wrote a story or column for the newspaper, her words had to stand on their own, literally in black and white. If she left room for gray, her readers could get the wrong message.

She looked at her watch. She wasn't big on jewelry, but she splurged a year ago and bought herself a Movado Swiss watch. It looked delicate, even on her slender wrist. She had two hours in the air before a driver would meet her at LaGuardia and take her to the Lotte New York Palace, a historic landmark hotel in midtown Manhattan. There she could freshen up after picking up a change of clothes from Saks Fifth Avenue, which was only a block from her hotel. Then it was on to the Fox street-side news studios on Sixth Avenue in the west wing of Rockefeller Center. That iconic building was two blocks from her hotel. Her editors were trying to make things as convenient as possible for her.

She thought about closing her eyes and trying for a quick nap, but she knew it was useless. Instead, she pulled out her laptop and turned it on. If she could write a story and fire it off when she touched down in New York, it could still make it into tomorrow's first edition of her paper, and onto the doorsteps of Milwaukee and its suburbs by five-thirty a.m. She thought John Lawler's fast was interesting, and she was sure her readers would find it fascinating, too. She would make sure not to make any connections between the killings and the hunger strike, and she would make no mention of the Prairie du Chien newspaper's ongoing abortion count or the Christmas sermon. She would do her best not to compromise the ongoing murder investigation.

Chapter Forty-Five

Tina Sawyer drove her black 1999 Chevy Silverado down Baton Rouge's Florida Boulevard, heading west since leaving Airline Highway. She passed a used furniture retailer and a dollar store and thought she might want to stop at the dollar store on the way back from her errand. Tina's brother, Tom, rode shotgun, literally. He was in the passenger seat and a 12-gauge pump shotgun lay casually across his lap. Jim Picket was their friend and Tina's sometime lover, although sometime "humper" might have been a more accurate description. He sat in the bed of the pickup with his back against a wheel well.

Tom and Jim were twenty-three and Tina was nineteen. The guys wore tattered jeans and light flannel shirts with the sleeves cut off. Tom was nearly six foot tall and rail-thin, and Jim was five-eight with his weight north of two hundred and fifty pounds. Tina had on jean shorts and a red tube top that worked overtime to restrain her large breasts. The guys had battered LSU ball caps covering their shaved heads, and Tom wore his beard long. Jim preferred a goatee. Tina's long, bottle-blonde hair was snarled and frayed. It flowed out from under a faded Tulane cap. One thing the three had in common was they were all hopped up on crystal meth. Tina also drank a mixture of grain alcohol and lemonade from a plastic water bottle as she drove. She called it Louisiana Lemonade and it carried a kick. The boys drank warm beer out of longneck bottles. They'd consumed six apiece on their hour-long drive over from Loranger.

It was unseasonably warm, almost eighty degrees, and they drove with the windows down. The window between the cab and the bed was open, too, and Jim played imaginary drums while the Misfits "Green Hell" blasted back to him and anyone on the sidewalks.

Tina turned off the boulevard and down an alley. She pulled into the back lot of a one-story brick ranch-style building and nudged up against the rear steel exit doors of the Capitol City Women's Clinic. Then she turned and yelled back to Jim, "Give 'em hell !"

Jim reached down with his left hand and pulled a whiskey bottle out of one of the two full cases that sat by his side. The smell of gas was heavy in the air as they idled. He worked the fingers of his right hand to extricate a cigarette lighter from the pocket of his too-tight jeans. When he had the lighter out, he flicked it a couple of times until a flame sputtered to life. He lit the end of the rag that hung from the bottle and tossed it at the window of the building ten feet away. It exploded as it broke the window, raining liquid fire inside the building.

"Shit, yeah!" Jim shouted as Tina shifted into reverse and smashed the pedal down. Jim was still a little off-balance from his throw, the beers, and the meth, and he fell against the case of bottles closest to him. Nothing broke, but gas splashed inside the bed of the truck and all over his shirt. "Damn! Fuck!" he yelled. "You're gonna break my fuckin' neck back here!"

Tom laughed. When Tina stopped her backward progress by slamming the Silverado's rear bumper into a shiny new red Honda Civic, he pulled the shotgun to his shoulder and pumped three quick blasts of number four shot through the building's other window that faced them. The noise inside the cab was deafening and Tina yelled "Jesus fuckin' Christ!" Jim rolled almost to the tailgate when they collided with the Civic. He cussed a blue streak. Tina slid the transmission back into drive and roared out of the parking lot and down the alley the way they had come. She hurtled out into traffic and spun the wheel hard to the right. She fishtailed but made the turn and at the first corner, she made another hard right. Jim rolled around in the bed like cheap luggage, the bottles of gas splashing all over. Now they were in front of the building they'd just firebombed. Tina roared into the driveway and pulled to a stop by the front door. The door started to swing open, but when Tom pumped his first shotgun blast into the opening, the door closed again. Jim, still cussing, lit another bottle and flung it at the nearest window. He hit the side of the building and the flames licked harmlessly at the brick face.

"Christ sakes!" Tina screamed. "Cain't you hit nothin', ya stupid turd!"

"Fuck it!" Jim hollered back, lighting the next bottle. "Any dickwad can drive a truck, Tina! Try throwin' a bottle a' fire if ya think it's so fuckin' easy." He lit and tossed another bottle and it burst through the window and showered fire inside the building. "Get the fuck outta here!" he shouted.

Tom had reloaded and he pumped three more shots into the building as Tina backed up with a squeal of tires and got them back into traffic. She shifted into drive and they rocketed forward. "Shit, yeah," Jim hooted loudly as he watched the Women's Clinic of Baton Rouge billow smoke and flames.

Chapter Forty-Six

Cole walked to the front of the main conference room of the Crawford County Courthouse. The two-story sandstone structure housed the county sheriff's department and jail and, in a twist, Prairie du Chien's Police Department. The county and city decided they could save their residents some money if they shared space and collaborated more closely. It made Cole's job easier, too.

The conference room was long and narrow, with two simple, dark wood tables pushed together lengthwise. The tables were lined on both sides with matching wooden folding chairs with black faux leather padding covering the seats. A massive flat-screen TV was the focal point on one wall. Twelve area law enforcement agents filled the chairs closest to the front of the room and Cole had to move sideways at times to reach the blank whiteboard there.

As he picked his way forward he saw a framed mission statement. He'd been in a number of local law enforcement buildings and wasn't sure he'd ever seen one with its own mission. He scanned it quickly and the words that stood out were courage, honor, and integrity. Under the "Integrity" heading the statement read: *We are responsible for our conduct, both professionally and personally. We are honest, fair, and strong of character. We hold ourselves accountable to the highest standards of ethical conduct and endeavor to be role models for others.* Cole thought if everyone in law enforcement lived up to those words, their shared profession would be in a better place, and the world would be a better place to live.

He picked up a purple marker that was labeled "grape," but when he pulled the cap off and wrote his last name, "Huebsch," the pungent glue-like scent that caught his attention didn't smell like any grape he'd ever want to put in his mouth.

"Hello, everyone. I'm Special Agent Cole Huebsch with the Federal Bureau of Investigation," he said loudly, looking around the room. He'd invited the Prairie du Chien Police to this briefing, along with the county sheriff and his deputies. He'd also called in four state troopers who worked the area. Cole grinned a bit and thought that for the next hour or so, speeders in the county wouldn't get any tickets. He shook away the thought and continued.

"This briefing will be, out of necessity, brief…and low tech." His nose wrinkled involuntarily and he capped the marker and set it back on the ledge by the whiteboard. He squinted as he addressed the men and two women in front of him. The long fluorescent tube lights overhead washed the length of the room with a sickly yellow cast.

"I'm sure most of you, if not all, are aware of the two recent and separate murders of abortion doctors in the state, the first in Milwaukee and the second in Oshkosh.

"The killer fatally shot both doctors with 30/30 lever action Marlin rifles with four power scopes. He left his murder weapon at the crime scene both times, but that has led to dead ends or red herrings. We don't know much about the killer, but we believe from boot prints taken in the snow at the Oshkosh murder scene that he's a shorter male, somewhere between five foot even and five four in height, and around one hundred and fifty pounds in weight."

"Sounds like a short, stocky son of a bitch!" a heavyset young deputy in the back blustered, his face turning beet red when every eye in the room focused on him. When he reached up and covered his goatee with a big hand, Cole thought he might be trying to obscure his identity.

"Right now, based on the best data we have, we think we're looking for a short, kind of chubby fella," Cole diverted the attention back his way.

"We don't have much on the killer, but we suspect he lives in, or at least has close ties to, Prairie du Chien." That caused a buzz in the room.

He picked the marker back up absently and walked down the right side of the room. He was wearing a charcoal gray pinstripe suit with a white button-down shirt and a blue and gray striped rep tie. His black loafers made a clicking sound as he walked.

"Your former mayor is staging a hunger strike a couple blocks from here. Two blocks from there, the editor of your local newspaper is running a count on the front page of each edition of his paper that provides an estimate of the number of abortions committed in this country since the Supreme Court handed down its Roe v. Wade decision. Both the hunger strike and the paper's abortion counter began a couple weeks before the first murder.

"If this was a town with a population of a million people or so it would strike me as more than odd that two different people who weren't colluding would start protesting abortion in two very different ways. In a town like Prairie, with a population south of six thousand, it's way too big a coincidence. I've spoken to John Lawler and Grant Grae, and both told me they were inspired by the pastor of St. Gabriel's, Father Wagner, and his Christmas sermon. I think the shooter was in St. Gabriel's Catholic Church here, in Prairie du Chien, on Christmas morning. I think he was likewise inspired by Father Wagner's homily, but he took it in a more deadly direction."

Cole made his way back to the front of the room and turned to face the officers again. "Our best theory right now is that the killer is a member of St. Gabriel's parish. If he's not a member, then someone related to a member. A lot of people who go to Christmas Mass are people who grew up here but moved away. They come back to be with family for Christmas. Unfortunately for us, there are probably more non-parishioners and other irregular attendees in church on Christmas than any other day…except maybe Easter Sunday. In order to run this down, we're going to have to get a number of things done and done quickly, before our bad guy pulls the trigger again.

"First, when I leave here, I'm going to have a talk with Father Wagner. I plan to lay this all out for him and get his cooperation. Second, I will want a shortlist, pun intended, of any adult males in the parish ages sixteen through seventy who are shorter than five-six and between one forty and one hundred and sixty pounds. I can't believe there are going to be more than a few guys who fall into this group, and I want deep background checks and bios on anyone on this list. This has got to be a priority. We don't know for sure if the killer is working alone, and something could always have gone wrong when we developed the physical description of the boot imprints in Oshkosh, so we're going to need to cast the net wider.

"Next, I want a diagram made, a grid that shows every pew on both sides of the main aisle at St. Gabe's, and we need to place on that grid every person who was in Church on Christmas morning. We need a parish directory and we need to begin calling the names on that list to populate our grid. Every time we get a new name and drop that onto the grid, we call back here and update the master grid. Ask the parishioners if they were at Mass Christmas morning and where they sat. Ask who was ahead, behind, and on the sides of them. If you're Catholic, you know that they share the sign of peace, a handshake, or even a hug, right before Communion. You get a pretty good idea of who's around you. Also, ask them if they saw other people they recognized on their way into or out of Church, or while Communion was going on. Finally, at some point in Father Wagner's sermon, he asked people to stand and be counted if they were ready to make a difference. We know that Grae and Lawler stood up at this point. They've both admitted this to me. I want to know if the people in the pews saw anyone else stand up.

"I'm asking the police chief and sheriff to work with the Highway Patrol to divvy up the assignments." Cole took a deep breath then and paused. He took a slow look around the room and made sure his gaze took in every person present. When he began again his words were slower, measured, and deliberate. All eyes in the room were on him. "Every assignment is big. In cases like these, it's getting the little things right that catches the killer. Work fast but don't cut corners. We need everyone on this; nine-one-one dispatchers, clerical people, everybody can pitch in. Thank you and good luck."

Chapter Forty-Seven

As Cole worked his way out of the room, a policewoman in her fifties reached to shake his hand. She had short, blonde hair and pleasant features. "Agent Huebsch, I'm Ann Mara, Prairie du Chien's Chief of Police. I hope you're wrong about the killer being from our town."

"I grew up here and I wouldn't like it much either, but one way or another I want to find him soon, no matter what his hometown is."

Cole felt a tap on his shoulder. He turned to see another hand extended. He shook it and the big trooper said, "I'm Sergeant Art Clark. I'm the lead for our contingent of state troopers working this case with you."

Cole said, "I'm glad to meet you both and to have your help. I don't like to fight over jurisdictional issues. We're all on the same side and our only objective is to get the killer as soon as possible. Can I assume we're on the same page?" Both nodded their assent.

"Good. Is the Sheriff here?" Cole asked.

Mara shook her head. "When you called and asked us to pull our teams together, the sheriff was out on a call. The dispatcher said a farmer outside Soldiers Grove called in a report this morning that someone stole three of his hunting rifles. The sheriff's like me. We both like to take calls to show our guys we don't mind getting our hands and boots dirty. Soldiers Grove is at the furthest end of Crawford County, so he was nearly fifty minutes away when we told him about this meeting. There are a lot of back roads between here and the Grove."

Just then the door opened and a short, square man in a sheriff's uniform strode in. When he saw Cole his face lit up and he lengthened his stride.

He yelled. "Whoa! Cole Huebsch! The man! The myth! The legend! Finally come home to see his brother!" Sheriff Fwam Vang reached Cole and wrapped him in a bear hug, lifting him off his feet.

"Ooofff! I had twenty-four good ribs before that hug," Cole laughed, as Fwam set him down on the tile floor. "Good to see you, Fwam."

"Man, Cole, where have you been? Lotta people miss you around here," he said. He looked at Mara and Clark and said, "This guy is a damn hero. He was a big deal in Prairie, the biggest deal ever in our high school. And not because of being maybe the best wrestler Wisconsin ever produced. But because of who he is in here." He pointed his index finger at Cole's chest for emphasis. "Biggest heart of any dude I've ever known. In high school, he could've pushed other kids around or picked on 'em, but he did the opposite for guys like me. I had two strikes against me. I was short and I was Hmong. I looked different from all the other kids. I was a year behind Cole in school and he made me feel like somebody…called me by name in the hallways. The rest of the kids didn't look at me funny after that, and nobody, no matter how big or old, would push you around if they thought Cole was your friend."

Fwam's eyes were getting leaky and Cole's face was turning red. "You're full of it, Fwam. I noticed you back then because we needed a one hundred and one-pounder on our wrestling team. You were one of the few guys in school who could make that weight and had potential."

"Bullshit," Fwam said. "You did talk me into going out for wrestling, but not for yourself. That was to help the team and even more to help me, I think. You helped me get stronger and learn to defend myself. I got so much confidence from the sport and from you that it completely changed the direction I was headed ."

"You were good." He looked to the others. "He made it to state twice and lost a close one in the finals his senior year." Cole nodded to Fwam. "I was proud of you. To have never wrestled until your freshman year and to work so hard that you almost won state. Unheard of."

"Well, I had you to thank for it. And it took some of the sting out of that last loss at state when I saw you up on your feet clapping for me. Coach said you skipped practice at Marquette to cheer me on."

He looked at the police chief and trooper again and said, "It wasn't only me, though. Cole made everyone feel like he was your friend. I remember having a typing class with him his senior year and Cole made a point of sitting next to Mary Fuller. Mary was the shyest girl in the whole school. She always looked down when she walked. Couldn't make eye contact. And she hardly talked to anyone. But Cole got her to open up. The first time he got her to laugh out loud the whole class stopped for a second, even the teacher. But after that, it became pretty routine. Mary came out of her shell and blossomed." Fwam nodded at Cole and said, "Keep in mind he was pretty much just a kid himself back then."

Cole was trying to keep from blushing and mostly failed. He said, "Yeah, well, you were always telling stories and I think you might be stretching this one a bit. But I'll take any kind words I can get."

Fwam looked at Cole for a moment. "You know, Mary and I ended up getting together. You had something to do with that. You weren't around for it, but we got married twelve years ago. Still together. Best thing I ever did."

Cole took a step back and sized his old friend up. Fwam looked like he was maybe five three and one fifty or so, a lot of it muscle. He couldn't help but think that Fwam fit their current description of the killer perfectly. He knew Fwam would figure that out, too, when he was read in on the briefing by his deputies. He said, "I wish I was back in town for pleasure, Fwam. It's anything but."

They shook hands all around again and started heading for the door when a police officer rushed in. "You're gonna want to turn on the news!" he shouted excitedly.

"Which channel?" Chief Mara asked her officer.

"I don't think it's gonna matter," he said.

Chapter Forty-Eight

The chief grabbed the remote from one of the tables and hit the power button. A male CNN reporter in a plaid blue blazer and purple paisley tie came on, talking into a microphone in front of a single-story building that was ablaze. The Louisiana sun, the heat from the blaze, and the realization that he was covering the story of his career combined to cause the reporter's face to perspire as he spoke too soft for those in the conference room to make out. Scrolling along the bottom of the screen was the breaking news of the clinic firebombing in Baton Rouge, Louisiana. Mara nudged the volume bar up until it seemed the reporter was shouting his story right at them.

"...at least one dead here on the scene and more potential casualties in other parts of the city caused by the firebombers," he said. "Reporting live from what's left of the Capitol City Women's Clinic, I'm Andrew Sennett."

A television studio set came on the screen and the camera zoomed in on a handsome anchorman seated behind a desk. "Thanks, Andy. Besides the alleged death at the clinic, there are reports of more casualties caused by the firebombers. Law enforcement hasn't confirmed that, but we're hearing from witnesses on the scenes. Thanks to all those calling our tip line at 225 'GOTNEWS.' From what we've pieced together so far, an unknown number of assailants set the Capitol City Women's Clinic on fire shortly before noon this morning. Shots were fired at the clinic and one person is believed to be wounded and possibly dead. We don't know if the shots were fired by the assailants or from inside the clinic by security or other armed individuals. The assailants fled the scene in a large black pickup truck, headed east on Florida Boulevard at a high rate of speed. A parish sheriff's vehicle is reported to have crashed a few blocks from the clinic, but at this time we have no update on the condition of the occupants of that vehicle. The pickup is reported to have taken the ramp and headed south on Airline Highway, again at a very high rate of speed. We've heard reports of an explosion or accident and Airline Highway southbound lanes have been shut down beginning at Florida Avenue."

A view of the Airline Highway scene from above came on the screen courtesy of the station's rented helicopter. Like the national viewers, Cole and the others in the conference room could make out the battered remains of a vehicle at the base of a bridge. It was an inferno. "That's all we have at this time," the announcer said. "We will bring you live reports as we have more."

Mara clicked to the other news stations. It was more of the same, including on the national networks that had broken away from their normal broadcasts. Mara clicked off the remote and everyone looked at Cole.

He took a moment before addressing them with a half-shrug. "From my perspective, this doesn't change anything we talked about regarding our next steps here…in Wisconsin, in Prairie du Chien, or in this room. We have no idea if this is related. When I leave this building, I'm going to walk the few blocks to St. Gabe's Parish and see if Father Wagner is in the rectory. If he is, I'm going to have a conversation with him."

"You want me to give a quick call and see if he's there?" Fwam asked.

"No. I don't think there's much chance he's directly involved in the shootings, but I want to be careful. I like the element of surprise when I have a conversation like the one we'll be having. I don't want answers rehearsed, and I don't want to give him even a five-minute heads up that I'm on my way."

"I can drive you over there if you'd like," Fwam offered.

"Thanks, but it's only a few blocks and the cold and the walk might help me get my head together. There's been a lot of pressure on everyone involved in this case from the minute the shooter pulled the trigger in Milwaukee. The president, the media, members of Congress, and almost all the heads of law enforcement have been frothing at the mouth to get this solved. This was a hot mess to begin with, and the blaze just got hotter." He nodded at the big blank screen of the television. "There's nothing like a little Cajun seasoning to add more heat to the stew."

Chapter Forty-Nine

Father Wagner sat at his desk preparing his homily for the coming Sunday's Masses. The scraps of paper that made up his notes were laid out before him like a jigsaw puzzle. His brow was furrowed in concentration when the door chime pulled him out of his reverie. It wasn't that long ago that someone else would have gone to the door to greet the visitor. Housewives from the parish used to take turns volunteering their time to provide housekeeping services, but the parish had fewer overall members now and almost all the parish women who weren't long since retired worked outside the home. He grabbed his tepid mug of lemon-laced green tea and went to see who was calling.

Wagner's eyebrows arched when he opened the heavy wooden door and stood facing Cole. His expression went from concerned to puzzled when Cole showed his badge and introduced himself as FBI.

"May I come in?"

"Of course. I'm sorry I seem a little confused," Wagner said, clumsily reaching to shake Cole's offered hand while also working to open the door wider with his foot. His teacup tipped and a little of the green tea slopped onto the carpet. "Please, come in," he said. "It's not often I get visited by the FBI."

Cole surveyed the interior of the modest parsonage from his position in the little foyer while Wagner closed the door behind him. The pastor led him into his study and gestured to the couch. He declined Wagner's offer of tea or instant coffee.

"Father, you might not recognize my name, but I grew up in Prairie du

Chien. Our family was part of St. Gabe's parish. My parents passed away during my senior year of college. Except for their funeral, I haven't been back to visit."

Wagner shook his head. "I'm sorry I didn't recognize you right away, Cole. It's been more than twenty years since I helped bury your parents, and that was one of the hardest funerals we've ever had in the parish." Whatever anxiety Wagner felt, left him. He went from being on edge to being in his comfort zone. He felt the need to console. "No man should ever lose his roots," he said. "I can't imagine why you haven't come home before now. Seems sad."

"I suppose. But I'm an only child and there never seemed a compelling reason to return."

"No friends left behind? No high school reunions to attend?"

Cole felt almost like he was back in the confessional as a boy. "I'm not the only one who thinks high school reunions are overrated. And as a non-attender, I'm pretty sure I'm in the majority," he smiled. "I've only got a couple of friends left that live in Prairie these days and they know that if they hop on Highway 18 going east they'll eventually run into Milwaukee."

"But that's not why you came back to town or stopped in to see me. Is it?" Wagner offered the question softly, bringing the mug of tea to his lips and taking a sip.

"No, Father. It's not. I need help solving a couple murders and, more importantly, help in preventing more murders."

Wagner's face clouded as concern and confusion fought for their place as the dominant emotion again. "I don't, I don't understand," he said.

"It's all right, Father. I have some questions I need your help with. That's all. For instance, do you know that one of your parishioners is staging a hunger strike at City Hall? I left him a while ago and if I'm any judge of character, he's going to starve himself to death if abortion isn't made illegal…which means he's written his own death certificate."

"I heard about John's hunger strike but I didn't take it that serious. I heard that his son, Matthew, was going to talk him out of it. I hope you've misjudged how far John is prepared to take this."

"I don't think I have misjudged, though. When I went down to City Hall and talked to Mr. Lawler, his sons, Matt and Luke, were at his side, offering their support. And how about the *Courier Press*? Did you know that the editor is now featuring a running count of the estimated number of abortions that have taken place since Roe v. Wade...in every edition of the paper? I believe he's a member of your flock also. What do you make of that?"

"I applaud it!" Wagner said, his tone growing louder and gaining confidence. "It's about time we focus attention on the outrage, the tragedy, which is abortion. I couldn't be prouder of Grant. He lost a third of his subscribers because of it, but he hasn't backed down."

Cole leaned forward on the couch. "And how do you feel about the guy who's murdering abortion doctors in our state?"

Wagner's forehead became a sea of creases and furrows and he shook his head slowly back and forth as he tried to make the connection. "What are you talking about? I heard about the murders, but they took place in Milwaukee and some city north of there. Ach, I can't recall exactly which town right now. But what does that have to do with Prairie du Chien and why you're here?"

"Because I think there's a very good chance that all three things are related. John Lawler and Grant Grae both tell me it was your sermon that moved them to try in some way to make a difference. I think one of your parishioners was moved by your Christmas sermon, not to stage a hunger strike or to make the magnitude of the abortion issue more public. If I'm right, this guy was moved to take more direct action, to pick up a rifle and stop the doctors in a cold, sure way."

"I don't believe that," Wagner said. But the way he sank deeper into his chair and tried to rub the wrinkles from his forehead belied the point.

"Father, you know better than I do that people have committed murder in the name of religion as far back as the history books go. The Catholic Church and its support of the Crusades is one example. That was a thousand years ago and ended up with over a million people dead, slaughtered over a piece of ground."

"The Holy Land," Wagner nodded.

"The Holy Land," Cole repeated. "Looking back, you have to wonder what Christ thought of the whole thing. More than one million of his people killed over land. I don't think that's something he would have endorsed."

"I know that," Wagner agreed. "But I still don't see how any of this ties to me and my Christmas sermon."

"Father, I know you were trying to do the right thing. I noted that more than a million people were lost during the Crusades, but because of legalized abortion nearly a million of God's children are lost every year in the U.S. alone now. They're killed before they even get a chance. But I believe you inadvertently caused at least one member of your church to take the law into his own hands...to personally stop abortions by killing those who commit them. If you don't think people in today's times can be persuaded to take lives in the name of their God, then think about the radicalized Muslims and the jihad they're waging. People want to believe the jihadists who embrace holy war are ignorant, uneducated poor people. The scariest thing about the movement is that many jihadists are smart and well educated, often at American universities. I think the power and conviction of your words and delivery tipped someone past the point of no return. That someone is out there right now plotting how to kill a third doctor. And likely more."

Father Wagner looked down and rubbed his forehead more urgently. "This, this is not what I intended. A good man like John Lawler taking his own life and another possibly killing physicians. I don't know what to do."

Cole leaned forward and lifted Wagner's chin so that he made eye contact with him. "Father, you can start by telling me about that Christmas Mass. I especially want to know about the sermon itself, word for word. And what made you write it, give it...everything about it."

"Okay. Okay. I have nothing to hide," Wagner said, looking straight at Cole. "But this could take a while and I'm getting hungry. What if I make us a couple of braunschweiger sandwiches?"

Cole broke into a smile, a memory of the smoked liver sausage coming to him from his past. "Father, I haven't had a braunschweiger sandwich since the second to last time I was in Prairie. That time I had a braunschweiger sandwich and a glass of milk with my dad before I headed back to school at Marquette."

Chapter Fifty

Cole and Father Wagner sat at the dark round walnut table in the rectory's kitchen. The buttery colored walls warmed the room. The two men ate their sandwiches with dill pickle spears and Fritos from a bowl set in the middle of the table within easy reach of each. The priest filled Cole in from the beginning, telling the story of how he got into the priesthood and how he'd grown stale and begun to doubt his own faith. He walked him through the events of the past Christmas Eve and described that night as his own metanoia, or transformation.

"Metanoia is a powerful word," Wagner explained as he chewed on a bite of the thick marble rye bread he had slathered braunschweiger on. "In the secular world, psychiatrists might use the word to describe the process of experiencing a psychotic breakdown and the subsequent re-building or healing process.

"To Catholics, it means an almost seismic spiritual transformation, the most famous example is Saul being struck by lightning and becoming Paul. In the Bible, when Saul is struck by lightning he has an epiphany. His hard heart breaks open and he becomes filled with the joy of the Lord.

"A metanoia is a radical transformation. It's a powerful answer to a typically anguished prayer…and it demands a response." Wagner's eyes were full of fire as he defined the meaning of metanoia and began to detail his own personal transformation.

"If Sigmund Freud or one of his contemporaries watched from the couch out in the other room on Christmas Eve, I'm sure he would believe he witnessed a psychotic breakdown. In truth, it was my salvation and rebirth."

He smiled and held up his glass of skim milk. "Until that night I couldn't stand milk. After I left the farm I lost the taste for it and my preference for beer grew over the years, as I became more and more dispirited.

"But I haven't had any alcohol since the night of my metanoia, other than the wine during Mass, which we believe is the actual blood of Christ. You should have seen the look on Bower's face when he came to replenish my beer stock the first week and all of the bottles were still full. I'm sure he's been telling more than a few people about that."

Cole was enjoying the conversation but felt the need to get to the point. "Tell me about the sermon," he said.

"Well, I told you how this transformation is like a prayer answered that requires a response. You see, my Christmas sermon was my response. I sat down to write it and my hands were shaking, but the words poured out. That homily almost wrote itself, but they were my fingers gripping the pen that flew over the paper. On Christmas Day, in the sacristy getting ready for Mass, I lost my surety. I was shaking, I was so nervous. But once I began walking down the center aisle, I didn't feel old and tired. People told me after Mass that I looked radiant. My voice rang out, clear and reverberating. Everything I did was effortless. When it came time for the homily, I didn't look at my notes. Not once. And as I spoke I felt the deepest, warmest love at times, and at other times the most righteous anger."

Cole studied the priest. "I know how strongly you feel about abortion, but I need your cooperation if we're going to prevent more physicians from being killed. Will you help me?"

Wagner was quiet. Slowly he nodded. "Yes. I despise the work these abortionists are carrying out, but it's not right to take their lives. We need to let God judge them. What can I do?"

Cole asked for a diagram of the inside of St. Gabriel's Church, one that showed the layout of all the pews. He told Wagner his plan to blow up the diagram and put a name in every seat. Wagner got up and Cole followed him to his den. There was a tall wooden butter churn filled with rolled-up tubes of architectural drawings. "I found this old churn in the attic of the farmhouse I grew up in," he said. "I think what you're looking for is in here."

There were at least a dozen rolled-up tubes of paper in the churn, each held closed with a rubber band. There was a sticker on the outside of each that gave a brief description of what was inside. As Cole scanned the labels he saw interior and exterior elevations and schematics. When he came upon one labeled "interior layout," he grew hopeful. "This could be exactly what we're looking for." After getting Wagner's approval, he started sliding the rubber band to the end, but it was brittle and broke halfway there. The date on the label said it was from 1966, the last time the church had seen a major renovation. He took care unrolling the paper, which had also become stiff and fragile over the years.

Cole had the diagram mostly open, though it had been rolled up so long it had a mind of its own and wanted to retreat into that shape. The size of the paper, three by four, was a pleasant surprise. "This should be big enough to work from, and it's got all the pews laid out the way they're situated today, I presume," Cole said. "If you're okay with it, I'm going to take this with me and make a number of copies. We'll keep a master copy at the courthouse that we'll fill in. The group we have doing interviews will each get one to use as reference."

He let the paper roll itself up again and asked Wagner for another rubber band. He produced one from his desk drawer and Cole secured the paper with it. "I'll also want a list of all your parishioners and any contact information you have on them. We'll start interviewing people and filling up that diagram with names as soon as possible. When I get the diagrams copied, I'm going to send someone back here to interview you. You said you were up and down the aisles, and greeted people before Mass started. I'm hoping you can give me a head start on people in pews, even if you don't remember the exact pews they were in."

"I can do that, and I have a list of our parishioners and their contact information on my computer. It's on a large spreadsheet. If you want to wait, I can print out a copy and give it to you now."

"Tell you what, Father. Here's my card," Cole said, handing him his official Bureau business card. "That has both my email address where you can send me a copy of the spreadsheet, and my cell phone in case you ever need to get a hold of me. I'd better head back to the courthouse now and see what else I can get done today."

"Do you want a ride?" Wagner asked

"No, thanks, Father. "To be honest, it felt good to walk down Beaumont Road again. Even with everything going on right now, it brought back some nice memories."

"You know, Cole, I remember your parents," Wagner said. "Sitting here talking with you was like talking to your dad. I'm sure people have told you that you look like him. I used to admire your parents' faith. I knew that your dad closed up the Blue Heaven at two a.m. on Sunday mornings and probably didn't get home until after three. But every Sunday he and your mom were here for nine-thirty a.m. Mass. Every Sunday. And when you came along they brought you, too. I don't remember much about their funeral, to be honest, other than the fact there were so many people there to show their love and support."

Cole remembered the funeral and the bleak feeling that enveloped him at the gravesite. It had been a warm, sunny day, yet he had never been so chilled. He could picture a younger Father Wagner making an effort to console him, and his eyes welled up again. He walked toward the rectory's front door, carrying the rolled-up layout of the church in his left hand and discreetly wiping his eyes with the back of his right.

As he got to the door he turned to Father Wagner and asked, "Any chance you have any of Bower's beer left in the fridge that you won't be needing anymore?"

Chapter Fifty-One

Cole didn't head directly back to the courthouse when he left Father Wagner. As he shut the rectory door, he was drawn to the large stone church. He walked over and tried the side entrance. The big wooden door opened smoothly. Cole didn't know if they kept it open for visitors or if it had been inadvertent. Either way, he stepped inside.

He walked toward the main entrance and over to a side table. In the dim vestibule, he made out holy cards and copies of last Sunday's parish bulletin. A shallow wicker basket filled with small metal crucifixes sat in the middle of the table beside a wooden offertory the size of a shoebox. Cole picked up one of the crucifixes and examined it. He reached into his right suit coat pocket and retrieved its twin, holding them up side by side to confirm it. He put five dollars into the charity box and opened an inner door to the church, the carved door groaning as it gave way.

Inside, he dipped the fingers of his right hand into the holy water font and made the sign of the cross. Memories of long ago Sundays flooded through him. There was a time he felt loved and protected in this solemn building. He walked down the long center aisle toward the altar and the large figure of Christ nailed to the wooden cross that hung on the wall behind the altar. When he got to the end of the pews, he genuflected and sat down in the first row, feeling a little odd carrying the beer and the rolled up church diagram. He lowered the kneeler, knelt and bowed his head. He thought of his parents and felt their loss anew, his loss magnified in this town, and even more in the old church.

At a table far to the right of the altar, rows of flickering candles swayed with the movement of unseen currents of air. Cole had been baptized shortly after he'd been born. On that day his parents and Godparents had committed to raising him in the faith. Later, when he was a junior in high school, he stood up and accepted the faith as his own during his Confirmation. *That was one commitment he hadn't lived up to very well,* he reflected. This was the first time he'd been in a Catholic Church since his parents' funeral Mass. The candles wavered again and he remembered that candles symbolized light in the darkness of life, especially in an individual life. Light also represented illumination, and Cole realized that right now he needed to be illuminated, about the case, and maybe more about his feelings for Michele.

He said a prayer that his parents were in a good place and asked that they watch over him and keep him in their hearts. And he said a prayer for Michele. As strong as she was, she was also wounded somehow. He asked the Lord to heal her and give her hope. Then he rose and went over to the table of candles. He picked up a stick match from a small box, struck it, and lit two red candles and a white one. He blew out the match, the dark smoke curling heavenward and the burnt match smell reminding him of incense. He put twenty dollars in the offering box there and walked toward the nearest door. Just short of the exit, he stopped and looked back at the entire church in all its quiet grandeur. Then he pushed through the door and out into the cold.

Chapter Fifty-Two

When Cole reached the courthouse it was five p.m. He called everyone in the building back to the conference room and walked through his detailed plan for identifying each person who attended the Christmas Mass. He gave the layout of St. Gabriel's Church to Fwam and asked for at least thirty copies. He asked that one be labeled "Master" and be kept in the conference room, updated in real-time as information came in. "I want all changes in pencil," he said, "because I suspect we'll have some differences in recollection since the Mass took place more than four weeks ago."

He surveyed the room. "I didn't pick up any new facts regarding this case from Father Wagner. What I *did* pick up on was the passion and the fire he brought with him Christmas morning. It doesn't take a leap of faith to see someone on the edge being swept over it by that sermon. I'm confident we're on to something here, and I can't tell you enough how important the work is that I am asking you to do. Thank you and good luck."

Cole grabbed Fwam on his way out of the conference room and asked if there was a place in the building he could hole up and make some phone calls. His friend set him up in an empty office that Cole could only describe as spartan. No paintings or photos hung on the walls, and there were no personal touches or knick-knacks to be found. But it had a chair and a desk, decent lighting, and a landline.

He closed the door and sat down in the leather manager's chair. *Nice,* he thought, resting his arms on the armrests and leaning back. He lowered the seat until it was the perfect height. He tapped his password into his phone and placed his finger on the screen to access his secure Bureau email account. He read the early reports on the clinic bombing in Baton Rouge and also the latest from the major news outlets, both print and electronic. He shook his head. Maybe it shouldn't surprise him, but he found it humorous that the reporters often dug up a lot of facts before law enforcement did. From a distance, nothing about the Louisiana clinic firebombing tied it in any way to the physician killings in his state. Jeffers, however, thought enough about it that he and an entourage had taken off in a Bureau jet from Chicago within a half-hour of the earliest incident reports to take a first-hand look. Cole knew some of the men and women in the New Orleans FBI field office and thought they were more than competent. They dealt with some pretty hairy stuff in the Delta. But Jeffers felt a road trip was in order. Cole wondered if he just had a hankering for some authentic Cajun food.

Cole wanted more information on the firebombing, but didn't want to get in Jeffers' way. If he called anyone in the New Orleans field office it could get back to Jeffers and lead to a fight Cole didn't want or need. He also didn't have confidence that Jeffers and his Chicago gang would come up with anything that the local Bureau hadn't already uncovered. Instead, he googled Baton Rouge and found out it was in East Baton Rouge Parish. A county in any other state was known as a parish in Louisiana. He found a number for the parish Sheriff's office and punched it into his cell phone. A receptionist picked up and after Cole identified himself she rang him through to the sheriff. Beau La Bauve answered with a gruff, "What else you want?"

"Whoa, Sheriff. I don't think we've ever spoken. I'm Cole Huebsch with the FBI's Milwaukee, Wisconsin office."

"Listen here! I been pretty much kicked off the bombing case by you Feds and then you rub salt in the wound by commandeerin' half my men and women to do the scut work you think you're too important to do. How do you think that makes me feel?"

"Probably not happy. But your feelings aside, I'd like some cooperation. I've got a person or persons up here who've already shot two doctors to death, and I don't think he or they will stop until they're either behind bars or dead. I need your help to figure out if your bombers also did the sniping up here or if there's even a connection at all."

"Well, hell, I personally talked to your guys from the New Orleans office and then later some dickhead from your Chicago field office. They wasted more'n two hours of my time. Why don't you talk to them for Christ's sake?"

"Cause it's like that game of telephone you played as a kid. The further away from the source you get, the less accurate the story becomes. I won't take up a lot of your time, but I'd like to hear the details from you. Directly. Can you do that for me...one officer to another?"

"Go on," the Sheriff sighed.

"Walk me through what happened there, in your own words."

La Bauve chuckled. "Who else's words would I use?" Cole could almost hear La Bauve collecting his thoughts before he continued, "This afternoon a young, big-titted blonde girl and her brother drove into our fair city of Red Stick from their shack in Loranger, about an hour northeast of here. They had a..."

"Wait a minute," Cole interrupted. "You mentioned a city called Red Stick?"

"Baton Rouge, son. That's French for Red Stick. Anyway, Tina and Tom Sawyer... I know... It sounds like I'm makin' this stuff up as I go along. Maybe Huck Finn was there, too, right? But goddamn me if Tina and Tom Sawyer didn't indeed ride into Red Stick. Another dimwit named Jim Picket rode along in the bed of their pickup. They pulled into the back lot of our one and only abortion clinic and threw a Molotov cocktail through a back window, started a fire that sealed off the rear exit of the building. Someone in the truck, probably Tom Sawyer himself, then fired several shotgun blasts into the clinic windows. They backed out of the lot in a rapid manner, caving in the front of some poor couyon's Honda Civic on the way. Then they wheeled around to the front of the clinic big as you please, and lit up the front entrance in a similar manner. The guy in the back hit the side of the building on his first throw, but he got the second bottle through the window well enough and they effectively sealed off both main exits. We don't have toxicology reports back yet, and I don't know we ever will. But from eyewitness accounts it sounds like the three were all drunk, high, or both. They still executed their plan pretty well."

"I heard you had a fatality at the clinic."

"Yes, sir. The one and only security officer," La Bauve said. "A retired cop. He was comin' out of the building with nothin' but a heavy flashlight in his hand and he took the brunt of a shotgun blast in the chest. Knocked him right back into the building. He was near to dead when he hit the linoleum. But he had enough life left in him to scream like a lobster hittin' the boilin' water when the fire started cookin' him. I didn't see him, but they tell me there won't be an open casket."

"Nobody else hurt at the clinic?"

"Miraculously, no. Staff did a nice job grabbin' fire extinguishers and dousin' the flames long enough to get everyone else safely out a side window. But they couldn't get the security officer out before the whole building was engulfed. By then the fire department was on the scene and they contained the fire. The clinic's pretty much gone though."

"From the reports I've seen it sounds like the trio committed a little mayhem after they left the clinic," Cole said.

"Mayhem," the sheriff spat. "That's too nice a word for what those scum did. They killed one of my deputies and another one is still not out of the woods."

"I'm sorry for your loss. All I've heard or seen is that two officers were injured."

"We can get away with holdin' back some details from the press down here a little better than you fellas seem to be able to. Once the three drove away we were on 'em pretty quick. Two deputies were right behind 'em a few blocks after they fled the clinic. They were too close, though. They took one of those Molotov cocktails to the windshield goin' eighty miles an hour and they veered off the road and hit the corner of a local savings and loan. The bank building didn't give at all and the cruiser became an accordion in the blink of an eye. One of my men died at the scene and the other doesn't have much of a chance."

"I'm sorry, Sheriff."

"Yeah, thanks for that. It hurts even more that the idiots in the truck ran over a couple of innocent bystanders in their mad dash to Airline Highway. That's why we figure they were out of it, because the hag at the wheel had a hard time steerin' a straight line. Couple blocks from the highway she wandered over the curb and took out an older couple walkin' down the sidewalk. Mercifully, they both died right then and there."

"Jesus," Cole whispered into the phone.

The sheriff sighed heavily again. "One other thing that pisses me off is we didn't get to take these monsters down. They got onto the highway and made a beeline for Highway 12 and the quickest route home. The staties were maybe six car lengths behind 'em, inchin' up at more than a hundred per when the truck ignited. Went up in a big fireball. The techs on the scene think these guys had two cases of their homemade firebombs in the bed of their truck, and we're pretty sure they'd only used up four or five bottles. The troopers on the scene say as many as twenty bottles must've gone up all at once. The guy in the back of the truck was engulfed in the blink of an eye and he dove out of the bed. At a hundred miles an hour he bounced on the pavement quite a ways. Not quite the recommended *drop and roll* technique they teach at the academy. Anyway, the flames shot into the cab and the Sawyers both got hot quick, too. Our Tina got a might distracted by the fact that her flesh was burnin' and she drove 'em smack into a bridge abutment. No seat belts. Not pretty."

"Sounds gruesome. But I'm guessing folks won't be too broke up about that part of this whole mess."

"You'd be surprised. There's Bible thumpers in this area who'll say those three should be considered for sainthood."

"Speaking of Bible-thumping, did your guys find any small crosses at either the crime scene or the site of the crash? My person or persons of interest left a small metal crucifix, about an inch high, at the sites where he killed the two doctors. That's one tidbit we haven't shared with the press yet. He also sprayed deer blood where he made the kill shots from. I doubt you've heard that either."

"I haven't heard anything about a cross or crosses being found, and nuthin' about deer blood. I guess it would've been sprayed at the clinic, if it happened. I'll make sure my guys are on the lookout for such. But they ain't big items and both the clinic and crash sites are like, well, bombin' zones. It'll be like lookin' for a needle in a haystack. But we'll go over everythin' with a fine-tooth comb. We'll keep it quiet, too. The other Feds I talked to never brought this up."

"Yeah, maybe it comes back to haunt me. The FBI isn't always big on transparency. We typically like to keep things close to the vest, but I think you need to know about it," Cole said. He considered explaining the difference between a crucifix and a cross but let it go. "Anything else you can tell me about what these three were like? Any thoughts on their motivation?"

"Not yet. This is the one percent of the one percent of the South that makes us all look bad. Put the characters from *Duck Dynasty* in a blender with knockoffs of the old *Dukes a Hazard* and you pretty much got an idea of what they were like…except the DD boys and the Dukes never really hurt anyone good from what I can see."

"Sounds like an episode of Good 'Ol Boys Gone Bad," Cole quipped, regretting it immediately.

"What?" La Bauve said.

"Nothing. I was talking out loud while I was thinking," Cole backtracked. "Thank you, Sheriff. You've been very helpful. I know you're still in the middle of it and you've lost men, so I appreciate all the help you've given me. If you come across anything else you think I might find useful, if you think of a connection I might not be making, hell, if you ever need anything…I hope you'll call me direct. Your assistant has my contact information, but remember the name Cole Huebsch. Is there anything else I should know from your end?"

"Well, I don't know if it matters, but this ain't the first time somebody threw a Molotov cocktail at an abortion clinic in our fair state," La Bauve said. "Could be our specialty, like shrimp gumbo and jambalaya. A few years back a couple threw one at a clinic up in Shreveport. But their aim was for shit compared to our Red Stick fuckups. No damage done to either person or property in Ratchet City. The woman involved told the police it was a memorial lamp for an abortion she had there. She got six years."

"Memorial lamp, hmm."

"I'll leave you with this. The screwiest thing about this whole thing is that all three of these nuts in our parish were smoking camels...maybe to soothe their nerves. It's apparently a dropped butt that set off their funeral pyre. So, I guess cigarettes really do kill folks. Enjoy the rest of your day."

Chapter Fifty-Three

Cole had barely hit the "end" button on the Baton Rouge call when his phone's ringtone came on again. He saw that it was "Milwaukee FBI" and he took it. "Cole, here," he said

"Cole, it's Li. I've got you on a speakerphone and Lane and Ty are with me. So don't blurt out something stupid like 'Ty walks like he's got a corncob up his…'"

"STOP right there, Li," Cole interrupted. "I think you know I'd never say anything like that about young Ty. And I think it's his business where he keeps his corncobs."

"Words of wisdom, boss," Lane chimed in.

"Anything new from the home front?" Cole asked.

"J. Edgar and Company found a connection between SW and Agnes Jones," Li said.

"Who?" Cole asked, rubbing his temples. The long day was catching up with him. He leaned back in the chair and put his feet up on the desk.

"The budding star of the Raging Disciples and the elderly drunk lady from Nekoosa. The two people we matched to the cigarette butts found at the scene of the Martin murder," Li said. "We knew that Smith's older brother was being held at the Boscobel Supermax, and we learned today that Agnes' son is there, too. Quite a coincidence."

"What's her boy locked up for?"

"He's serving four consecutive life sentences for four counts of murder one. He was a pretty big dealer in central and northern Wisconsin. Turns out if he didn't like a customer he would mix a little rat poison in with their coke order," Lane answered.

"Seems like a nice enough guy," Cole deadpanned. "Momma must be mighty proud. I wonder if the kid drove the old lady to drink or dear old mom drove the kid to deal and murder. Lovely family portrait to be sure."

"That's a chicken or the egg question," Lane said.

"Nice analysis, Laney," Cole said.

"Jeffers has some of his agents and other law enforcement conscripts looking at every Supermax employee and every visitor who's been to the Boscobel prison in the last two months," Ty said.

"How about deliveries, or law enforcement dropping off or picking up prisoners?" Cole asked.

He could hear the rustle of notes in the background before Ty answered, "I don't see that Jeffers has spread the net that wide yet."

"Every prison in the state is smoke-free now," Cole said, "but I'd bet the majority of visitors to the Supermax smoke. I can picture them walking up from the parking lot to the main doors, puffing on cigarettes, and then when they get to the doors they flick them into the, ah…the cigarette receptacles."

"Cigarette receptacles? Maybe outdoor ashtrays," Li offered.

"Ash urns is the term I think you're both searching for," Lane said.

"Whatever," Cole continued. "They flick their butts by the door into the thing with sand in it. Or hell, they throw the butts on the ground and proceed on their merry way into the building. I doubt that crowd frets too much over littering. Maybe our killer discreetly grabbed a few stray butts as he was walking into or out of the building. Who would notice or watch for something like that? Maybe they think it's nice the guy's picking up litter."

That thought hung in the air while the Milwaukee contingent waited to see where Cole was headed. "It doesn't make sense that a guard or another Supermax employee took those butts to plant at the murder scene. Because finding the butts and tying them back to the prison doesn't throw us off their scent…it would *lead* us to them. Every step of the way the killer has tried, with great success by the way, to confuse us. Would he set out the crumbs that lead right to his front door? No. Our focus here should be on visitors and law enforcement from other areas who are transporting prisoners to or from the Supermax. Even though the Supermax holds over five hundred inmates, there's not a lot of coming and going there. You get sent to Boscobel and you're typically there a long time. No short stays in the Supermax.

"We should see if they have cameras on the main visitor entrance," Cole continued. "I'm sure everyone has to sign in and out, too. See if you can run the list of visitors, both public and officers of the law, from December twenty-fifth until the night of the Martin murder."

"Will do, boss," Li said. "Why Christmas Day, though? You on to something ?"

"I think so. The Catholic priest here gave a sermon on Christmas morning that called for his parishioners to do what they can to stop abortion. In a town with less than six thousand people, we've now got a former mayor who's staging a hunger strike, and a newspaper editor who's running an updated count estimating the number of abortions since Roe v. Wade in every edition of his newspaper. Both told me they were inspired by their priest's Christmas homily. If I'm right, then someone else in church that morning got similarly inspired, but he picked up a 30/30 rifle instead."

"Really?" Ty asked. "No offense, but is that plausible? I mean, I can see someone skipping a few meals or writing something in a newspaper after hearing a good sermon or speech, but going from law-abiding citizen to physician killer because of one sermon? I don't care how compelling the sermon, that seems kind of far-fetched. Again, Cole, no offense."

"None taken. But how is it any different from someone in Iraq or Afghanistan strapping on a bomb and detonating it in a crowd after a few choice words from their Imam or Mullah? Our guy doesn't even have to sacrifice his own life."

"True, but the jihadists are taught that the West is evil from the time they're born. They aren't radicalized after one stirring speech," Ty countered.

"Fair enough. But we've had instances of Americans becoming radicalized jihadists in a matter of weeks over the Internet...without ever having face-to-face contact. And remember, I was born a Catholic and raised in Prairie du Chien. We're taught from the time we're little that abortion is murder.

No gray areas. If you believe that in your heart and at your core, then the reproductive rights physicians are taking innocent lives, and lots of them, every day."

"It sounds like the most promising lead we have," Li said.

"I agree," Lane added. "Want us to saddle up and ride out there?"

"Saddle up? No," Cole said. "Keep your posse right there. I've got local and state law enforcement helping me, so I don't have to go to Jeffers. We're identifying everyone who attended that Christmas Mass so we can see who matches what little of a description we have of the killer. It should be a, shall we say, 'short' list...pun intended."

Cole heard the groans from the others. "I'll take those as groans of admiration," he said. "I'll actually take whatever I can get at this point. Anything else on your end?"

"We're wondering if you think there's a possible connection between Baton Rouge and our guy," Ty asked.

"No. Our guy's exploits might' ve triggered the rampage down south, but I don't think they're related in any other way. When you called I was wrapping up a conversation with the parish sheriff down there."

"You called Baton Rouge?" Ty asked.

"Yeah. I did. I wanted to check in with them."

"Jeffers thought there was enough in Baton Rouge to warrant taking a crew down there on a Lear jet," Li said.

"And to each his own."

"Wanna hear something sweet about Jeffers?" Li asked. "You won't find it in any of the official reports."

"Are you going to make me beg?"

"No. That would be unbecoming of you. Jeffers directed law enforcement in Wisconsin, Iowa, Minnesota, Illinois, and Michigan to roust every gun show in their states..."

"Wait a minute. That's a lot of resources he's tying up."

"Yup. There can be upwards of ten to fifteen gun shows any given week in those states, and that doesn't include one-off sales like the one our killer took part in at the La Crosse VFW," Li said. "Anyway, Jeffers had them on the lookout for a guy wearing a big green army coat, in a wheelchair or with a walker, who has a beard and big glasses. An Iowa State Trooper found a guy that fit that description to a T in Des Moines and Jeffers flew directly there. Apparently, he sweated the guy for two hours trying to get him to confess to the murders. Turns out the guy really did lose the use of his legs in the service of his country. A Purple Heart recipient. So Jeffers basically abused a decorated military veteran. His legend grows."

"Couldn't happen to a nicer guy. Anything else?"

A chorus of "No's" was the Milwaukee answer.

"All right. Let me know if something else comes up on your end. I'll do the same with you if anything more turns up here. I feel like we're about to catch a break."

Chapter Fifty-Four

Cole got up, stretched wearily, and walked out of the office, closing the door behind him. Fwam was still in the building and he argued with Cole to come over for dinner with he, Mary, and the kids and to be their guest for the night. But Cole insisted he would not impose on his friend. He settled for a ride to the Dousman Hotel.

Two hours later, Cole lay on top of the hotel bed's plain white comforter. The grand three-story hotel was located on St. Feriole Island, with great views of the Mississippi River. The sturdy brick building was more than a hundred and fifty five years old and had been neglected for more than two decades before being recently rehabbed to its former glory and reopened.

He was stripped-down to his boxers, T-shirt, and socks. He'd hung his suit in the closet and his dress shoes sat neatly at the side of the bed. After the sheriff dropped him off at the hotel, Cole checked in and headed for the workout room. He shot for four hard workouts a week, alternating between biking and running, throwing in a long swim when he really needed to think. He longed for a lap pool. Instead, he rode a stationary bike for an hour and then ran five miles on the treadmill at a six-and-a-half-minute-per-mile pace. After a quick shower, he lay on the bed. The TV was on and he flicked the remote, flitting from channel to channel. He skipped through a couple minutes of a *M*A*S*H* rerun, the *Property Brothers*, and the day's sports highlights. Thanks to Father Wagner he had a four-pack of Toppling Goliath's King Sue double IPA. He had just drained the first when he heard two sharp raps on the door. He groaned as he rolled out of bed and went to answer it. After a quick look through the peephole, he opened the door enough to grab the pizza from the delivery kid, and gave him twenty bucks for the sixteen dollar pie. By the time he closed the door and got situated on the bed again, this time sitting up with two pillows propped behind his back, the national Fox nine o'clock news was coming on the air. He had cracked open his second pale ale when his ex-wife, Janet Stone, came on the screen. It was a tight close-up and she looked beautiful. Cole shook his head. She hadn't aged at all in the past five years. Only gotten better looking. Her full medium-length blonde hair framed her face, letting viewers admire the effect of her high cheekbones, delicate nose, and full red lips. He was still drawn to her large, round, sky-blue eyes. She was confident and witty when they'd been together and, as she introduced the news lineup for the evening, he could see she still possessed those traits. If anything, she was even more self-assured. In a lot of ways he still missed her. There was a reason they fell for each other and got married all those years ago. He was starting to feel sorry for himself when she announced her first guest and the camera panned back to show Michele Fields across the desk from his ex.

Some people's good looks don't translate well to television, but the cameras on the Fox set loved Michele Fields as much as they did Janet Stone. She looked gorgeous, and intelligent at the same time. She had discarded the navy suit she'd worn earlier in the day and was wearing a deep red dress that was both modest and sexy. Cole grinned, thinking of her trying on different dresses in Manhattan before heading for the bright lights. He was proud of her, and excited, too.

A guy could do worse than to end up with either of those two women. Cole realized he'd been lucky to have a chance with one and wondered what it would be like to have a chance with the other. He wondered even more if he could do better this time. He munched on a slice of pepperoni, sausage and green olives as his ex-wife brought up the topic of the physician murders in Wisconsin. She congratulated Fields on the outstanding coverage she was providing not just Milwaukee and Wisconsin, but to a riveted national and world audience. She asked Michele to describe how the murders took place and what law enforcement was doing to apprehend the killer or killers. Michele was also able to talk about how these killings were both similar to and different from other abortion violence that had taken place in the nation's history. She then dropped the bombshell that the killer had emailed her twice to explain his reasons for the murders.

Janet leaned forward in her chair, engrossed in the conversation. "How did you feel when the killer reached out to you directly to tell his story?"

"It was unnerving. Unsettling. Those are the best words I can use to describe my response," she said. "He feels righteous and is sure these killings are the will of God. He thinks he's saving innocent children. He wants to be understood, but what he's doing is incomprehensible."

"Do you think the clinic firebombing in Baton Rouge is related to the murders of physicians in Wisconsin?" Janet asked.

"I haven't been read in on the firebombing today," Michele said. "I was traveling much of the day and all I've seen of that city's tragedy is what I was able to see on your station before coming on with you tonight. My heart goes out to the victims' families and to the state of Louisiana."

"But, from what you know, do you see a link between the abortion violence in these two disparate geographic regions of our country?" Janet pressed.

"It's conjecture on my part, ill informed maybe…but I'd say no. I don't see any similarities between the Wisconsin shootings and today's Louisiana firebombing…aside from the fact that both involve the cold-blooded murders of dedicated health care professionals."

Janet leaned even further across the desk and locked eyes with Michele. "There's one more question I need to get out there and it's not an easy one. You've been forced to work closely on this case with the lead FBI agent in Milwaukee. Is your relationship with that agent, Cole Huebsch, strictly professional?"

Cole choked and spat out a mouthful of beer as the question was put to Michele. He lost the handle on his second slice of pizza and it fell topping-side down on the white comforter.

In New York, the camera came in tight on Michele, her face full in the lens. Her head was cocked to the side and she had a quizzical look on her face. She shook her head side to side slowly and squinted. "What?"

"I asked if your relationship with FBI agent Cole Huebsch is strictly professional," Janet repeated coolly.

Michele went from startled and confused to angry as if a switch had been flipped. She tried to control it. "Are you asking this as a news anchor or as the FBI agent in question's ex-wife?"

Both women's faces moved quickly from pink to crimson. Janet responded, "If one of the lead agents in this historic investigation is distracted, it could be catastrophic. I think the question's relevant."

"Our relationship is strictly professional," Michele said, her eyes never breaking contact with Janet's. "Which is more than I can say for this interview."

Janet turned to look directly into the camera. "We'll be right back after a commercial break," she said. Michele unclipped her microphone and was getting up from the desk before the camera cut away.

Chapter Fifty-Five

Cole got out of bed and picked up the slice of pizza he'd dropped. Buttery cheese and marinara remained on the white comforter, even after he grabbed a tissue and scraped up all the obvious pepperoni, sausage, and green olives. If the plate-sized colorful stain that remained were a Rorschach test, at that moment he'd have to say he was looking at the Grim Reaper holding an Uzi. "What do you make of that, Dr. Rorschach?" he said aloud.

He threw the ruined pizza slice into the small garbage can beside his door, then took out some of his frustration by crumpling up the pizza box with six untouched slices inside and cramming it into the same garbage can. The TV interview he'd just witnessed made a great appetite suppressant. He felt like throwing it all through the window, but he gritted his teeth and restrained himself. Instead, he shut off the TV and the light in the room and sat down at the small antique desk that looked out onto the Mississippi. It was dark outside and he couldn't see much, but the few lights that dotted the riverfront parted the gloom in small cones of diffused yellow haze. He saw desolation. He heard the bleat of a train whistle and thought of the iron tracks that ran north and south, cleaving the town in two. He grew up a block east of the train tracks, and both the familiar horn and the vibration of the trains rocked him to sleep as a boy. Tonight it was noise and distraction.

He lay his head down on the desk, anger and frustration pushed aside by a toxic blend of exhaustion and despair. His investigation was sliding from a simple hot mess into the biggest shit storm in the history of the Bureau. And that was saying something. It was bad enough that he was caught in the blowback, but now Michele was being smeared.

His phone rang. He'd had the volume on high so he could hear it amid the commotion of the hectic day, and the iconic original ringtone seemed to bounce off the walls of the hotel room. He looked at the phone and considered not picking up. It said 'Janet Wifey.' He'd never bothered to change it. It appeared his ex-wife had kept his number, too. He picked up. "Hello?"

"Cole, I'm really sorry. I don't know what to say," Janet began. "I want you to know I caught up with Michele in her dressing room after our interview and I apologized. I know you're both going through a lot right now and I just made it worse."

"I'm told admitting you have a problem is the first step on the road to recovery," he said, taking a large gulp of the ale to avoid saying too much.

"It's just that Jeffers called me right before we went on the air and told me that you were being unprofessional with Michele," she said. "I believe the precise words he used were, 'He's boning the reporter.'"

"The man always did have a charming way with words."

"I'm sorry," she said. "I mean it. I'm really, really sorry. I tried to keep my composure and I had it for most of the interview, but I couldn't stop myself at the end. It didn't help that she's so damn beautiful and younger than me."

"Really? I never noticed."

"You always were a shitty liar, Cole."

"Yeah, well, what the hell made you believe Jeffers?" he asked, his voice rising as he sat in his boxers staring out into the bleak darkness. "You really think I'm either that callous or that irresponsible?"

"No. I don't," she said softly. "That's why I'm so sorry." A moment hung between them before she said, "Oh, I wish Jeffers were here so I could break his nose again."

The comment caught Cole unprepared and he lost the anger he'd built up. He laughed out loud. "Well, that I'd like to see. The first time you broke that beak of his was one of the highlights in my life," he said. "You breaking Jeffers' nose ranks above any wrestling victory I ever had and it's right up there with the feeling I had on our wedding day."

"That wedding day meant a lot to you, too?" she asked hopefully.

Caught off-guard again, Cole struggled for something to say. An awkward silence separated them even more than the thousand miles of highway between them.

"Michele told me that this case and going back home hit you pretty hard," Janet said. "I always wanted to go back to Prairie with you but..."

"Why would you care if I was attracted to Michele?" Cole interrupted. "What hold do you think you have on me? I'm not much on *Entertainment Tonight* or the gossip rags, but even I've seen stories linking you with a number of A-list actors."

"That's mostly my publicist trying to get my name out there," Janet said quietly.

"Mostly?"

"Yes. Mostly," she admitted.

Cole stood up and walked over to the window. He could feel the big river's pulse as he imagined its muddy water flowing steadily south toward the Gulf. God knew what secrets it carried with it, along with all the sediment.

"For what it's worth, Cole, I think Michele really cares about you. And I want you to know that I think you're a good man and that you deserve to be happy." She hung up.

Chapter Fifty-Six

Cole continued to stare unseeing out the window, as unsettled by his ex-wife's call as her interview with Michele. He wanted to call Michele and see how she was handling things but didn't know if she'd speak with him. He hadn't even had a chance to sort out his own feelings. His phone rang again and the screen lit up. Against his iPhone's original clown fish wallpaper, "Gene Olson," appeared at the top of the screen in clear, white letters.

Cole sighed as he picked up. "Hello, Gene."

"Hey, Cole. How's the investigation coming along on your end?"

Cole let his guard down. Maybe Olson hadn't heard about the Fox interview yet. He'd rather face that in the morning. Or never. "We're on to something in Prairie du Chien. There are too many connections to be random. I think we'll find the answer to the abortion murders here.

"From the early reports I saw, your analysts in DC don't think the Wisconsin murders are related to the Louisiana firebombing," Cole continued. "I agree. There's nothing that really ties them together and a lot that's different. Our guy up here is a true believer doing what he thinks is God's work. The bayou boys down in Creole country seem like losers...haters. Our guy up here is smart. I know the three in Baton Rouge killed a number of people, but it wasn't thought out."

"Bayou boys? Creole country? When did you develop this love of alliteration?" Olson chided. He paused a moment and a seriousness that Cole recognized immediately entered Olson's voice when he continued.

"I'm not only calling to catch up on your take on the case. I'm also calling to see how you're doing."

"I'm not sure how to answer that. I'm getting along with Jeffers as well as I can, mostly by staying out of his way and pursuing leads he hasn't. I'm sure he let me poke around Prairie du Chien today because he and the yes men and women he's surrounded himself with don't see much of an interest here. Jeffers thinks nothing exciting could ever happen outside the lights of a big city."

"You really believe that's how everyone on his team feels?" Olson asked.

"I don't know. I do know Jeffers took at least seven agents down to Baton Rouge on a Lear with him. Those are seven pretty good minds distracted from a complex case. You've already got an army of law enforcement officers down there led by FBI leaders we both know are top-notch. And they're all tied up now, looking over crime scenes where the perps are already out of business forever.

"The firebombing in Baton Rouge was a drunken stunt," Cole said. "Those hicks were maybe inspired by our shooter and the widespread coverage he's gotten, but just as likely they were set off by cheap whiskey and pills. They can't hurt anybody or anything from here on out, unless you count the land pollution when their charred remains are interred."

"How do you really feel?" Olson asked.

Cole smiled to himself. "I guess that's Olson-speak telling me I'm being too blunt in my assessments as I get older."

But Olson was neither amused nor deterred. "You didn't answer my question, Cole. How do you really feel…about the reporter?"

Olson had deliberately caught Cole off guard and he fumbled his reply, "What?"

"How do you feel about the reporter? The woman you're working with? Michele Fields? How do you feel about her? It's a simple question," he pressed.

Cole switched gears. "I feel she's been helpful. Incredibly helpful. She made a connection that a thousand professionals in DC, Chicago, and other places with access to a lot more tools and information never did. That's how I feel about the reporter." He stiffened, waiting for Olson's response.

He didn't have to wait long.

"Well, after the catfight on national television tonight, that's all anyone seems to be talking about in New York, DC, LA and everywhere in between. There are a lot of people interested in the topic here at the J. Edgar Hoover building and over at 1600 Pennsylvania Avenue. You know that place, right? It's where that big white house sits."

"It caught my attention, too," Cole said, softening. He realized the pressure Olson was under to get these crimes solved. "I was sitting on my hotel bed here, eating pizza and drinking a beer. When Janet popped the question to Michele, well, let's just say Jeffers is going to have an extra cleaning bill from this hotel stay. When you drop a big slice of pie that's halfway to your mouth and it lands upside down on a white bedspread, it makes a mess. I know that now from first-hand experience."

"Does Janet have anything with her line of questioning?" Olson probed. "As I recall, she's more than a pretty face with a smooth voice. A lot more. She's a damn good reporter with better instincts for reading people than ninety percent of our agents."

"She does have good instincts," Cole said, his speech accelerating and getting louder, a locomotive picking up steam. "But a reporter' s only as good as her sources. In this case, her source was rotten. It's the same bullshit I've had to deal with while trying day-in and day-out to catch this killer. Collin Jeffers dropped the juicy bombshell on Janet right before she went on the air tonight."

An uncomfortable silence separated them, and Cole felt himself deflating. "Ah, crap," he said. "First, you know you can believe me when I tell you that the reporter and I haven't been physically intimate. It's been, to answer Janet's question directly, 'strictly professional.' I haven't so much as kissed her cheek. You want to hook me up to a lie detector, that's what you'll get. But between you and me, two friends who've had each other's back a long time; I'll tell you that I'm drawn to Michele somehow. She's bright and she's good at what she does. But she's also got a vulnerable side."

"So, what are you saying?"

"I'm telling you that I will not cross the line from working relationship to something more…at least not until this case is behind us."

"You're saying you won't take the reporter to bed until after the case is put to bed. Do I have that right?"

"In a manner of speaking," Cole answered. "Jeffers could assign someone else to liaise with Michele, but we've developed a relationship that works. I said before, she helped draw the connection to Prairie du Chien with access to nothing more than Google, when the analysts at J. Edgar with all their supercomputers didn't."

"Maybe because there isn't a connection to be made," Olson mused.

Cole smirked. "You betting on your machines and the robots who work with them over your own boy now, Gene?"

"No, I'm not," Olson admitted, letting Cole know he still had faith in him before he cut the connection.

Cole set his phone on the desk and got up from the chair. He paced and thought about Michele. He looked at the phone in the dim light. Half of him wanted to hear the familiar ringtone and see her name pop up on the screen. The other half was afraid he wouldn't find the right words if she did. He picked up the phone again and walked to the window, looking out into the dark night…trying to see what couldn't be seen.

His phone rang, and he answered. "Hello?"

"Cole! This is Frau Newhouse. I saw on the TV. Is it true that you've found a girl?"

Cole shook his head and couldn't help but laugh as he evaded the question. "You can't believe everything you hear on TV. But I do know I'm coming home tonight. If you hear me sneaking up the stairs in a couple hours don't be alarmed." He had made the decision in the moment. They talked a bit about their day and he said goodbye and ended the call. He didn't know if either Uber or Lyft drivers were available in the small town, so he chanced a call to Deputy Hubbard.

"Evening, Deputy. Any chance you'd give me a ride out to the airport? I'm at the Dousman Hotel," he said. When Hubbard told him he had nothing better to do, Cole thanked him and called the airport. Then he reached his pilot on his cell and told him to get back to the plane and warm it up. They were heading back to Milwaukee.

Chapter Fifty-Seven

Cole snuck down the stairs and into the garage of the home he shared with Frau Newhouse. He figured his stealth was improving since she didn't wake up and try to talk him into staying for breakfast. Then again, it could be the fact that it was just after four a.m. It had only been three hours since he'd slipped into his warm bed. Now, he wore sweatpants over his swim trunks and an old Marquette sweatshirt under his winter coat. He carried his suit, shirt, and tie for the day, along with a gym bag.

He hung his suit up in the backseat of his car and threw the gym bag in beside it. He settled into the driver seat and fired up the Charger, backing out and heading for the YMCA. During a major case his sleep, diet, and exercise were all catch-as-catch can. His stomach rumbled, but he almost never ate breakfast. No three squares for him. His eating habits were more like a wolf's or a big cat's. He might not eat on a schedule, but when he did stop to eat, he didn't hold back. It might not be "dietitian recommended," but it worked for him.

His sleep was more haphazard when he was in the middle of a big case. He could get by on a couple hours' a night for several weeks on end, seemingly no worse for wear. But when a big case ended, he crashed. Then he slept most of forty-eight hours straight, waking to go to the bathroom and maybe get a drink. Now he craved exercise, and not the fast-paced running and biking he'd done the night before. He turned into the underground parking lot of the downtown Y and found a space near the door. He grabbed his clothes and bag, punched in the electronic code at the employee entrance, and let himself into the building.

At four fifteen a.m., Cole had the massive structure to himself. Management liked having him around and let him have the run of the building. He paid his dues and made a nice annual donation on top of it, and he made good use of his "before-and-after-hours" access on days like today.

In the dim safety light, he headed straight for the sauna after stowing his suit and gear. He wanted to feel the dry heat and the closed-in feel of the small wooden confines. The cavernous building's thermostat was set at fifty-five degrees in the off hours and would automatically kick up to sixty-eight degrees at five-thirty a.m. Cole was a little chilly in his swimming suit and he savored the wall of heat as he opened the sauna door. He shut the thick wooden door behind him and it closed with a *shhhhhh.* He sat on a bench in the softly lit room and it brought back memories of being in the confessional years ago. It made him wonder if he should press Father Wagner harder. The killer could have confessed the murders to the priest and he would be unable to share that with anyone according to the laws of the Catholic Church. At least that's how Cole remembered it. He had begun to trust and even like Father Wagner, but he made a mental note to ask the priest about it directly to see how he reacted.

He rinsed off in the shower before slipping into the Olympic size lap pool. He lifted his head and leaned back, drifting for a moment. The massive round clock on the north end of the pool read four thirty-five. The sun was still almost three hours from rising as he shook out his arms and shoulders and adjusted his goggles.

He began a steady crawl toward the deep end of the pool. The slap of his cupped hands knifing the water and the splash of his feet were rhythmic white noise easy to ignore yet soothing at the same time. The pool area was lit by murky overhead lights, and the pool itself by oval lights that ringed the water's edge and shimmered a foot or so below the surface.

He reached the deep end and pushed off with his feet back in the opposite direction. If his goggles didn't leak in the first length, the seal would be okay for the next sixty-nine he planned to churn out. Seventy lengths, or thirty-five laps, put him over the two-mile mark and brought him to a level of exhaustion or weariness that stripped away his normal thought process. The monotony of the swim, the rhythm of his strokes, the cadence of the splashing…all had a way of allowing his mind to wander and to shift focus at the same time. Like a good athlete *letting the game come to him,* he pulled through the water waiting for the answers to find him.

He made four strokes for every breath he took, eating up the laps. His mind finally felt almost anesthetized as he counted off the laps, navigating by the painted line on the pool bottom. His eyes stared at the thick line, seeing and unseeing. He sifted through key chunks and tiny fragments of the case while he pulled himself through the water.

The first crime scene came into view, with Smith's body heaved over the snowbank. The second scene followed, with the pool of blood spreading out from under Dr. Martin, thick and sticky. He saw the rifles, the cigarette butts, and the deer blood. He tried to picture the killer, short and thick. He couldn't help but see his old friend, Fwam Vang, but he forced that image away. He was halfway through his sixty-eighth lap when he first noticed boot prints faintly on the pool's bottom. The Y must have completed maintenance on the pool recently. *Maybe they drained the pool and scrubbed the bottom,* Cole thought, *probably with some kind of strong bleach or cleaner*. In the dim lighting, the prints of the worker's boots were barely visible. Still, the prints crowded out Cole's other thoughts, as he started on his last two laps. He tried to pick up the tread pattern, but couldn't make it out in any detail. He reached, kicked, and breathed and tried to focus. He sensed the importance of the moment and tried to slow his breathing, to relax, and let a conclusion come to him. The prints were narrow, so much so that they must be pulled over a bare or stocking foot.

He touched the wall after his final lap, took a deep breath, and sank slowly to rest on the pool's bottom in just three feet of water. They had matched the boot prints found at the second murder scene to a pair of L. L. Bean's Snow Boots in a woman's size seven. The treads matched exactly. The Bureau had checked every other style that L.L. Bean made and no other boot matched the tread. So, what had they missed? Still sitting on the bottom of the pool's shallow end, Cole surveyed the boot prints once more. He imagined the guy who cleaned an empty pool wore rubber boots without liners...and an idea came to him. What if the killer took out the big felt liners before pulling on the PAC boots?

He stood, his lungs drawing in air, water streaming down his chest and arms. He thought about it more, absently moving toward the ladder and out of the pool. He got into the shower and cranked on the hot water. If the killer wore those L.L. Bean Snow Boots without the liners they would provide little more protection from the cold than the liner-less boots the pool cleaner had worn. And it was cold the night of the Martin murder. The temperature was close to zero. If the killer wore those boots without the liners, Cole reasoned, his feet might freeze but he would leave a boot print in the snow that would be several sizes smaller than his real boot size. Maybe they should be looking for a guy who was a little taller and quite a bit thinner.

It felt right. It wouldn't be practical to wear PAC boots without the heavy liners in the winter, especially if you might need to stay still for an hour or more in freezing weather before taking your shot. But that's exactly why the shooter would have done it, to throw off the FBI and others trying to stop him. That was the one constant in this case; everything the killer did was designed to send his hunters away from him.

Cole excitedly toweled himself dry and dressed. He checked his phone for messages as he shut his locker. Michele had texted him minutes before.

I have another email from the killer.

Chapter Fifty-Eight

Michele lived alone in a condo on the twentieth floor of a newer downtown high-rise. She couldn't afford the lake views, but her city views were pretty spectacular. Not that there was much to see at six a.m. in the winter. She dressed for the day and took the elevator down to the rear entrance. There were parking spaces in the lower level of the building, but they were pricey. She didn't mind parking on the surface lot out back; it was well lit and crime wasn't much of an issue in the area.

She pushed through the heavy glass door and paused under the halogen floodlight outside. She thought she'd heard someone whisper her name. "Miss Fields," it came again nearby, from within the tall arborvitae trees that lined the building's exterior. "It's me. It's me…the shooter."

She froze with fear and her hands began to shake. She held her keys and they jangled uncontrollably. Her heart pounded in her chest and she tried to decide whether to try to get back into the building or make a run for her car. But she couldn't move in either direction.

"I'm not here to hurt you," the voice whispered. "I would never hurt a woman. I've never hurt anyone who wasn't hurting someone else."

Michele tried to find her voice and swallowed hard. "Then, then why are you here? Why are you stalking me?"

"I don't mean to scare you; I just want you to understand me. I thought if you could listen you might come around and help my cause. At least stop attacking me." The voice was still a whisper, but it was becoming agitated. "I sent you an email earlier this morning, did you read it ?"

"I, I did read it," she stammered, leaning to look closer at where the voice was coming from. Though she was still afraid, she thought if she could see him, she would be able to describe him and help put him away.

"You need to know that those people who set that clinic on fire in Louisiana aren't working with me. They're scum. They weren't careful and good. Honest people were killed."

"I believe you," she blurted. "I said as much on national television last night."

"I didn't know," the voice said. "Thank you for that."

Michele wanted to jump into the thick evergreens and tackle the person there. He was supposed to be a smaller man, although maybe heavier and powerful for his size. She might not be able to subdue him, but if she could claw him and get his DNA under her nails, even if he got away they might catch him. She tried to will herself to charge into the darkness of the arborvitae but remained rooted to the walk.

"I don't know how much longer I can do this," he said. "But I want you to know that I am not a bad man."

"I never said you were," she said, swallowing again. A breeze came up and the cold sunk deeper. If she didn't try something soon, she knew she never would. She slipped her car key between her right index and second fingers and tightened her hand into a fist, the teeth of the key jutting out like the blade of a knife. She bit down on her lower lip, tensed, and jumped into the arborvitae. Something akin to a growl rose from her throat. She pushed through the dense evergreen limbs, slipping on ice, stabbing at the darkness in front of her. Snapping through the tender branches, she smelled red cedar and her own fear. Out of breath, she reached the end of the arborvitae and stumbled out of them. The killer was nowhere to be seen.

Chapter Fifty-Nine

In his car, Cole called Michele to see where she was, and when she didn't answer he raced the few blocks to the *Journal* building. A security guard signed him in and he ran up the stairs to her floor. The combination of the swim, his exercise from the night before, and a lack of sleep had him breathing hard when he got to Michele's cubicle. He pulled up short when he saw her. Her face was in her hands and she was sobbing.

He touched her shoulder awkwardly. "Michele. It's okay. No matter how bad his emails are, his words can't hurt you."

She looked up at him, her eyes red and wild as she dabbed at the mascara running down her face. "He came to my condo this morning. He was waiting as I stepped outside to go to my car." Her voice was uneven and rising.

"Did he hurt you?" Cole said. "Are you okay?"

"He didn't touch me," she snuffled.

Cole looked up at the ceiling as he shook his head. "I can't believe I didn't see this coming. Jesus, what's wrong with me? He sent you multiple emails for Christ's sake. When you didn't respond the way he'd hoped, then he would obviously try to reach out to you again."

Cole rubbed his eyes, trying to massage away his sleep deprivation and the residual chlorine from his morning swim. "Hang on a minute," he said to Michele. He pulled his phone from his suit jacket and punched the screen. "Li: The killer made contact with Michele this morning at her condo. He spoke to her from the row of arborvitae that runs along the back of the building. Send techs to the scene to see if they can lift any boot prints. Also, have them check to see if the condo's security staff caught our guy on their cameras." He was about to end the call when he added, "And get a security detail on Michele this morning. Have them come to the *Journal Sentinel* building. I won't leave 'til they get here. If you can't find agents, then call the U.S. Marshalls. They owe me."

"I don't need protection," Michele said in a low voice, still staring down at the floor.

Cole reached down and lifted her chin so she was looking at him. "I'm so sorry, Michele. You could have been hurt or worse. I failed you." He felt impotent. "But I need you to allow us to protect you now. Please."

Even in the dim light she could see the tears form in his eyes and run down his cheeks before dripping onto his dress shirt. It touched her, and she reached up and touched his wet cheek with her slender fingers, wiping away the tears. "Don't make this about you," she smiled sadly. "This should be my moment."

"I know," he agreed, with a sad return smile. "I don't suppose you took his picture while he stopped to chat you up."

"Not quite. He stood in the shadows of the trees and spoke to me. I tried to go in after him but I was so scared." Her lower lip trembled but she stopped herself from crying again. "I wanted to jump in and grab him so bad, but I was paralyzed. By the time I went into the trees to try to get him he was gone."

"You went into the trees to get him?" Cole's head was tilted and he shook it. "I can't believe you did that. I don't know many men who would do that, even those in law enforcement."

"I know that's bullshit," she smiled. "But it's making me feel a little better."

He put his hand on her shoulder again and squeezed gently as his eyes bore into hers. "It's not BS. It was incredibly brave. But from now on you don't go anywhere without one of our agents until this thing is over."

"Okay. Thank you. Now maybe we can get back to work." She nodded to her computer screen where the email was up. Cole read it for the first time while Michele read it for the third.

It wasn't me. I am not connected in any way with the vile people who firebombed that clinic in Louisiana. They didn't stop a murderer...they killed innocent people.

The security guard at the clinic should have known better, but he never killed any babies. And they are reporting that he was a former police officer. He didn't deserve to die like that. They killed two innocent bystanders and also critically injured two deputies. Those killers are not related to my cause. They are subhuman. It's not that I didn't understand when I started this that I could be a spark that ultimately ignites righteousness across America. But when my thoughts drifted in this area I thought it would be other soldiers of Christ like me, who fight evil and protect the innocent. MY WHOLE FOCUS HAS BEEN ON SAVING INNOCENT LIVES! *The people who threw the firebombs weren't trying to fight for those who couldn't. They killed blindly. Indiscriminately. From the stories your fellow reporters around the country have been airing, the three were also full of liquor and God knows what else. They weren't doing the Lord's work. They were doing the Devil's!*

I have prayed for the security guard and for the unlucky pedestrians who died, the first in what he saw as the line of duty and the last by chance or providence. I am praying still for any burn victims who made it out of that clinic alive and for the brave deputies who are fighting for their very live .

Please tell people that I am fighting alone for the innocents, and that those evil people who carried out today's drunken rampage do not fight alongside me! Please tell them. It's the truth and it's your job to print the truth. Right?

Michele waited for Cole to finish. He looked up at her, shaking his head as she handed him a warm cup of coffee in a *Journal* mug with the words "Pulitzer Prize Winner" under its masthead.

"What do you make of it?" she asked as he took a big slug of the coffee.

"It tastes like it's been sitting on the burner for more than a few hours. It has an ashen quality with notes of burnt plywood." He smiled at her over the rim of the mug, savoring the return smile as much as the warmth he felt in his hands cradling the mug. They'd been together just yesterday, but to Cole, it seemed like much longer. They hadn't spoken since before last night's Fox interview and he would have liked to ask her about it. If not for the killer's morning contact, it would have been the elephant in the room.

"I'll give you credit for maintaining a passable sense of humor at a time like this, but I'm looking for your thoughts on the words on the screen here."

She gestured to her monitor.

"I know. My attempt at a joke was diversionary, meant to gain me invaluable seconds to better frame my thoughts."

"And those thoughts are…"

"I tend to take him at his word. His anger, his outrage at what happened in Red Stick, ring true to me."

"Red Stick?"

"Baton Rouge is French for 'Red Stick.' I'm surprised you didn't know that," he grinned. "Okay, I learned that yesterday from a sheriff down there who's been pushed aside in the investigation by my Bureau colleagues."

"You really are stalling…"

"Moving on, then," Cole continued. "I think he's telling the truth when he says the clinic bombers aren't connected to him. He's also adamant that he's working alone. Maybe I'm a big sucker, but that feels right to me, too. I don't see multiple gunmen. He comes across as a lonely guy. A loner and a lone gunman. Again, that's just my feeling."

"Anything else?"

"One more thing, but I want to ask you not to use it for a while."

She nodded. "Okay. I won't use it until you tell me I can."

Cole bent to the keyboard and scrolled up, pointing excitedly. "Look at how he writes about the security guard. Notice how sensitive he is to the fact the guard used to be a police officer? He said the former officer 'didn't deserve to die like that.' He also described the deputies as brave. Seems to me he's giving police officers and deputies a great deal of respect. When we have acts of domestic terrorism like this, the perpetrators typically rage against authority figures like law enforcement. They don't go out of their way to revere them. After his line about the firebombers seriously injuring two deputies, he goes on to describe the perps as 'subhuman.'"

"I see what you're getting at. He even said he's praying for the deputies," Michele said. "But what does that tell us?"

"I'm not sure, of course, but the guy could have family in law enforcement. Maybe he's part of the establishment in some other way, like he served in the military. Maybe he's even a cop himself…"

Chapter Sixty

Cole drove to his office after leaving Michele at the *Journal Sentinel* building. He finished catching up on the reports coming in from their offices in Baton Rouge, Chicago, and DC when his cell phone came to life.

"Huebsch, here."

"Mornin' Agent Huebsch. This is Sheriff La Bauve from Red Stick."

"Hey, Sheriff. Hope your day is off to a better start than yesterday."

"Don't see how it could be worse," La Bauve said. "Neither of my deputies made it. I spent the night with two young wives who both have kids with no daddies now. I never seen so many tears in my whole life. Not ashamed to say I cried a few myself."

Cole was quiet a moment and thought about how he'd feel if he lost Li, Lane, Ty…, anyone under his watch. He said, "It maybe won't mean much to you, Sheriff. But I can't tell you enough how sorry I am. The only other thing I can think to say is that you, your team, and their families are in my prayers."

It was a few seconds before La Bauve could go on, but it seemed far longer. "It means something, Mr. Cole. It means something."

Cole could tell the sheriff was composing himself. "I'm calling to tell you we didn't find any medals or blood at the crime scenes. Most of it was a charred mess, but we picked through everything real good. We ran metal detectors all around the outside of the clinic and had lots of false alarms, but no medal. And not a trace of blood outside the security guard's. I'm just closing the loop with you."

"Thanks, sheriff. Please know that I meant it yesterday when I told you to call me if you ever need anything. It's nice in our line of work to know that you've got a friend or two somewhere out there in another area of law enforcement. You never know when you might need them. I feel like maybe I've got one now in Baton...ah...Red Stick."

"That you do," La Bauve said. "*Laissez les bon temps rouler.*"

"What?"

"I said, 'Let the good times roll. Now, go get you a killer."

Cole had barely set down his cell when his desk phone began chirping. He picked up. "Huebsch, here."

"Cole, it's Father Wagner. I've been thinking about our conversation yesterday and I'm worried about what I may have started. I don't know what I can do to stop the killer, but as soon as I get done with this call I plan to pay John Lawler a visit. I'm hoping to talk him into eating again."

Cole thought of his conversation with the former mayor before answering. "I appreciate the effort, but I think Mr. Lawler has made up his mind. And from what little time I spoke with him, I must say I admire that mind of his. Seems like a good man."

"A good man who I may have convinced to take his own life," Wagner said quietly.

Cole knew he couldn't erase the priest's feelings of guilt, but maybe he could ease them. "John Lawler is a man of principle, and he's of sound mind. If you talked him into his hunger strike, you didn't talk him into something he didn't already want to do. It doesn't take much of an introduction for a person to see that Lawler is his own man."

"Thank you, Cole. I'll let you get back to your work then."

"Wait, Father. There's something I need to ask you. Before I ask it though, I want you to know that I appreciate the way you opened up to me yesterday. You're a good man and a better priest than you give yourself credit for."

"What is it, Cole? I don't think anything will shake me more than I've been shaken this past month."

"Could you tell me if the killer confessed to you?" Cole asked directly. "Would the rules of the Catholic Church allow that?"

"No. They would not. Inside the confessional or on a street corner, if a person confessed the most heinous murder, I could not divulge that to you or anyone else. Not even a serial killer. If I were to break the sacred seal of confession, I would be subject to excommunication from the Church."

"I see," Cole said, purposely letting that comment echo between them.

"But it's a little more nuanced than that," the priest continued. "If the killer confessed to me that he planned to kill again and mentioned the name of his next victim, then I would call you immediately and tell you who to protect. I couldn't tell you the name of the killer, but you would know something that could help you. Also, if nothing has been confessed, I can tell you that. And so far, the killer hasn't confessed to me or reached out to me in any way. You have my word on that."

"Okay, Father. I appreciate that," Cole said, meaning it. "And please tell the Lawler family that they're in my prayers. I find myself saying that a lot more since we talked yesterday."

"I'll do that. And thank you for saying that."

Cole went back to the reports and finished them without learning anything new, except that the techs found nothing useful at Michele's condo. The row of arborvitae ran under a clogged rain gutter and a hard sheet of ice along the side of the building prevented useable boot prints. The building had exterior cameras on the exits, but the killer had avoided them. Cole scrolled through his emails, replying where he needed to. His door was ajar and a slender arm snuck through the opening, waving a wrapped submarine sandwich. Li's most seductive voice floated to Cole from the other side of the door, "Care to exchange a few minutes of your time for a fifteen-inch Cousin's sub?"

"Li, if that's a veggie sub that door is going to get slammed in your face and you may lose your right arm in the process," Cole said loudly.

"How does a steak and cheese sound?" she cooed, still hidden by the door.

"It sounds like 'open sesame,'" he laughed, and Li, Lane, and Ty all piled into his office. They took seats around the table and started in on their subs.

"Have we gotten anything new from the profilers?" Cole asked as he sat down and unwrapped his sandwich. "The killer's latest email sure makes it seem like he's fond of law enforcement, like he sees himself as one of the good guys."

"Nothing new yet, but the day is still young," Lane said between bites.

"Well, do me a favor and check in with the first suspect we ruled out, the guy from Centralia. I want to know if he ran into any law enforcement when he was in Wisconsin right after Christmas."

"I'm on it," Lane said, licking his lips.

No rays of sun were able to split the cloud-laden skies, so the blinds were fully open. Everyone ate hurriedly. Ty finished first and asked, "You feel pretty strongly the killer was in Prairie du Chien and heard that Christmas sermon?"

"I do," Cole answered, wiping his mouth with a napkin. He rolled the napkin in the sub wrapper and crushed it into a ball before tossing it at the wastebasket near his door. It bounced off the rim of the basket and rolled into a corner.

Lane had the second half of his sandwich up in front of his face and he whispered, "Too bad the killer doesn't have Cole's aim. We'd be referring to him as the shooter instead of the killer."

"I heard that," Cole said, retrieving his miss and dropping it in the basket.

Li wrapped up the remains of her seven-inch sub and tossed the wadded wrapper at the basket without looking. It hit low on the door by the hinge and bounced in. "If the shooter had Cole's aim we wouldn't even be on this case. It might be a misdemeanor."

"You guys should go into standup," Cole said. "But, yes, Ty, I do think the answers lie in Prairie." He reached behind him and grabbed two large sheets of paper from his desk. They were copies of the most recent grids he'd received from Chief Mara back in Prairie du Chien. He laid one out between himself and Ty and handed the other to Li. She laid it on the table between her and Lane.

"This is the layout of the inside of the church," Cole said. He pointed to the small rectangle that symbolized the altar and ran his right index finger in a straight line to the front doors of the church. "This is the main aisle, and the diagram shows twenty-six pews on each side of the aisle. Mara said that one pew was ripped out a few years ago, long after this diagram was printed, to make room for wheelchairs. Those pews hold from eight to ten adults each, depending on the size of those adults. So that's..."

"That's anywhere from four hundred and eight suspects to five hundred and ten," Lane finished for him.

"That's right, Mr. Smarty Pants analyst," Cole said, looking at Lane, raising his eyebrows. "But these two squares behind the walls on either side of the main aisle are both cry rooms."

"Cry rooms?" Ty asked.

"Those are rooms where parents take their babies when they start acting up in church, so they don't disturb other people," Cole said.

"In the world of grownups they're called 'infant care rooms,'" Li said.

"Whatever. I grew up going to this church and at good old St. Gabe's, we call these cry rooms. Each of them has an official occupancy limit of twenty people, which is forty additional suspects," Cole said the last quickly. He looked at Lane and smiled. "Not quite as fast on the draw that time, huh Rainman?"

"You want credit for twenty plus twenty equals forty?"

Cole shrugged and winked at Lane before continuing. "There's also a balcony or choir loft."

He pointed to a smaller diagram in the corner of the layout. "The balcony has six smaller pews on each side of the choir pit. Mara said the twelve pews in the balcony each hold maybe six people."

"Seventy-two," Li broke in.

"We're fighting over twelve times six now?" Lane complained.

"And the choir pit itself has twenty chairs and another spot for the director," Cole said.

"Five hundred and forty-one to six hundred and forty-three suspects total." Everyone stared at Ty, who blurted out the answer. "Sorry?"

"I'm impressed, Ty," Cole said. "But the total number of bodies in the church is even higher, since a number of people came in later and couldn't find a place to sit."

He pointed to the back of the church and the two side aisles. "People were standing against the walls along the entire back of the church and maybe a quarter of the way down each of the two side aisles. Mara is estimating another fifty to sixty additional. Anyone?"

Lane was about to answer when Ty said quickly, "Five ninety one to seven hundred and four suspects in all."

Cole looked at Lane with a pout on his face. He raised an eyebrow, put his right pinky to his lips, and did his best Dr. Evil impression. "No more, Rainman? No, Laney? Gonna cry?"

Everyone laughed out loud and Cole took a long sip of water. "Let's say six to seven hundred total. Now we're getting somewhere. Probably half are going to be women and maybe another quarter of the total will be kids under eighteen. Which takes us down to an even more manageable list of suspects. Another half or so of this group will be taller than five eight, which gets them off our suspect list. We're down to seventy-five to ninety or less adult male suspects if I'm right, without even subtracting others based on weight, elderly, etc."

"Back up the bus, Cole," Li said. "From the boot prints, we figured this guy was probably somewhere between five even and five foot four. Why go to five-eight with our suspect list now? Just being careful?"

"Maybe. This morning I asked myself what would happen if the killer bought a pair of boots like those we matched his prints to, but he took out the thick liners and wore them over nothing more than a thin pair of socks."

"What would have happened is he would have frozen his damn feet off," Ty said. "It was freezing up in Oshkosh that night he shot Martin, below freezing in fact, if I remember right."

"I'm pretty sure his feet wouldn't have fallen off exactly, but they could have been damaged by frostbite," Cole admitted.

"That would have sent us looking for a shorter, heavier killer, with what we all thought was hard evidence," Li said, nodding. "That's exactly the kind of thing our guy would do."

Chapter Sixty-One

Father Wagner walked down the sidewalk. It was only five blocks from the rectory to City Hall, so he opted for the exercise. It was out of character, but he was trying to be a better man. Most of the sidewalks were cleared as well as they could be, but that still left an inch or so of hard-packed snow to walk on in spots. It was cold enough that Wagner's shoes made a metronomic crunching sound as he walked.

He looked up at the heavens. A weak funnel system had moved in during the day, starving for moisture, and the earlier sunshine had been replaced by partly cloudy skies. Wagner was certain he would walk headlong into snow flurries on his walk home later, maybe even a full-blown winter storm. Five blocks. *You could do that in a blizzard,* he reassured himself.

A snowbank rose six feet on his left, piled up over the past few weeks by repeated passes of snowplows. The bank ran the length of the road and was so high Wagner couldn't see over it.

Still two blocks away from City Hall, he came upon the throng of people who showed up to support John Lawler's cause since Michele's story broke and statewide and even national media began running with it. Heavily bundled folks clogged the sidewalk on Blackhawk Avenue, and spilled into the main thoroughfare, rendering it a one-lane street.

Some carried signs with pro-life messages, while other signs read simply "Thank You, John" or "We love you, John."

Wagner shouldered his way through the crowd and finally up the steps and into City Hall. His collar and his persistence moved him ahead of the people lined up to pass along words of encouragement to the man willing to die for unborn children he would never know. Wagner nodded to a couple of his parishioners as he passed, but didn't recognize most in the crowd.

He saw Matthew standing at the end of the hallway, his back against the wall, and assumed John was sitting beside his son. Wagner was still twenty feet away when Matt saw him. Matt stepped forward and put his hands out in front of him. The crowd pulled back a foot or two and he said loudly, "Please, make way for Father Wagner. He's my father's priest."

A narrow path opened in front of Wagner as the well-wishers sucked in their chests and stomachs and flattened themselves as much as possible against the walls.

Wagner approached John Lawler and saw the peaceful smile that lit his face. He had a radiance about him and the priest didn't know if it was the patina of death or of everlasting life.

Matt pulled a plastic chair over for Father Wagner. The priest thanked him and sank onto the chair. In a soft, gravelly voice he leaned down near the elder Lawler's ear and said, "John, what's going on here? You have a lot of people upset and worried."

Lawler met his gaze and spoke in a voice weak from malnutrition. "I'm doing what you said, Father. I'm trying to put the spotlight on the murders that are taking place every day in this country. I've still got a little faith in my fellow man. I believe in my heart that if people can open their eyes and see what's really happening, that they'll step forward and put an end to it. I guess you could say an old man is trying to make the scales fall from their eyes."

"That's noble of you, John, but misdirected. The Good Lord frowns on his followers taking their own lives. It doesn't matter if you do it quickly or, in your case, in an agonizingly slow manner." He nodded his head up and down a couple of times, trying to coax acknowledgment or, better, assent from his parishioner.

"Father. My life is coming to an end anyway. I'm not taking it, the Lord is. He's calling me home. I'm doing something useful with what's left of my life, this precious life God gave me."

Wagner was becoming exasperated. His voice rose slightly, but his words could still not be heard by anyone but John Lawler. "I can't let you do this. It's not right and it's not holy. When I called out the congregation on Christmas morning, this is not what I had in mind!"

"Settle down, Father. Know clearly that you did not make me do this. I do it of my own accord. If you're here because of your conscience, then please, go in peace." He said this last with a hearty twinkle in his eyes.

"Your words did move me," Lawler continued. "I won't deny that. But I believe you were no more than the Lord's sound system on that wonderful morning. I've listened to your sermons for more than thirty years now and, to be perfectly honest, you never inspired me before. It seemed to me you were going through the motions most of the time, like you weren't sure if you even believed half of what you were telling us."

Father Wagner's face flushed deep crimson as Lawler spoke his mind, averting John's eyes and looking down at the floor.

"I'm sorry, Father. Forgive me. Maybe my hunger has given me an edge. I didn't mean it to come out the way it did. I want you to know that I'm responsible for my own actions here, and aware of what the consequences of those actions will be." He ran his hand through his sparse white hair and said, "Whew. I do run on, don't I?"

Wagner looked at him again and shook his head. "No, John, you're a man who speaks when he's got something worthwhile to say."

John broke into a faint smile again and any tension dissipated. "I suppose that's right." He licked his dry, cracked lips. "I don't know how much longer I'll be able to launch into one of these diatribes."

"I wish you'd given me that personal homily a decade or two ago," the priest said, rising stiffly. "The part about me coasting through life. But maybe I wasn't ready to hear it back then." He started to leave but turned and looked into Lawler's eyes. "You'll let me stop by again soon and give you the last rites?" His eyes held back a wave of tears.

John nodded. "I'd have it no other way." He paused and said, "I love you, Father."

"I love you, too, John. Thank you." The priest leaned down and gently hugged Lawler. He turned around then and the crowd parted before him.

He pulled his coat close to his body and headed home.

Chapter Sixty-Two

The next morning a little before seven a.m., the sun was nowhere to be found in Rockford, Illinois, an hour and a half drive southwest of Milwaukee down first I-43 and then I-90. The cloud cover brought the temperature up to thirty degrees Fahrenheit, which felt like a heatwave given the recent cold snap. A light, damp mist partially shrouded the home of Dr. Aarav Sadana.

Sadana graduated from King George's Medical University in Lucknow, India twenty-three years ago. The state of Illinois was the sixth friendliest to Foreign Medical Graduates, so after passing his United States Medical Licensing Examination, he matched with Southern Illinois University's OB/GYN residency. He completed his training there in four years. His accent was heavy, and he initially had a hard time connecting with his patients. So he was thrilled when he landed a job at the Rockford Center for Reproductive Health. He took over as medical director three years into his practice and had served as the clinic's lone physician the last fifteen years. His English improved over the years, and he knew he could build a busy obstetrics practice. But he felt the center's patients needed him, and that kept him at the clinic.

Sadana had a good life. He lived on Sinnissippi, a private golf club built on the city's east side more than ninety years before. He was introduced to the game while in residency and became hooked immediately. He was also a runner and six days a week he left his house at seven a.m. and completed a four-mile route on mostly asphalt-covered cart paths inside the country club grounds.

The FBI had assigned staff to protect all abortion providers within three hundred miles of Milwaukee. It took a lot of manpower but, with two separate physicians murdered within the last four weeks, nobody was taking chances.

Sadana had on black running tights and two thin top layers under a grey SIU fleece. He also wore a black stocking hat and gloves. The five foot seven Sadana did a couple quick stretches alongside the six foot two agent who'd been assigned to him, and they headed out behind his house at a brisk jog.

The path was clear for the most part, but occasionally they had to steer around ice or snow to avoid a spill. The agent led the way, his head on a swivel to spot potential trouble early. He wasn't crazy about the morning runs, knowing two other doctors within a couple hundred miles had been gunned down recently. But Sadana was running with or without him, leaving the agent little choice but to accompany him. The agent was in superb shape, but he had to admit the smaller doc pushed him.

Chapter Sixty-Three

The shooter waited roughly two miles from Sadana's back door. The spot he chose was fifteen feet off the cart path, on the backside of a massive oak whose trunk was nearly ten-feet wide. He settled into an indentation in the trunk, where wind or ice had ripped off a lower limb in the tree's youth. The oak swallowed him up.

The shooter was nervous, more nervous than when he shot the first two doctors. He knew that with every abortionist he took down, the heat was building and the circle was closing more tightly around him. Like a noose. It was inevitable he would be caught. At least one FBI agent was getting warm. He wanted to take out as many of the murderers as he could before that happened.

A light breeze kicked up but the shooter paid it little attention. He wouldn't be shooting at a distance this morning, so he needn't take the wind into consideration when making this shot. Today's work would be up close and personal. His first two kills had gone off without incident, and he was taking a chance by altering what worked. But he didn't want to be predictable. He wouldn't make the Feds' job easy.

He held the 12-gauge Remington pump shotgun against his body, butt down, barrel up, minimizing its profile. He would be visible to anyone coming down the cart path toward him, but he'd watched the path the last two mornings and Sadana was the only one he saw jog this route. And Sadana would come from the opposite direction. Two days wasn't much of a sample size, but his time was running out.

The shooter's nose dripped, leaking over his lips. He wiped it with the back of a gloved hand. A chill ran through him and he shuddered. He was antsy and willed himself to calm down. He breathed in and out slowly, watching wisps of steam rise and disperse. He wanted to get this over with and go home.

The branches above the shooter groaned as a bigger gust of wind pushed against them. He shook his head, realizing the wind could be a problem if it kicked up even more. He wasn't worried about it knocking his shot offline, but it could potentially conceal the sound of the runners' approach.

The thought was pushed away by the rhythmic slap, slap, slap of running shoes on asphalt. Faint at first but steadily increasing in volume. The shooter glanced to make sure the red edge of the gun's safety showed, letting him know it was ready to fire. Adrenaline coursed through his body, warming him and spiking his heart rate. He welcomed it. He didn't need to be calm and accurate at close range. He needed to be fast. Violent.

When they were so close that he could hear their breathing, loud and nearly synchronized, the shooter pushed away from the oak and faced them. He brought the gun to his cheek in one motion, just as they were even with the tree. Their heads began turning at the sudden movement, but the shooter pulled the trigger before either saw anything. The roar of the gunshot shattered the morning and the agent went down hard, hit in the left side of his chest and ribcage. The shooter stepped toward the runners as he pumped a new shell into the chamber. He pulled up and shot the agent again, this time high in the back as he lay sprawled on the pavement.

Sadana stared at the fallen agent. He knew he was looking at a dead man, but he heard the agent moaning and struggling to breathe. He should see blood, but there was none. He processed it all in the span of a millisecond, noticing the two bean bags on the ground by the agent, and realized the gunman he hadn't seen yet had fired non-lethal rounds.As a wave of relief flooded the doctor's system, the shooter jacked another shell into the chamber, aimed at Sadana's center mass, and jerked the trigger.

The first two shells were bean bag rounds, but the third was a number four buckshot load. Twenty-one large lead pellets tore through Sadana's back and out the other side. He died instantly, his heart and lungs shredded.

CHAPTER SIXTY-THREE

The shooter pumped his last shell into the chamber, realizing even as he did it that he was done shooting for the day. He slipped the safety back on and reached down to collect the three empty shells he'd ejected. He turned to leave but stopped and turned back toward the doctor. He closed the two steps between them as he reached into his jacket. He pulled out a small metal cross and tossed it on the doctor's bloody upper torso. He pulled out his catsup bottle and sprayed it at the doctor's feet until it declared itself empty with a wet "blat." He looked at the agent and saw that he was breathing raggedly with his eyes closed.

The shooter turned and began his own jog on painful feet through a short patch of woods, the shotgun heavy in his right hand as he slogged through brittle ice-covered leaves and twigs. He climbed over a low fence and emerged at the back edge of a Dunkin' Donuts parking lot. His Blazer was backed into a stall ten strides from the tree line where he stood and as far from the retailer's entrance as possible. He pressed his key fob and unlocked his truck. He set the shotgun down before stepping out of the woods and raising its rear hatch.

He retreated to the tree line and retrieved the shotgun. After looking around to make sure nobody was watching, he walked back to his vehicle with the shotgun shielded as much as possible at his side. He slipped the gun into its cloth case and shut the hatch. He opened the driver's door, got in, fired up the truck and pulled slowly out of the lot.

A Dunkin' Donuts coffee sounded mighty good to him, but he didn't want to push his luck. He thought he heard the sound of a siren in the distance but couldn't be sure. As he turned right out of the lot and headed north, Mick Jagger shouted "I can't get no satisfaction!"

"Ain't that the truth," the shooter mumbled.

After a thirty-five-minute drive due north up I-90, the shooter pulled into a McDonald's in Janesville, Wisconsin. He went through the drive-thru and ordered two sausage McMuffins and a large cup of black coffee. He sat at the far end of the parking lot and made quick work of the McMuffins, carefully sipping the hot coffee in between bites of the sandwiches. On his way out of the parking lot, he pulled up to a big trash can, tossing in his crumpled McDonalds bag containing wadded-up paper wrappers and napkins and three spent 12-gauge shotgun shells.

Chapter Sixty-Four

After reading urgent text messages about the Sadana shooting, Cole jumped in his car and headed toward Rockford down I-43. It was only an hour and a half at normal driving speed, interstate the whole way. But Cole wasn't driving normal. He planned to be at the murder scene in an hour.

He tried Jeffers' cell phone, leaving a voice mail letting him know he was on his way and requesting a return call. Jeffers got back to him a half-hour later, just as Cole screamed past the exit for Lake Geneva, Wisconsin at a hundred and twenty miles an hour.

"Cole, here." He kept his hands on the wheel and utilized Bluetooth and the car's speakers.

"Yes. I know that, since I called you and you answered."

Cole fought back a harsh comment. "Just letting you know I'll be on the scene in a half-hour."

"No. You won't. I'll be there and I'll have everything and everyone I need there before you hit the Illinois border. Turn around and head back to Milwaukee."

Cole pounded the dash. "Olson told me to stay close to this, to help out in any way I can. We need to work together."

"They put me in charge, Cole, and I don't need you in Rockford. We've got *competent* people on it. So head back. This isn't a request."

"Listen. I know I can help!"

"Head back," Jeffers repeated coldly, then hung up.

Cole came up to a turnaround in the median used by state troopers and emergency vehicles. He glanced in his rearview mirror and rode his brakes hard when he saw nobody immediately behind him. The car shuddered to a stop in the middle of the turnaround. The Dodge was idling, but his mind was racing. He was at a crossroads. He could keep heading to the murder scene in Rockford and have it out with Jeffers in front of a horde of agents and reporters. He could head back to Milwaukee and sulk. Or, he could head to Prairie du Chien where he was becoming convinced the answers lay.

His nerves were shot. One of the things that made him a good agent was his ability to keep his cool when others became unglued. But the twists and turns of this case combined with Jeffers's attitude were wearing on him. Toss in the small doses of fitful sleep he'd been getting and he felt like he was losing it. He took a couple of deep breaths and did a slow Y turn that had him aimed southwest again. At the first break in traffic, he jumped on the gas and shot onto the interstate. He knew that two exits down he could get off and connect with US Highway 11 heading west toward Janesville. From there he would head north, skirt west around Madison, and then make the straight shot west to Prairie du Chien.

Chapter Sixty-Five

Ty, Lane, and Li huddled in a Bureau conference room linked up with Michele at her *Journal Sentinel* office for a conference call with Cole. It was noon, three and a half hours since Sadana's body had been found. The shooter had yet to reach out to Michele.

She had her laptop open with her email account enlarged to full screen. Her eyes kept darting down to the screen, expecting and dreading a message from the shooter at any moment.

"I can't believe Jeffers," Cole said, his voice raised. "Who would pull a power play like that in the middle of an investigation as big as this one? My God! He's so full of himself. He's afraid we'll contribute something and he'll have to share a little credit with us."

"Not us exactly," Ty said. "I don't think he's got anything against me or Michele. And I don't think he dislikes Lane or Li. It's just you who seems to piss him off so much."

"You're probably right. But that pissing off thing goes both ways. He's such a moronic dick!"

He was just getting started on trashing Jeffers when Michele cut him off. "What do we know about this morning's events? Is it our guy?"

Highway 11 was a two-lane and Cole was making great time on it until he slowed behind a battered red pickup, tooling along ten miles under the posted fifty-five miles per hour limit. It was straight road. He saw an opening and floored it, crossing two yellow lines to rocket around the pickup with little room to spare before a semi blew by him heading in the other direction.

"Cole, do we even know if the Rockford shooter is our guy?" Michele repeated.

He took a couple deep breaths. "Yeah. I'm pretty sure. It was well planned; it's in the radius we've mapped out, etc. I know we have differences like shotgun versus rifle, close versus distant, but this is our guy."

"Cole, this is Lane. A report just came in saying they found a small metal crucifix and blood that wasn't the doctor's on the scene. They aren't saying it's deer blood yet, but what are the odds? It's our guy for sure."

"What else do you have?" Cole asked, putting the pedal down again, grateful for a stretch of open road.

Lane continued. "The shooter used a 12-gauge shotgun from close range, ambushing Sadana and the agent assigned to protect him. They warned the doctor about the obvious exposure of going out on a run, but he insisted."

"Did the agent die, too?" Ty asked.

"No. They're still working the scene, but it looks like the shooter put the agent down with two bean bag rounds and then fired one shell of four-ounce buckshot at the doctor. From a distance of a few feet. It made a hole in Sadana's chest the size of dinner plate."

"Tell me the agent was able to give us a good description of the shooter," Cole said, pulling down his visor as brilliant sun broke through the clouds. "A reliable eyewitness right now would be a welcome break in the case."

"No eyewitness," Li said. "The agent says he didn't see the shooter at all. He said he saw motion to his left out of the corner of his eye. Before he could turn his head he was hit in his left front side by the first bean bag. It knocked him to the ground and he'd barely kissed the pavement before the second bean bag hit him in the upper left side of his back. The pain was crippling."

"I didn't think bean bags could do that," Michele said.

"They can do that and worse," Li said. "Bean bags aren't really non-lethal rounds. 'Less lethal' would be a better way of putting it. They cause one death or more a year in the U.S. You'd feel a lot better getting hit with a bean bag than buckshot obviously, but you still wouldn't enjoy the experience.

"Paramedics on the scene are pretty sure the agent has two broken ribs.

That's one of the ways people get killed by bean bag rounds. They get shot in the chest from too close and their ribs splinter into the heart. Game over."

"Have they found the shotgun?" Michele asked. "The killer left the rifles at the scene the first two times he pulled the trigger. I'm assuming he left the shotgun at this scene?"

"Nope. I don't see anything about that in the early reports," Lane said. "It was at a golf course though, so he could have dropped it somewhere on his way out of the woods. They might find it later."

"Why keep the shotgun?" Michele asked. "Why not leave it at the scene like he did with the rifles? Are there two or more guys in on this?"

"Good questions," Cole said, slipping on a pair of sunglasses. "It was a 12-gauge, which I'm pretty sure is the most common shotgun gauge made. Our guy doesn't go for exotics in his weaponry. Most every sportsman in the Midwest is likely to have a 12-gauge in his house. It's good for hunting ducks, geese, grouse, woodcock, and even rabbits and squirrel…though you'd want a good headshot on a squirrel with a 12 or you'd ruin what little meat it has on it."

"Do people really eat squirrels?" Michele asked, shaking her head in disgust as she sat at her desk.

In the Bureau conference room, Ty looked like he'd bitten into something sour, too.

Cole laughed. "Oh, you pampered city folk. Of course, people eat squirrel. It's a delicacy. But that's not the point. The point is the twelve is such a popular shotgun with so many uses that our suspect list is as big as it was before."

"I've heard of guys who even hunt deer with 12-gauges. They use solid slugs instead of buckshot," Lane said.

"Now you're with me, city boy! But you'd only use a shotgun with slugs for deer in real brushy areas, where you'd only typically get an open shot at fifty yards or less. It's not the most accurate."

"Again," Michele interrupted. "Why didn't the killer leave the gun behind? That's been his M.O."

"M.O.? Does anyone say that anymore?" Cole asked.

"Yeah," Ty deadpanned. "Mostly in law enforcement, which seems to be outside your area of expertise at the moment."

Cole was working on a smart-ass comeback when Michele cleared her throat loudly over the phone. "Last chance; why not leave the shotgun behind?"

They were all quiet, searching for answers when Cole finally said, "Why not?"

"Why not?" Ty asked.

Cole was smiling now as he neared Janesville and raced onto the I-90 ramp leading north toward Madison. "Why not indeed."

Michele noticed that Cole's voice came alive, got larger, when he became excited. She liked it, she realized.

"The thing is," Cole continued, "if the shooter keeps one of the 30/30s and we find it in his house, car, whatever, down the road, then ballistics will match the rifle to the bullets found at a murder scene. That ties the murderer to a killing. He takes a bigger risk keeping the rifles versus dropping them at the scene.

"But ballistics can't tie buckshot to a specific shotgun. The shell casings maybe, but I bet our guy was clever enough to pick those up before leaving the scene. So if we catch up to him later today and he's got the shotgun, it ties him to nothing. He's no more a suspect than any of the other tens of thousand 12-gauge owners out there. Anything else going on?"

"You should know that things are heating up at the clinic where Smith was killed," Li said. "The three older ladies we saw on that television report are long gone, probably playing Canasta at a senior living center. And the students are gone, too...one would hope back to the classroom, but more likely to the campus taverns. They've been replaced on both sides by seasoned, hard-core activists. Some look to be professional, read that paid, protesters. This is now seen as ground zero for the reproductive rights battle. NARAL, the National Association for the Repeal of Abortion Laws, has brought in a rental physician to keep the clinic open until they can find a permanent replacement for Dr. Smith. The far fringe of the pro-life movement is looking at the drop in abortion providers and people seeking care at the clinics and they're emboldened. Even with a visible police presence at the clinic, everyone watching expects things to boil over and lead to violence. And that same scene is being played out at many of the abortion clinics still open across the country."

They were digesting that when Michele said nervously, "His message is here."

Chapter Sixty-Six

Michele read the killer's email out loud, her voice quavering.

"I apologize if I scared you when I approached you outside your condo. I didn't mean to; I just need you to understand. I'm not sure how much time I have left to do God's work. Not much, I imagine. I'm not the enemy, but I'm being hunted like one. And when our law enforcement agencies work together to take someone down, they're pretty good at it. Your friend is one of the best. If he wasn't on this case, I might have more time to remove more evil from the world, to protect more infants from slaughter. But eventually, they will catch up to me regardless. My best hope is that after I fall, others will pick up the cross that I now bear. I've read your stories about abortion shops across the country shutting down out of fear. It has given me strength to know I've made some difference. But if others don't hear and heed the call that I have, then it will only be temporary, a blip of sanity in an otherwise insane world. You have not printed my emails, but I assume they will eventually be printed...either in your newspaper or in your memoir. Either way I am confident they will be widely circulated around the world in other publications, news and social media. In the end, you will help me more than you can ever know, and more than you have wanted. For that, I thank you."

Nobody said anything for what felt like an eternity. The only sound was the ambient noise of the Charger eating up the miles.

Li broke the silence with a weak, "Sounds like you've got an admirer, Cole."

Michele was struggling with the killer's notion that her reporting was contributing to more deaths and potentially a near-complete loss of access to reproductive health care for women. Panic and guilt clouded out other thoughts.

Cole tried to clear his own mind. Jeffers was the FBI's face and voice on this case, but the killer wasn't referring to him when he mentioned the reporter's "friend." Li picked up on that, too. The killer's reference to Cole indicated he somehow had inside information on the case. That supported Cole's earlier contention that the killer was potentially in law enforcement himself.

Cole veered off onto Highway 18 as he neared Madison. The beltline skirted around the capital, leaving him two hours of driving at posted speeds to get to Prairie du Chien. He would beat that, but the last sixty miles from Dodgeville on was all two-lane. Cole was passing a village of ice fishing shanties on Lake Waubesa when Lane yelled, "We got the location of where the email came from! It was sent from a burner phone somewhere between Verona and Mt. Horeb, just west of Madison."

"Jesus, he's running home to Prairie du Chien for sure. He knows we're on to him," Cole said, weaving around cars. "He can't be more than an hour ahead of me. " Cole realized there was no way he would get to Prairie before the killer, especially given the long stretch of two-lane ahead of them. "I've got a call to make," he said, clicking off.

Chapter Sixty-Seven

"Sheriff Vang."

"Fwam, it's Cole. I'm headed your way."

"Cool. We have the church diagram pretty much filled in." He hesitated then before adding, "I penciled in me, Mary, and the kids. We came in ten minutes early and all the pews were already taken. We stood up in the back of church. So, I was standing the whole time. I know how that must look..."

"It looks like you were in Mass that Sunday along with a lot of other people. I know you, Fwam, and I don't see you as a suspect. Plus, I think the killer misled us with the boots he wore for the Martin murder."

"What do you mean?"

Cole filled Fwam in on his theory that the killer took out the liners of the winter boots he wore in an effort to mislead. He thought the killer might be five-six to five-eight or so and in the neighborhood of one hundred and fifty pounds. "Sorry, buddy, but you aren't that tall or that svelte."

"Hell, it was damn cold the night Martin was shot. You'd have to be a tough son of a bitch to sit there with nothing between your feet and the frost but a little rubber and a thin pair of socks. You could get frostbite and maybe lose a couple toes."

"I've been thinking about that. I'm convinced the killer is in law enforcement. We got another email from him that reinforces that. I also believe the killer was in St. Gabriel's for that Christmas sermon. And now I'm convinced the guy is five foot seven and one fifty give or take. Remind you of anyone?"

Fwam blurted, “Randall Hubbard. My deputy.”

“It fits. When he picked us up at the airport, he had on big orthopedic shoes and kind of shuffled. He had either just shined the hell out of those shoes or they were brand new. Has he always worn big, cushiony shoes like that?”

“Come to think of it, no. I mean, I don’t go around looking at people’s shoes all the time, but I’d notice that. Plus, there’s never been anything wrong with the way Deputy Hubbard walks. If he’s shuffling now, it means something’s afoot.”

“Pun intended?”

“What?”

“Never mind.”

“Damn. I hope you’re wrong about this,” Fwam said. “Hubbard’s not the most social guy, but he’s smart, tough, and loyal. He’s had my back in more than a few bad situations over the years and he was always rock solid. No weak knees with Randall when the shit hit the fan.”

“Which means he’s got all the makings of our killer. The guy who took down Drs. Smith, Martin, and Sadana was smart and wicked tough. Loyal? That’s probably a good description, too. He’s loyal to his cause and to the God he believes called him to this work. But we have to stop him .”

“Yeah. You know, you said a minute ago you think the killer is in law enforcement and that’s got me thinking. Specifically, I’m thinking about the deer blood. You wouldn’t have to kill a deer with a bow or rifle to get your hands on deer blood if you’re in law enforcement around here. There are twenty thousand car, deer collisions in the state every year. This past year we had one hundred here in Crawford County alone. My guys get called out to the scene typically. The driver who hits the deer can legally claim it these days, but they rarely do. So a lot of time it’s officers like Randall or me who end up gutting the deer and either keeping it or giving it to our local food pantry. If he wanted to save deer blood over the past month he would’ve had opportunity.” He sighed. “What do you need me to do?”

“I’m going to be there in less than an hour and a half,” Cole said. “Check your payroll and see if the deputy was off on the days of the three murders.

Then bring Chief Mara and the State Troopers up to date. In an hour, quietly pull together eight or so of the best officers you have combined. Wait for me at the courthouse. I think Hubbard is still on the road, thirty minutes or so outside of Prairie. Don't call him. If he comes into the courthouse then see if you can take him into custody without anyone getting hurt. But I don't see him making it easy for us."

Chapter Sixty-Eight

Cole averaged over one hundred miles per hour on the four-lane from Madison to Dodgeville, where he roared past the huge buildings of retailing giant Lands' End. He would have pushed the pace more, but in spots, the wind blew snow onto the road and it got dicey on corners. Orange plastic, hip-high webbed snow fencing strung along vast open stretches of farm fields helped, but enough grains of snow were blasted onto the road by the wind to make it lethal if he wasn't careful.

Cole liked a wide range of music, but only occasionally listened to classical. Occasions like this. Something about this case made him pop in a CD he'd made of his favorite classical songs, and Aaron Copland's *Fanfare for the Common Man* came on. The song was five minutes long, but the entire CD was close to an hour. He planned to be in Prairie du Chien before the final notes played.

As he drove he thought about how the toughest cases he'd ever worked resembled the parts and rhythm of a symphony. This case had started with an allegro or brisk pace, then dropped to an adagio or slower pace. The minuet, the old courtly dance movement followed, back and forth. He felt the case now building to a crescendo and, hopefully, its finale. The base drums pounded and the trumpets sounded as he barreled through Montfort, population seven hundred. Twenty large white wind turbines, each towering two hundred feet tall, waved him on with their gigantic arms. They looked like they'd been planted in the middle of long harvested cornfields, the straw-colored stalks chopped to a foot high pushing out from the snow. His ringtone sounded and he glanced at the phone. "Collin

Jeffers," it read. He kept driving.

He dropped down to under thirty before reaching Fennimore, when he came up fast behind a black buggy pulled by a sturdy black mare. Water from melting snow was spun into the air by its large spoked wheels. A big orange yield triangle hung on the back of the Amish rig. Pachelbel's *Canon in D Major* tried to soothe Cole's nerves without success. Any other time he would have basked in the grace of the music combined with the snow-covered fields and the stark beauty of the black buggy against that backdrop of white. Instead, he punched the gas when he saw an opportunity and roared around the buggy and quickly through the town. Jeffers called again, and then again. He left voicemails both times. Cole drove.

He knew there would be consequences for not answering Jeffers's calls. Olson made it clear from the start that Jeffers was in charge of the investigation. He owed him a report. He wondered if ignoring Jeffers was worth losing a job he mostly loved. When his ringtone went off again, he picked up. "I'm sorry," he forced himself to say. "I must have somehow put my phone on vibrate."

"What? It's me, Lane. I've got that intel you asked me for on the Centralia guy. The guy we originally thought purchased the first murder weapon."

Cole blew out a long breath. "What do you have?"

"He was pulled over by a county sheriff's deputy on the outskirts of Prairie du Chien," Lane said. "The guy said he was speeding and admitted he drank a few beers before he left the fishing derby. He told me he thought he was good to drive but was nervous anyhow when he saw the lights come on behind him. He's had two other speeding tickets in the past twelve months and was surprised when the deputy let him off with a verbal warning."

"Did he get the deputy's name?"

"No," Lane said. "But he gave me a description. He said the deputy was a bit on the short side and skinny."

"Thanks, Lane. That helps complete the picture. Do me a favor and call up the Boscobel Supermax. Ask them if a Deputy Hubbard from Crawford County either brought them a prisoner or picked one up since Christmas."

"Okay. Hey!" he said, with growing excitement. "You think the deputy pulled over our Centralia guy and made a copy of his license. And the same deputy was in Boscobel and picked up those cigarette butts. You think this Deputy Hubbard is our killer!" Lane said.

It wasn't a question, but Cole answered, "I do," before thanking Lane and disconnecting the line.

Strauss's *Blue Danube* waltzed Cole past Mount Hope, its two hundred residents, and the town's iconic top-heavy water tower. Five minutes later, he dropped down Patch Grove hill. The spring movement of Vivaldi's *Four Seasons* carried him through the long, winding valley and over the two bridges that crossed the chasm carved by the Wisconsin River. Bach's haunting *"Air on the G string"* filled the Charger as he drove into Prairie du Chien and made his way to the courthouse. The rise and fall of violins magnified his emotions; he felt their bow strings drawing back and forth against his nerves. A text message from Jeffers lit up his screen.

Don't fucking confront the suspect until I get there!

Apparently, his team was filling Jeffers in as he'd directed.

Another text appeared, this one from Lane.

Deputy Hubbard dropped a prisoner off at the Supermax on December 28th.

Chapter Sixty-Nine

John Lawler came out of the unisex hallway bathroom, his wife, Kathy, clutching an elbow to keep him upright. The people who had come to support the cause or the man pushed themselves against the narrow hallway to allow passage. John and Kathy shuffled to the end of the hall, John's head bowed, and they made their way to the chair Matt had dragged out of an office for him to use. John reached out and grabbed an armrest, steadying himself as best he could, and with great effort and gentle assistance from his son and wife, settled into the chair.

Lawler didn't know the date or the time. He didn't know either that at that very moment tens of thousands were gathering eight hundred miles away in Washington DC, readying to march in a show of support for life and rallying to end abortion. He was unaware, too, that thousands of others were gathering in the same nation's capital, demanding that women's reproductive rights be protected. Both rallies and marches were expected to draw larger crowds than the annual marches held less than two weeks earlier to mark the anniversary of Roe v. Wade. The spate of abortion violence had increased tensions on both sides of the issue in every part of the country.

Lawler also no longer noticed the dozens of colorful flowers in vases crammed around his chair or the way the walls of the drab, sterile corridor were papered with cards and letters from well-wishers and supporters. When they first trickled in, the staff shared them with Lawler and the family. But now they were flooding in at an overwhelming rate and piling up in a storeroom unopened.

The bottoms of Lawler's pajamas had ridden up to his emaciated calves, and Kathy bent and pulled them down to his ankles. She covered him with two heavy blankets. The longer he went without food, the more the cold affected him. She stood looking at him, her clear hazel eyes catching and holding his, and she took both his hands in hers and held them. "You know you can stop this if you want to." Her eyes were watery but still smiling. "I know how stubborn you can be. But nobody will think less of you if you want to go home with a pretty girl like me. Maybe we could stop at Culver's and grab a butter burger and some cheese curds on the way. How does a turtle sundae sound?" There was more twinkle than moisture in her eyes as she said this.

"Your parents should have named you Eve instead of Kathy, the way you're trying to tempt me. It wouldn't be hard to turn my back on an apple, but a Culver's butter burger and cheese curds? A turtle sundae?" He bowed his head further and kissed her hands. It was hard for him to talk for long, but he whispered, "I can resist any food, but I never could resist the cute girl who's standing in front of me."

Kathy turned away so her husband wouldn't see the tears rolling down her cheeks. She nodded at the followers and the cards. "Looks like you've got a lot of admirers. Maybe I should be jealous."

He chuckled and rasped, "Ha. I don't think you need to worry about that." He grew serious again and squeezed her hands feebly. "I do think what I'm doing here has struck a chord with some people; made them stop and consider things." He looked down and was quiet, then struggled to lift his head and catch her eyes again. He was trembling. "Do *you* think I've made a difference?"

She bent over and put her arms around him, pulling his frail body tight to her own. He was sobbing softly, with little moisture or energy left to expend. Her embrace shielded him from the onlookers as she kissed the top of his head and said, "You've made all the difference to me."

Chapter Seventy

The deputy sat at the picnic table in his backyard. He'd brushed the snow off the top and benches and placed two bags of Kingsford Charcoal on the top as a rifle rest. As Cole parked his car in the alley behind the deputy's house, he watched Hubbard calmly sip coffee from a steel mug and caress the rifle that lay across his lap.

Four squads pulled up behind Cole's Charger and as the men and lone woman got out, he reminded them to be careful. "We think he's working alone, but don't assume that. I want two of you to go through the front door and work your way to the back. Clear each room before you settle at the back door and focus on the deputy. Watch for tripwires or other booby traps. I don't expect them, since he sees you all as good guys. But we need to do this right so we all walk out of here in one piece when it's over."

Cole wiped his forehead, the sheen of sweat contrasted with the firm, steady tone of his voice. "I'm hoping we don't fire a shot. Deputy Hubbard hasn't killed anyone he didn't perceive as a murderer, a serial killer of sorts. I don't believe he wants to kill a cop, even a Fed like me." He eyed the deputy, "He's holding a high-powered rifle though, so there is that.

"He could be a suicide by cop candidate, and might like to make himself a martyr for the cause. If that's the case, he'll threaten me and may even shoot wide of me. Hold fire unless you see me go down." He scratched distractedly at the Kevlar vest he had layered over his dress shirt at the courthouse, and looked at the faces around him. He read the nervousness and anxiety written clearly on each. He nodded. "Stay focused and we'll all be okay."

Fwam took one of his men around to the front of the house, while Chief Mara set up the remainder of the team. Cole gave Fwam enough time to get inside and make sure the deputy was alone. Then he slowly started walking toward Hubbard, the twenty-five yards he had to cover looking more like the length of three football fields. The deputy set his coffee down and brought the rifle up, resting the forestock and barrel on the charcoal bags.

Cole moved carefully. The shooter had made shots a lot more difficult than this. At this range, he could hit a quarter, or take out Cole's eye. He pushed that thought away, and each baby step he took carried him a foot closer to the deputy.

The sky was bright and cloudless and Cole approached the shooter with the sun at his back. This was standard operating procedure when confronting an armed suspect, but Cole second-guessed himself as he shuffled forward. The shooter would be squinting. He would be uncomfortable and fighting to keep the glare from obscuring his sight in the scope. He was more than an adequate marksman, but under these conditions, his aim could be compromised.

"We aren't going to hurt you," Cole called to Hubbard in a loud, clear voice. He wanted to sound commanding and authoritative. "We're going to take you in and talk about what you're involved in and what you believe."

The deputy had the rifle aimed at Cole's head and Cole was mulling the position of the sun and his next words when the deputy fired. He felt like he'd been tapped high on his forehead as the report of the 30/30 shocked his ears. He staggered to a stop, wondering if he'd been hit. He shook off the thought and shouted, "Don't shoot! Do not return fire!"

He fought a quiver in his lips and added even louder, "Deputy Hubbard will not shoot me! He's a good man who doesn't want to go down in history as a cop killer!" He moved forward again. Slower. Ten yards from the deputy he noticed how soft the ground was. The sun was melting the snow and the ground was spongy with moisture.

When Cole was no more than four yards from the shooter he tried to concentrate, but he wondered now if he really understood Hubbard. What if he misjudged him? Would he kill him in cold blood? In the span of one small, slow stride, images of a coming spring, death, resurrection, and blooms crowded his thoughts, competing for space in his brain with images of Michele. If he died now there was so much about her he would never learn, so much he wanted to tell her and maybe give her that he never could.

"Stop right there or I *will* put a bullet in you," Hubbard said, not much above a whisper. The law enforcement personnel whose guns were all trained on the deputy from behind the relative safety of their vehicles and the back door couldn't hear and likely didn't notice the slight movement of the deputy's lips.

The words were clear enough to Cole. He held up and tried to focus on breathing slower and deeper.

"I was making a difference," the deputy said, keeping his eyes tight to his scope and his rifle trained on Cole. "The number of abortion doctors going to work has gone down the past few weeks, and not just in Wisconsin and Illinois, but across the country. No surprise, right? You'd figure a bunch of baby killers for cowards. They can't spend all that money if they're not breathing."

Cole stood on the soggy lawn, bathed in the harsh sunlight reflecting off the melting snow. He could tell the deputy had more to say, so he stayed quiet, taking another deep breath and swallowing hard.

"I knew you'd catch on to me sooner or later, but I was hoping for later. Shooting defenseless murderers isn't fun, but trying to protect the innocent, the unborn, those who can't fend for themselves, well, that's been a noble calling. I've never felt like I made much of a difference before, but lately, I have been. It was never about me. It's been about the children. It was always about the children."

Cole felt his head get warm, but not from the sun. His brain was warming up from the inside, not the outside, with a familiar gentle pulsing. He tensed, wanting nothing more than to leap out of the way and maybe keep running until he got back to Milwaukee. Instead, he held his ground and started to tell the deputy he understood when the 30/30 fired a second time. This round, from close range, slammed into the meat of Cole's left shoulder and spun him around. He cried out as he tumbled to the slush. He thought to yell not to shoot, but the sound of eight guns barking deafeningly from the vehicles and back door drowned out the notion.

Cole rolled painfully to his side and looked toward the picnic table. The deputy had been hit, dropped his rifle, and was sliding under the table.

"Stop!" Cole croaked. *"Stop firing!"* His voice cranked up.

It was quiet as Cole scrabbled on his three good limbs to Hubbard, who lay awkwardly on his back, his legs pinned under him. The deputy had multiple chest wounds and his life poured crimson from his body. He gasped, "Forgive me," and stopped breathing.

It dawned on Cole that maybe it wasn't him the shooter wanted forgiveness from. It was *Him*.

He rolled onto his own back in the wet snow and shut his eyes to the sunlight, feeling more than hearing the cops and EMTs rush over.

Chapter Seventy-One

A desk lamp was the lone light on in the *Courier* offices this night. The dim bulb cast strange shadows on the walls of its editor's office. The paper's few employees had left earlier, leaving the building empty except for Grant Grae. He and his staff published twice a week, on Tuesday and Thursdays, and the crew left early on Fridays.

Grae leaned back in his desk chair, his hands locked behind his head. His feet were stretched out and crossed at the ankles, heels resting on the edge of the roll-top desk. He groaned and sat up straight, dropping his head a bit to squint at today's *Courier Press* front page. Deputy Hubbard's death ran above the fold under the paper's masthead and a huge banner headline screamed *Local deputy dies in shootout*. A sidebar story also ran above the fold, and the related story's background was shaded to set it apart from the main story. It ran under the headline, *Deputy is Alleged Abortionist Killer*. Below the fold ran yet another banner headline that read, *Former Mayor's Fast Ends in Death*. The subhead in smaller type read, *City Mourns His Passing*. At the same time Deputy Hubbard took eight rounds to his upper body, John Lawler drew his last breath. The reporter noted that the time of death recorded on the death certificates of both men read exactly fifteen hundred, or three p.m. Central Standard Time. It didn't take a religious zealot to know that Christ was supposed to have died on the cross at three p.m. If this didn't sound like a *Ripley's Believe It Or Not* story, then Grae didn't know what did.

Lawler's son, Matthew, was quoted in the story saying that his father "Died for our sins."

Grae looked up from the paper. Michael stared down at the editor from above, his thirty-six points and beams casting bizarre, ghoulish shadows on the wall. Grae never told the FBI Agent or the reporter that he'd named Michael after the archangel. It never came up. He leaned forward and reached into the upper left-hand drawer of his desk. He pulled out an old paperback Bible and turned to the Book of Daniel, verse 12…the end times…

And at that time shall Michael stand up, the great prince which standeth for the children of thy people: and there shall be a time of trouble, such as never was since there was a nation even to that same time: and at that time thy people shall be delivered.

Grae looked up at Gabriel, the deer he'd named after another archangel, and which shared its name with the Catholic Church a few blocks north. In the New Testament, Gabriel is referred to as "the angel of the Power of God," and the words most used to describe him are "great, might, power, and strength." In Christian teaching, Michael is the angel of judgment while Gabriel is the angel of mercy.

The gun cabinet behind Grae was open, and he reached in and pulled out his Marlin 30-30. He rested the butt on his right thigh, the barrel pointing up at an angle toward the ceiling. He fingered the hickory stock. It seemed like he was being drawn through a thick, heavy fog, called to pick up the cross from the fallen deputy and to continue his work.

He felt the same pull earlier, but instead, he picked up his pen, which he wielded with even more power and precision than his rifle. The result was the editorial that lay within today's paper. It told the tale of two men who heard a call and who had the courage to answer. A tale of one who wrongly fought murder with murder, and another who humbly and quietly sacrificed his own life in an attempt to save others. With the editor's help, the second man's ultimate sacrifice would draw the attention of his community, and maybe even the world, to reexamine one of mankind's most divisive issues… even if only for a moment.

The editor got up stiffly and put the rifle back in the metal cabinet. He locked it and then switched off the desk lamp before walking out of his office and into the night.

Chapter Seventy-Two

Cole's eyes fluttered open and he tried to figure out where he was. Light streamed through a window and from the corner of his eye he made out the IV in his wrist and the tubing that snaked up to a pole holding a bag of some concoction that dripped into his system.

He was in a hospital room. Even groggy he figured that out. He felt a dull ache in his left shoulder and realized he'd had surgery to patch him up after Hubbard's bullet put him down. A painkiller messed with his system, but he tried to focus his thoughts and piece things together. He remembered being shot and pulling himself over to Hubbard's fallen body, his clothes sopping up the killer's blood as he heard his final words. Not long after the paramedics determined there was nothing they could do for Hubbard, they looked after Cole. He lay on the ground while they stopped his bleeding and immobilized his arm. They wanted to move him onto a stretcher, but he waved them off. Fwam helped him to his feet, and when he stopped wobbling, the two joined Chief Mara in making sure the scene was secure and everyone else was okay. He asked to be taken to the airport so that he could get back to Milwaukee and they shot him up with a sedative for the trip. And now here he was. He was almost certain he was at St. Joseph Hospital on Milwaukee's north side.

He thought about getting up from his hospital bed, but a hand on his good shoulder caught him.

"You doing okay, bud?" Sheriff Vang asked. "Your surgeon told me a 170-grain bullet tore a nice chunk of muscle out of your shoulder. He said it blew away part of your deltoid, but didn't hit anything too vital. Said you had plenty of deltoid muscle to spare. You won't win any lift, clean, and jerk competitions in the near future, but that's more my area of expertise anyway." He smiled at his old friend.

"You're a good man," Cole said, returning a crooked smile. "Nice of you to sit here with me. I'd hoped for a beautiful woman, but beggars can't be choosers." He licked his lips; his tongue and throat felt dry and raw.

Fwam noticed and handed him a tall Styrofoam cup filled with ice water and a straw. "Try this. I'd give you a cold beer if I had one."

Cole scooted into a partial sitting position, grimacing, and slurped from the straw. The ice-cold water felt good going down, but Fwam pulled it away when he was halfway done. "Slow down, big fella. Ease into it. Give your stomach a chance to reset."

Before Cole could ask Fwam when he'd picked up his nursing diploma, Collin Jeffers burst into the room, with two hulking, young agents behind him. He dismissed Fwam with a curt, "Out. Now."

Fwam looked at Cole and then back at Jeffers. He was about to snap at Jeffers when he felt Cole's hand on his forearm. "It's okay. I'll be all right. We can talk about old times later." He gave his friend the best smile he could manage. "Thank you again for being here."

The two agents left the room with Fwam and closed it most of the way shut behind them. Jeffers looked at the door and then back at Cole. "What the fuck part of 'Don't confront the suspect until I get there' did you not understand?" he screamed.

"You're a Goddamn cowboy. Walking up to a killer who's holding a rifle on you might seem brave, but it was actually stupid. Fucking stupid!" he shouted. "This is the kind of fuckup that will keep you in a shithole like Milwaukee for the rest of your career. And that's only if I can't personally get you kicked out of the Bureau this afternoon." He sneered, "Trust me, I will hang your ass over this."

Jeffers felt emboldened seeing Cole in a hospital bed. He was slow to notice the color flushing into Cole's cheeks and extremities. He continued his tirade. "And your unprofessionalism with that cunt reporter? I'll submarine that bitch's career, too!" Jeffers' voice bounced around the room and carried into the hall.

By now Cole was crimson and struggling to a full sitting position so he could launch himself at Jeffers. It was one thing to attack him, but he wouldn't listen to Jeffers' vulgar attack on Michele. Just as he was about to grab Jeffers by the throat, another loud voice barked out.

"Cole! Cole! Relax." Gene Olson had entered the room and he looked directly at Cole. "I've got this." He turned to face Jeffers, his eyes hardening along with the tenor of his voice. "You don't know how lucky you are, Jeffers. I just saved you from getting your ass kicked by a little person, and now I'm saving you from getting your ass handed to you by a drug-addled agent with one good arm. I've heard everything you said in here and I'm giving you two options. Either put in for a demotion and transfer to the FBI field office in Anchorage, or resign on the spot here and now. I'm giving you a chance to gain a little perspective. Stop looking in the mirror all the time, worrying about how you look and how to advance your career. Spend more time thinking about what you can do to help others. Try to help the Inuit or Eskimos for a while and see if that changes your mindset.

He looked at Cole . "What's the proper term? Eskimo? Inuit? "

Cole shrugged his good shoulder. "No clue."

Olson looked back at Jeffers, stepping into his space. "It doesn't matter. You either go to Alaska and get your act together or resign. If you don't take one of those options then I'll fire *you* before the day is out. You couldn't have mucked up this investigation more than you did. Then you come to this hospital room and threaten the two people who did the most to break this case? It shows me that we messed up with you. Right now, you're an imbecile and unfit for service in the Bureau. Alaska, quit, or fired. Got that?"

Jeffers was shaking. He nodded.

"Then get the hell out of here and close the door behind you." Olson dismissed Jeffers and turned back to Cole. Jeffers retreated and the door shushed shut.

"He's not a little person..." Cole said, his throat dry and constricted again.

Olson cocked his head. "What?"

"Sheriff Vang. He's not a little person," Cole repeated. He grimaced again, reaching for his ice water. Olson handed it to him.

"I know," Olson chuckled. "I thought telling Jeffers he almost got taken apart by a little person might sting more. Damn, it felt good to call him on the carpet. He's had it coming for a long time. I hope he takes this opportunity to turn himself around. He does have some talent."

"I never noticed," Cole said, smiling back at Olson, not sure if the smile was due to the painkillers that coursed through his system or because of the scene that had played out in his room.

Olson took the seat next to Cole's bed that Fwam had vacated. "You and the reporter did great work," he said. "You're a hero for walking into a hail of bullets in an effort to apprehend the subject without taking his life. The official story is that he shot at you, trying to kill you at close range. Other law enforcement officers who were on hand for the arrest returned fire. The killer died at the scene."

"Not exactly how it went down. He *meant* to wing me. It was textbook suicide by cop. He shot twice. Not what you'd call a 'hail of bullets.' The first time he missed on purpose; hoping everyone would open up on him. But our guys held tight. When he hit me with the second bullet, they had to return fire. That's what happened."

"Not according to all the official reports that have already been written and accepted," Olson said. "See, if it looks at all like he was gunned down by an army of law enforcement officials, it could be viewed that he went out in a blaze of glory. Maybe others around the country see him as a martyr and take up his crusade. Frankly, we can't chance that. He tried to kill you and that makes him a cop killer, or at least a wannabe cop killer. That's the official story. Not much sympathy for cop killers out there, even amongst his ilk. We're hoping it discourages others who might otherwise try to follow in his footsteps.

"The director himself is outside your room, waiting to come in and congratulate you. Then, after you get cleaned up a bit, we'll wheel you down to the lobby and he's going to pin a couple of medals on your chest."

"Medals? For getting myself shot?"

"Ah, well, yes, partly for getting yourself shot. But mostly for stopping the killer," Olson said. "You're getting the FBI Star for sustaining a serious injury in the direct line of duty. And you're also getting the FBI Medal of Valor for exceptional heroism in the direct line of duty. In your FBI career, you've already received the Bureau's Medal for Meritorious Achievement and the Shield of Bravery. That's about all we've got to give, son."

Cole slumped lower into the bed and turned away from Olson. "Why don't I feel like a hotshot hero then?"

Olson put his hand on Cole's undamaged shoulder. "I don't know. But I read the director's speech on the plane on the way here. I think he's got it about right. There's a part where he says, 'But for the grace of God and Special Agent Huebsch's superior reflexes, the name Cole Huebsch would be etched onto the FBI Wall of Honor, the 37th service martyr in the Bureau's history.' To be honest, I don't think he's overstating things."

"I feel like a fraud."

"Bullshit," Olson said, taking on a sterner tone. "I was being soft on you because you're in a hospital bed. But don't lie there and tell me you didn't know walking up to that deputy that he was going to shoot you. It's Geno you're talking to. Don't forget that. I know about your ability to see a guy's move before it happens. That little warm glow you get in your head or whatever. Before that second shot was fired you could have stepped left, then reached in and grabbed the rifle away. The deputy had a lever action for Christ's sake! No way he gets another shot off. But you took one for the team because you knew if you didn't, he might be seen as a cult hero and others might follow him. So, yeah, you're a bona fide hero. Almost two billion people were involved in World War II on one side or the other. I'll bet during the whole war someone took a bullet meant for someone else or jumped on a grenade to save his buddies less than ten times. That stuff mostly happens in movies. You took a bullet to save lives of physicians you not only don't know, but who you think don't represent the best mankind has to offer. So, doing the math, ten in two billion is, what, one in two hundred million? You're not a one in a million hero, you're one in two hundred million. Heroic shit indeed!"

Cole turned and smiled again. "Did you rehearse that speech?"

"Maybe a little," Olson admitted. He got up. "We aren't doing an autopsy. And no ballistics checks. I figured a number of the team you lined up to help bring in Hubbard knew him personally. They don't need to know who hit the mark and who didn't. They'd feel crappy either way."

"Thanks for that."

"Now, I'm going to get a nurse and tell her to come in here and get you cleaned up…but not too pretty," Olson said. "It's going to help the optics if you keep that pasty complexion for now and the mussed hair. And that bloody gauze on your shoulder is the convincer. A little theatrics maybe, but we need to sell this a bit to keep more murders like these from happening again any time soon."

Before he got to the door he turned around and appraised Cole again. His eyes were watery. "We could've lost you, Cole. It was probably closer than you realize. I hope you know how much I think of you. From now on you can continue to work in Milwaukee and I won't try to transfer you to DC. But from time to time, I'm going to reach out to you to ask that you assist in special assignments. It won't be because you owe me. It will be because I need you."

He rubbed his eyes and then brightened a bit. "Think of me as Commissioner Gordon and you're Batman. Instead of shining a spotlight with a bat decal, I'll shine a big 'M' for Marquette or Milwaukee. That's when you come get my ass out of the sling. Deal?"

"Deal," Cole said, smiling.

Olson was at the door when he turned around. "There's one other small thing I forgot to mention. You're going to the White House next week. The President of the United States himself is going to pin the Medal of Freedom on your chest. That's our nation's highest honor. The icing on the cake is that he's sending Air Force One here to pick you up. Imagine that…"

Olson turned to open the door when Cole stopped him. "Wait," he said. "Gene, wait."

Olson looked back.

"This is really happening? The medals now? The White House next week?

And Air Force One picking me up?"

He was grinning. "Yes. It's really happening."

"And there's nothing I can say to you, the Director, or the President to stop it?"

"Not that I see. No."

"Then can I ask a favor?"

"Go for it."

"Give Grant Grae White House press credentials for the DC ceremony so he can cover the event. And let him hitch a ride on Air Force One with me."

"That seems easy enough to arrange," Olson agreed.

"Great. How many people fit on Air Force One, anyway?" Cole asked.

"I've only flown on it a few times myself, but I'm pretty sure it holds seventy people, give or take, besides the crew."

"Any way I can have Fwam and Chief Mara come along, too? Maybe the state troopers?" he asked. "Hell, it might be better to bring everyone in Prairie du Chien who was part of bringing down Hubbard to DC, along with Li, Lane, and Ty from my end. Michele, too. That way the President can tout the way city, county, state, and federal law enforcement all worked together to end the murders. That should look good for both him and the Bureau."

"You proud of yourself? You thinking of being a politician now?" Olson asked.

"No. But why waste space and fuel for a trip like that if you aren't going to make the most of it. Besides, I'm pretty sure my hometown could use a shot in the arm after this. Pun intended."

Chapter Seventy-Three

A week later Cole and Michele met for breakfast at Blue's Egg cafe. The popular diner in the 'Tosa suburb that picked up west where Milwaukee left off was packed as usual. He was seated when she walked in the door and stood as she approached his table. He longed to pull her to him, but tentatively reached out his hand instead. She hesitated before shaking it and sat down.

He sat down, too. "A handshake seems kind of lame after everything we've been through together." He tried to smile it off, but felt nervous and unsure. They hadn't spoken since before he'd been shot, and he wondered if this breakfast would determine if they might have a future together.

She nodded to his left arm, which was in a sling. "I'm sorry you got shot. I can't imagine that. I tried to see you at the hospital, but you were tied up with the director and others. By the time they said I could see you, my editors had sent me back to New York."

"I heard," he smiled. "The big time. CNN. NBC. CBS. ABC. And *The View*. You've been busy."

She smiled back at him and he melted. "But I didn't have the president fly me to the White House to tell the world I'm the biggest hero in the history of mankind. That was you."

"You can't say you weren't invited."

"I know. Thank you for that. My editors didn't think the optics would be good."

"That whole thing was a little over the top and put me in an awkward spot. I pushed back at first. But I gotta admit it was pretty cool to hang with the president for a while. I'm sure it'll all blow over in a couple days."

"I wouldn't be so sure."

"How about you?" he said. "I saw a report that said you're writing a book and signed with a top literary agency. That was fast."

Michele looked directly at Cole. "Was it your wife's report you saw?"

He reddened. "That would be my *ex*-wife and I don't remember."

A minute went by and neither spoke. It seemed longer. Snippets of conversations carried to them from nearby tables, mixed with bursts of laughter and the clink of porcelain cups meeting saucers. Cole sipped from his water glass. "I heard you won't be running the killer's last email."

"Gene Olson asked me not to. He's giving me access to other information that will be exclusive to me or that he'll hold for twelve months. That seems like a reasonable trade. But to be honest, I wouldn't have run it in the paper or used it in the book. I don't want to help recruit the man or men who might pick up this guy's torch now that you knocked it from him."

"*We* knocked it from him," Cole corrected. "Your book have a name yet?"

"The working title is *The Killer Sermon*, but it could change. I'm not married to it."

Cole considered before nodding. "I like it. It has a nice ring."

A waitress came to take their order. Michele asked for French toast with a side of fresh fruit, while Cole chose eggs over easy, sourdough toast, hash browns, and bacon. They both ordered coffee. Before the waitress could turn to leave Michele said, "We'll take an order of Monkey Bread, too."

"A woman after my own heart," Cole said, his smile coming naturally. "I had you pegged for the house special granola."

Michele was distracted and didn't respond. Cole could tell she had something important to say and he wasn't sure he wanted to hear it. If a rejection was on his way, he'd rather divert it with a lame attempt at humor. But he waited for her to say what was on her mind.

"This is a big story," she started. "One of the biggest that will ever be written in Milwaukee or Wisconsin. Did you ever wonder how I got to be the one to cover it?" Her eyes challenged him.

"I figured it was because you're a tenacious and talented writer," he said with an uneasy grin.

Her return expression was more of a grimace; he saw nervousness beneath it that he'd never seen on her before.

"Is everything all right? Usually my charm is the best weapon in my arsenal. It disarms people. Well, it doesn't literally disarm them, of course. Anyway, I seem to have put you on edge with it. I'm sorry if I said something inappropriate."

"I love the flattery, actually," she said, reaching across the table to take his hand. She was warmer and more genuine now, but still couldn't mask her fear or hesitancy. A deep sadness pooled in her eyes as well.

"I am talented, and tenacious with a capital T. But that's not why I got this story. I got the story because I was the first reporter on the scene." She looked down. "I was the first reporter on the scene," she repeated, hesitating, "because I was at the clinic when the killing occurred."

"Were you there covering a different story?" he asked, leaning forward.

She seemed to decide something then. She bit down on her lower lip and shook her head side to side. "No," she said firmly and clearly. "I was there because I had a follow-up appointment with Dr. Smith. He was going to examine me to make sure I was completely recovered…from the abortion I'd had the week before."

He'd been leaning across the table, listening intently. Now he looked at her, comprehension flushing through his face. He was stunned and involuntarily leaned back a little. She pulled her hands away from him, folding them awkwardly in her lap.

"That makes me a monster to you, doesn't it?" she said flatly. "You think I'm a heartless, selfish bitch who chose herself and her career over the life of her unborn child."

"No," he said, leaning toward her again. "I…I don't really know what to think. Maybe if I'm such a great investigator I would have seen this coming, anticipated it. But you blindsided me."

Her voice quavered in intensity as it rose in volume. "*You* were blindsided? I confess something very private and that's your reaction?

"Blindsided is what happens when you go out after work with a group of co-workers and let your guard down a little. When you have a couple drinks and are flattered that the cute guy from sports flirts with you. When you let him into your apartment thinking you might consent to a goodnight kiss and then he drugs you. He overpowers you. He forces himself on you! Blindsided is when someone causes you a level of pain and humiliation you never dreamed existed, even in your worst nightmares

"Blindsided is when the little strip of paper turns blue and you lose the battle to hold back the tears…when you learn for sure you're carrying a child you know in your heart you're in no position to raise ." She sat up stiffly in her chair, her body trembling.

Cole reached his hands back across the table, but Michele kept hers in her lap, strangling her napkin. "I don't know what to say, what I can say, to make this better," he said. "I can tell you're in a lot of pain and I feel helpless."

She shook her head again. "For you and people like you, abortion is an intellectual argument, another political topic you discuss off to the side at a cookout. For me, and a lot of women like me, it's not intellectual; it's intensely personal." She got up as the waitress was bringing their food, turned around, and left.

Cole's heart ached more than his shoulder as he dug his credit card out and handed it to the dumbfounded waitress. He wondered if he'd ever see Michele again.

Chapter Seventy-Four

A month later, Cole sat in the corner booth at the Sportsmen's Lounge. It was eight p.m. on a Friday and he nursed a mug of Paradocs Red IPA from Raised Grain Brewery. The beer tasted of citrus and caramel. Brewed nearby, it was the intended first course of his meal in liquid form. He licked his upper lip to catch a drop that had collected there and his tongue scraped the bushy mustache he'd glued in place before coming out for the evening. He looked up and caught his reflection in the large mirror that hung on the wall by his booth. A tattered blue and gold Marquette Golden Eagles cap covered the shaggy black and gray hair of his wig. With the mustache and bushy eyebrows, he hoped he could pass for a homeless person.

Cole shook his head and smiled to himself. The lounge didn't typically host guys that looked like him. The bar's website described itself as, "Diverse. Classy. Original." It encouraged its clientele to be stylish. "Don't just dress to impress," the website said, "dress to turn heads. Be classy. And do what feels right." His smile turned into a scowl when he considered the last part. He wished more people concerned themselves with doing what *was* right, instead of what *felt* right." That would make his job a whole lot easier.

A flash of light to his left caught his eye and he turned to catch the highlight on the 96-inch HD screen. It was late in the second half of ESPN's college game of the week and Marquette's men's basketball team was capping off another improbable comeback. Though nearly always undersized, MU's teams fought hard all forty minutes of every game, and often into overtime. Nothing came easy to them, but they got the job done. They often fell behind by double digits, but came back to win more than their share. Everybody underestimated them, typically to their own peril.

Maybe that's why I feel such an affinity to the team, he mused. *That, and the fact you got both your undergrad and master's degrees from MU,* he reminded himself.

"Hey, Old Timer…" The sportswriter, Dan Rippa, interrupted Cole's thoughts, as he leaned over him. "Why don't you belly up to the bar and let us have this booth," he said, gesturing to his two buddies who both had smug grins on their handsome faces.

"What?" Cole asked, looking startled. "You want to sit down? Okay, I don't mind the company."

Rippa looked at his pals and shook his head. All three of them wore dress slacks, nice sweaters, and wool sports coats. Their hair was fashionably long and styled.

"Ah, yeah, about that," he said to Cole with a fake smile, "this is kind of our booth and we have work to do. We're reporters at the *Journal Sentinel* across the street and this is where we hang out. My buddies work in the news/editorial section of the paper, and I'm in sports."

"Well, sit down here, then," Cole said with his equally fake but more convincing smile. He patted the Naugahyde-covered bench he sat on. "I love sports and used to play 'em some when I was younger."

Rippa was losing what little patience he had. He hovered over Cole, crowding him. "Look. I really wasn't asking you to move, I was telling you… although you weren't bright enough to pick up on that. This is my booth and I want you out of it. Now!"

Cole leaned closer to the sportswriter, invading *his* space and making it difficult for his entourage to hear his words. "I can see why you like this booth, what with the big mirror here," he gestured, "and the even bigger TV screen over there," he nodded with his head. "There's plenty of room here. You won't even notice me. I'll watch the rest of the game and SportsCenter, while you stare at yourself in the mirror." He winked at the sportswriter as he finished the last line.

Two minutes later the four of them had left by the bar's rear entrance and were now in the small employee parking lot behind the tavern. Even though it was cold, Cole could smell the sour odors emanating from the dumpster off to his right.

In the bar, Cole picked up on the fact that Rippa was right-handed. As he faced him, he put his own left fist up in front of his chin and his right fist close to his right ear. He looked awkward. The sportswriter broke into a grin as he saw Cole wide open for a hard right hook.

"Fair warnin.' I ain't got no insurance to cover ya," Cole blabbered, looking to confuse his adversary. He wasn't sure why he was adopting a hillbilly persona, but he didn't need to win an Oscar for this acting performance.

Rippa's grin faded and he bit down on his lower lip. Even without feeling the warm glow spreading in his head, Cole would have known he was gathering himself before knocking the old-timer down with one big punch. As Rippa launched his sweeping right hook with a grunt of effort, Cole stepped back. The right fist that would have caved in the left side of his face instead flew by, pulling its owner off-balance, twisting his body so that he was facing almost away from Cole. Big mistake.

Cole stepped behind the sportswriter, bending his knees and locking his arms low around his waist. Then he exploded straight up, lifting the bigger man off the ground. In the same motion, Cole leaned backward and twisted, propelling his opponent hard to the asphalt. As Rippa stretched out his left hand to break his fall, Cole slipped his own grip and caught the sportswriter's wrist and pulled it back into his body. Rippa's face was the first thing to hit the pavement, as Cole rode the other man to the ground. Cole felt the wet crunch of bones breaking and skin shredding as the man's head bounced hard twice.

Rippa lay face down, too stunned to feel the pain yet. Cole took his time going through the writer's jacket pockets and found a small bottle of clear liquid. He rolled him over, unfazed by the blood flowing from Rippa's broken nose and shattered teeth, or the ooze coming from his grated forehead. He could feel the two friends struggling to decide whether they should join the fight. The look of menace Cole gave them decided things, and they stepped back, though they were close enough to hear what Cole said next.

He held the bottle inches from the fallen sportswriter's face and said through clenched teeth, "If you ever drug a woman for sex again, I'll find out and I'll break more than your nose and your arm..."

As Cole straightened up he could sense Rippa's confusion. The guy knew his face was wrecked, but didn't feel any real pain in either arm. "Oh, yeah," Cole said, bringing his heel down with all his weight on Rippa's right wrist. The sharp crack of breaking bones was followed by the writer's scream. "Sometimes I get a little ahead of myself."

Cole turned and walked down the alley and out of sight as the two friends moved uncertainly to the aid of their fallen buddy. Cole wasn't sure if it was adrenaline or the Paradocs Red that helped get him through the quick brawl. His left shoulder was aflame and he would have sworn he'd reopened the stitches of his wound if they hadn't already been removed. He thought he'd feel like whistling *Ring Out Ahoya,* the Marquette fight song, after putting away the reporter. Instead, he felt hollow and empty. For nearly two months he'd battled the darkness and bitter cold outside, and now he confronted the cold darkness inside himself. He didn't intend to kill Rippa, but it could have happened. And Cole wasn't sure he would have regretted it. He thought of Michele, and how she would have felt seeing her rapist beaten. He swallowed bile, pretty sure she wouldn't have approved. He shoved his hands in his pockets and kept walking, wondering if he was any better than the late Deputy Randall Hubbard.

Chapter Seventy-Five

Another week went by and Cole sat alone at a table for two at the Calderone Club. It had pissed rain the entire day and that fit his mood. It was nine-thirty and the dinner crowd had cleared out. He'd ordered the Chicken Marsala entrée and was still picking at it. Michele had ordered it when he met her here the first time. He couldn't do the zucchini sticks though. The Fritto di Calamari was too good to pass up.

The Club's lighting was still soft and the soothing standards from Sinatra, Martin, Como, and others quietly played in the background, with an occasional song from the 60s and 70s thrown in for good measure. But he felt out of place here now. He felt alone and more than a little sorry for himself. It wasn't quite two months since his fatal confrontation with Hubbard, and it looked like it would be at least another three weeks or more before he would receive medical clearance to go back to his job.

He held his wine glass up to the light and stared at the ruby liquid inside, then took a long sip of the Kunde Reserve Century Vines Zinfandel. He kept the last drops in his mouth longer than usual, savoring the rich, velvety taste of the lush grapes. He splurged on the bottle tonight, a little higher on the price scale than he usually ventured. He wasn't completely sure if he was celebrating the end of the case or drowning his sorrows. He suspected it was a little of both. Dean Martin sang *That's Amore* in the background.

His cell phone vibrated in his suit jacket. Ty, Li, and Lane had called and texted repeatedly to check up on him. So had Gene Olson. They'd been acting like so many mother hens. Fwam and Father Wagner also reached out a few times to check inon him. It was almost too much. He wondered if they had a schedule. He tried to ignore the vibration, but couldn't make himself. If somebody needed him and he missed them, he'd regret it. He reached into his coat and looked at the phone. It was a text from Michele.

Can you meet for a drink?

He didn't know how people could type fast on a phone, but he did his best. *How about now? No time like the present. I'm at the Calderone Club. We've always got that.* ☺

He regretted the smiley emoji as soon as he hit send, but there was no pulling it back. He waited for the reply, wondering how a hero FBI agent could feel so much like a lovesick teenager. His waiter put a hand on Cole's shoulder, causing him to wince. He looked at him a little impatiently. "What is it?"

The waiter nodded his head toward a large window by the entrance. "Sir… "

Michele was outside tapping on the glass. Cole could see a tender smile and either tears or rain streaming down her face, as she looked at him hopefully through the window. He got up from the table and went to meet her. She was barely through the door when Cole reached her and pulled her to him. They hugged tightly and Michele laid her head on his good shoulder. He kissed the top of her forehead.

She looked up at him. "I'm getting you all wet. I should have taken off my coat."

"This is perfect," he said, hugging her tighter. The song *Fly Me to the Moon* drifted to them. Cole heard the last line, "In other words, I love you," and thought, *maybe I do*.

He realized they were moving to the music, dancing in the middle of the restaurant, as Linda Ronstadt sang *Different Drum*. Michele smiled up at him. "I looked up your name: Huebsch. In German, it means 'pretty.'"

His eyes crinkled. "I was wondering when you'd get around to noticing." He leaned in then and kissed her. They kept dancing.

A Note from the Author

Writers write to be read, and our readers make us or break us. If you like The Killer Sermon, please write a short review on Amazon, Bookreads. And if want to learn more about this book or coming releases, please visit kevinkluesner.net. You can contact me from there and I will answer any questions you have.

Acknowledgements

Thank you to all my early readers, who helped shape and reshape my story. Thanks to the Dames of Detection and Level Best Books for believing in me. Thanks to Dr. Julie Doniere, ER physician and tireless do-gooder, for her encouragement and medical review, and to Al Saibini, Retired Special Agent, U.S. Department of Justice, for making the story more authentic. Any errors in fact in this book are on me.

To Jeri Kluesner (Mom), for being my first reader and biggest fan. To Karri, Cole, and Ty (my kids), for their love and support. And to my wife of forty-one years, Janet, for lifting me up when I'm down, and for bursting my bubble when I get a little too full of myself. Love you tons!

About the Author

Kevin Kluesner holds both a BA in journalism and an MBA from Marquette University. He's worked as the outdoor writer for a daily newspaper, taught marketing and management classes at both the undergraduate and graduate level, and served as an administrator of an urban safety net hospital.

The Killer Sermon is his debut novel in the FBI agent Cole Huebsch series set in Wisconsin and the Midwest. Kevin might be the only person to claim membership in both the American College of Healthcare Executives and the International Thriller Writers. He lives in New Berlin, Wisconsin, with his wife Janet.

https://kevinkluesner.net

CPSIA information can be obtained
at www.ICGtesting.com
Printed in the USA
LVHW011155260122
709311LV00001B/31